ALL THE PATHS
TO YOU

Praise for *All the Worlds Between Us*

"This book is really sweet and wholesome and also heartbreaking and uplifting...I would recommend this book to anyone looking for a cute contemporary."—*Tomes of Our Lives*

All the Worlds Between Us "deals with friendship, family, sexuality, self-realization, accepting yourself, the harsh reality of high school and the difference between getting to tell your own story and having your own story exposed. Each character plays a vital role...and tells the story of this book perfectly."—*Little Shell's Bookshelf*

"If you're looking for an easy, quick cute f/f read, you should give this a try...This was a solid debut and I can't wait to see what else this author publishes in the future!"—*The Black Lit Queen*

"This book took me straight back to all of my gigantic teenage emotions and got right down to the heart of me. I'm not a swimmer and I wasn't out in high school, but I swear I was right there with Quinn as she navigated her life as a competitive athlete and a queer kid in high school. Experiencing love and betrayal and triumph through her story was bananas. Morgan Lee Miller, you ripped my heart right out with this brilliant book."—*Melisa McCarthy, Librarian, Brooklyn Public Library*

"I'm always up for fun books about cute girlfriends, and *All the Worlds Between Us* was certainly that: a super cute ex-friends to lovers book about a swimming champion and her ex-best-friend turned girlfriend...*All the Worlds Between Us* is a great rom-com and definitely recommended for anyone who's a fan of romance."—*Crowing About Books*

All the Worlds Between Us "has all the typical drama and typical characters you'd find in high school. It's a tough, yet wonderful journey and transformation. The writing is divine... It's a complicated tale involving so much pain, fear, betrayal and humiliation. *All The Worlds Between Us* is a terrific tale of taking what you want."—*Amy's MM Romance Reviews*

"Morgan's novel reiterates the important fact which should be repeated over and over again that coming out should always be done on one's own terms, and how this isn't a thing that any other people, straight or queer, should decide."—*Beyond the Words*

"Finally a sporty, tropey YA lesbian romance—I've honestly been dreaming about reading something like this for a very long time!"—*Day Dreaming and Book Reading*

By the Author

All the Worlds Between Us

Hammers, Strings, and Beautiful Things

All the Paths to You

Visit us at www.boldstrokesbooks.com

ALL THE PATHS TO YOU

by

Morgan Lee Miller

2020

ALL THE PATHS TO YOU

ISBN 13: 978-1-63555-662-9

This Trade Paperback Original Is Published By
Bold Strokes Books, Inc.
P.O. Box 249
Valley Falls, NY 12185

First Edition: June 2020

CREDITS
Editor: Barbara Ann Wright
Production Design: Stacia Seaman
Cover Design by Jeanine Henning

To Alex—this is the most I will ever talk about the sports.

CHAPTER ONE

This was my eleventh time being drug tested in the last year. That meant eleven times a stranger watched me pee into a cup.

The first time, I was sixteen, right before my first world champs in Barcelona. I was a shy pee-er, so I sat for what seemed like twenty minutes waiting for the minimum of ninety milliliters. Even though I was a minor and the Doping Control Officer stood on the other side of the bathroom stall, she was still there, getting paid to hear me pee. What an exciting job.

Now that I was an adult, the DCO had the pleasure of no barriers blocking her view.

By now, I was a pro. Technically, a professional swimmer and also a pro at drug tests. It came with the job, especially right before the Olympics. We all had to do it, but that didn't make it any less awkward. Nothing would ever normalize a stranger staring intently at my groin to make sure I didn't tamper with the pee.

I'd had to select my "vessel," which was just a creepy yet sophisticated way of saying "pee cup," and inspected said pee cup to make sure it was clean and no one had tampered with it. The DCO had instructed me to wash my hands with only water. Then she followed me into the bathroom and instructed me to pull my shirt halfway up my torso and my track shorts down to mid-thigh so she had a clear view. No matter how many times Officer Shelley fixed her gaze on me, I still couldn't look her in the eye. I held the cup halfway into the toilet and stared at one of the tiles on the floor. It was chipped and kind of looked like the state of Iowa. It only took about a minute to get myself to ninety milliliters under all that pressure. Then I had to secure the lid and follow Shelley into the back room where she would process the sample.

"Thanks, Quinn," Shelley said with a friendly smile. "Good luck at the games."

"If I pass my test," I joked, but it was clear that didn't sit well with her. Her smile faded, and she blinked. I thought it was funny because besides alcohol, I'd never smoked a cigarette, done weed, or popped any pill that wasn't an over the counter pain or allergy med. After all the drug tests at this very facility since I moved to Berkeley, Shelley should have known I was nothing but clean. "It was just a joke."

"Mm-hmm, stick to swimming. You're better at it. Gatorade isn't paying you to be a comedian." She held her firm scowl until she broke, offered me a wink, and just like that, we were cool again.

"See you in the fall," I said and waved.

Next stop: afternoon practice at Berkeley. Team USA had just come back from the Olympic trials in Omaha. Tapering had started, which meant practices were getting shorter and easier. It was also an interesting time because swimmers were a really awkward subspecies. For example, I wore three old suits that were barely still intact—see-through and holey—and purple tights. The only time I wore tights in my life. We wore extra layers to practice during tapering to increase drag, so by the time we shed the extra weight at the Olympics, we zoomed through the water. But it was also fun wearing ripped tights and very old suits to the point where they looked like we'd run them through a shredder. We walked out of the locker room to the pool deck as if we were on the runway and praised each other for whoever won the ugliest swimsuit competition.

But the weirdest, most awkward thing we did was not shave. Now that part I hated. It was a good thing my intense schedule made it almost impossible to form relationships outside of the pool because even if I had an ounce of free time to date, the lack of shaving would do a good job repelling all the women.

"Guys, the Tinder guy just asked me out on a date," Lillian said as we stepped through our house after practice. She showed his picture to me and Talia on her phone. He was in a tight, navy blue fireman T-shirt with baggy, sallow-colored fireman pants. Behind him was a firetruck, and I rolled my eyes at how corny the picture was. I could only offer her a shrug, then went to the fridge to enjoy my late afternoon meal while Talia took the phone to view the guy better.

This had been our lives since we'd rented the three-bedroom house a year before. Lillian and I had been teammates our freshman year at Berkeley, before she went pro at the start of our sophomore year, right after Rio. Once you went pro, you weren't allowed to swim for your college team anymore. We befriended Talia despite the fact that she went to our rival school, Stanford. All three of us were on the national team and went to Rio together. But unlike me, who got gold in the 4x200 free relay and took fourth in the 400-meter free, Lillian and Talia medaled in their individual events.

Living with my two best friends was great. They were like my sisters. The only thing that annoyed me was that they were too straight and talked about boys too much.

"Tinder Fireman?" Talia said with her tone rising in intrigue. She studied the phone. "Damn, he is gorgeous."

At least the guy had muscles. If my beautiful straight friends were going to date men, they had better date guys who were worthy of their sculpted Olympic bodies. But their fawning made me shiver in disgust as I ate a large spoonful of yogurt, hoping this round of straight talk wouldn't last too long.

"I mean, we've been texting nonstop for three weeks now, so it's about time," Lillian said. "He wants to go out tonight."

Talia grunted out of pure jealousy. There were a handful of rules during tapering. Because it was meant to preserve energy for our races, we couldn't even walk to the grocery store a few blocks down the street. And if we couldn't exert the bare minimum amount of energy to go shopping, sex was "strongly discouraged." The Olympics was like our Lent, except we gave up much more—like shaving, drinking, sex, going to the grocery store, or on a simple walk, every single unhealthy food imaginable, and only eating for fuel.

"God, I'm so jealous," Talia whined while plopping on the couch. "But good for you getting Tinder Fireman to finally ask you out."

Lillian let out an evil laugh. "Yeah, right as I feel jealous that you two are going to Tokyo and I'm not, I'm reminded that I can drink and have sex."

Lillian would have had to sacrifice those too if she hadn't torn her

ACL a year and a half ago while hiking in Yosemite. She fell five feet on an extreme trail and ruined her pursuit of the Tokyo Games. She was a breaststroker for the medley relay in Rio, American record holder in the 100 and 200-meter, and Olympic gold and silver medalist respectively. Breaststroke heavily relied on legs and knees, which meant that once her injury was confirmed, Tokyo was ruled out. She was depressed for a year while Talia and I had to reluctantly go to practice and she had to go her separate way to physical therapy. But in the last few months, when training and meal plans became stricter, a smirk found its way to her lips again while we envied her freedom.

"Okay, it's official," Lillian said after typing on her phone. "I have a date tonight."

Talia banged her head against the couch. "Gah. I want to have a date tonight. Not even a date. Just a rendezvous."

"Oh, shut it," Lillian said. "You're about to go to a buffet in a week. I don't even want to hear it."

"Ask him if he has any hot friends," Talia said, then glanced at me minding my business with my yogurt. "Both men and women. Help your two best friends out."

"Nah, I'm good," I said, spooning another helping.

"How are you good? When was the last time you went on a date?"

I looked up at the ceiling as I thought. "Like, five lifetimes ago, but I've already accepted the fact that I'm dying alone. You should try it. It's less stressful."

Talia grunted again and kicked her feet like a child. Lillian and I shared a laugh.

We made sure Lillian looked as elegant and hot as possible before lecturing her about texting us if she needed saving. Talia was always worried about her friends going out with people from dating apps. She watched too many *Dateline* episodes about dates gone wrong and convinced us to share our locations during the date so she could track us. It was sweeter than it was creepy. She was probably the most responsible one out of us, the mom of the group.

She glanced at her phone after the two of us made dinner, the recipe straight from our nutritionist. Baked chicken breast over brown rice, arugula salad with tomatoes, white beans, and minced garlic. Drizzled with olive oil and red wine vinegar. One of the four dinners we'd rotated on repeat for the last few months. I couldn't wait for the games to be over so I could indulge in a greasy slice of cheese pizza.

"They're at Louie's," Talia said with a judgmental scowl. "Louie's. That dive bar with those chicken wings we ate that gave us really bad—"

I raised my hand to cut her off. She didn't need to remind me of Louie's and the food poisoning we both acquired from their "famous award-winning buffalo wings" about a year ago. I wasn't sure how a bar with a consistently sticky floor won any awards, but we only started questioning that after it was too late.

"Talia, relax. She'll be fine. And stop watching those TV shows."

"You're right, you're right. I'm sorry." She flipped her phone over and stabbed her chicken with her fork. "I'm also trying to live vicariously through her."

"Oh, I know. But your time will come in Tokyo. You're a babe. It won't be too hard for you."

"I need it to be the second Saturday of the games. It's been a really long time."

"With your glowing tan skin and Hawaiian beauty, you will get the much-needed attention you've been craving and deserve."

"It's been five months."

"Ah, I don't want to hear it. Mine's longer."

"Why did we choose a really high maintenance and lonely sport?"

That was a good question. Training for the Olympics was a two-year commitment. We worked out six hours a day, four of those hours spent immersed in a pool, following a black line, and not talking to anyone. We spent a lot of time with our thoughts, and that definitely took a toll on our social life. It gnawed and pricked at Talia, but she was much more of a social butterfly than I was. I diagnosed myself at least seventy percent introverted, so being alone with my thoughts and having a bedtime of nine didn't bother me as much as it bothered her.

"I don't know, Tal," I said. "But the reason we did it will come to fruition soon, and then you won't be filled with so much dread."

"I wish I was like you, not fazed by all the stuff we have to give up. I know I'm being dramatic right now. Tapering gives you a lot of time and energy to overthink and make you feel like you're doing something wrong."

"Yeah, it does. You should binge *Stranger Things* with me. It seems like a thing normal people watch."

"God, I'm so antsy! I just want to take a walk or a run or freakin' go to a bar and have a drink. Or get laid. That would be nice."

"Again, don't complain. My dry spell has been longer."

"So, you've really accepted the fact that you'll be alone?"

"Pretty much. You tell me the last time I went out on a date."

She puckered her lips as she thought about it. "That one girl right after you and Alexis broke up."

After I thought for a moment, I realized she was right. That was a year ago, but that was just a dinner date and a one-night stand—rebound sex. I also didn't have the time to date after that, as the clock counted down to the Olympics.

"Sounds about right."

"Any plans on resurrecting the dating app after Tokyo?"

I shrugged. "I don't know. It seems as time consuming as swimming."

"Because you haven't tried. Haven't you only seriously dated, like, two women since you moved out here?"

"I wouldn't call Alexis or Bethany a serious relationship. Definitely not Alexis. Don't let our nine-month relationship fool you. She can't be tamed."

Alexis was the epitome of that Miley Cyrus song. She was this really hot blond tattoo artist with a full sleeve and five years of experience on me. How we lasted nine months still baffled me because looking back, the only chemistry we had was sexual. She was my longest relationship since I moved to San Francisco, but my four-month-long relationship with Bethany in college was more of a relationship than Alexis. At least Bethany acted like we were together. Alexis struggled to have a girlfriend. I don't think monogamy was meant for her. Since she had a wall up, my heart never fully opened for her, so when I broke up with her, I wasn't heartbroken. More relieved that we could stop trying to fit into something that wasn't meant for us. Being with her was more work than training for Tokyo.

"I'm not against dating," I continued. "I just don't want to waste my time if there isn't any chemistry. The free time I have is limited and valuable. If I'm going to date, I want to feel this thrill and excitement and have my stomach constantly on spin cycle while I'm around them."

"You've been on a lot of Tinder dates. No spark from any of them?"

No. After the Rebound Girl a few weeks after Alexis, I deleted the app. It was Tokyo crunch time. But before Alexis, I did go on quite a few dates. Only about three or four girls for a month or so, and then they got so fed up with my busy schedule that most of them told me they couldn't do it, and I didn't bat an eye. I understood where they were coming from. Dating someone training for the Olympics came with only a few spare days and nights.

"A sexual spark, yes," I replied. "A spark that runs deep? No. I haven't felt that way in a really long time."

She let out a long sigh. "Same. We should try the apps again after Tokyo."

"If we're going to date anyone, we should do it soon; we've got two years before we sell our souls to train for Paris."

She raised her water glass in cheers, and I followed her lead and clinked it. "Sounds good to me," Talia said.

After we ate, we checked in on Lillian to find her still at Louie's. She was alive and well after she told us she passed on the chicken wings and got a burger instead, so we knew she wouldn't die or suffer food poisoning.

Talia and I turned on the TV and settled on the couch to watch an episode of *Stranger Things*. Since we weren't normal people, we were only on the first season, trying to use all the available taper time to understand pop culture references. Lillian had been begging us to watch it so we could dress up as the gang for Halloween.

"You know, this show would be a million times better with a gay element," I said "I'm thinking Nancy would be good. She's cute."

"That's definitely not going to happen. She's with Steve and his hair. And come on, can you enjoy a show without a gay element?"

"Technically, I could, but it's not really preferred. I'm at that stage in my life where I only want to watch things that are gay...preferably when they don't kill the love interest literally the scene after they first have sex."

"Man, you're still pissed about *The 100*?"

"I'll forever be pissed about *The 100*. I devoted my life to it for them to ruin it completely. Plus, *Orange Is the New Black* got disappointing. *Orphan Black* got weirder and ended. So unless *Stranger*

Things becomes gay, it's not getting ahead of *Killing Eve*. I can't turn down an MI6 agent and a loveable female psychopath assassin being obsessed with each other. Sign me right up."

Right as I reached for my glass of water, my phone rang. The name that stretched across the screen sent my mind into a whirling spin of nostalgic disbelief. I nearly choked on the water as it descended my throat.

Speaking of dating, was this really happening? Was Kennedy Reed calling me?

"Oh shit," I said through an airy exhale. "What do I do?"

"What? Who's that? Why aren't you answering?"

I looked at her with worried eyes. "Dating…I dated her."

I couldn't even form sentences I was so taken aback. Talia picked up my phone, studied the name, and flashed it in front of my face. "Kennedy Reed? I don't remember hearing about a Kennedy Reed."

My heart hammered as if I was sprinting down the pool with full force. "High school girlfriend. The best friend," I said through the shortness of panicked breath.

Talia's mouth dropped, and then she tossed the phone on my lap as if it burned her fingers. "Oh God, what are you going to do?" She finally reached my level of panic.

"I don't know! I don't know!"

"Answer it! Answer it!"

I fumbled for the phone and pressed the green button.

Kennedy Reed calling me a week and a half before I left for the Olympics? All the history we shared exploded in my memory. My childhood best friend who gave me my first kiss the night before she moved to New York City when we were thirteen, came back to Aspen Grove sophomore year only to ignore me until our senior year, when she confessed the feelings she'd had for me since we were eleven. And then when we were able to move past that, we dated, and those five months were some of the most amazing of my life. She was my high school sweetheart. My first and only heartbreak. Why the hell was she calling me? She hadn't called me since…well…since we dated.

I sucked in a breath and planned on holding it until I got the reason she was calling. "H…hello?" Yup, I still had the amazing ability to sound like an idiot around her.

"Oh, hey stranger, long time no talk," Kennedy said with a chipper voice, and I could almost hear the smile.

All she had to do was say one sentence to send me flying back in time. "Hey!" I replied and hated myself for my tremulous voice. I scratched the back of my head as Talia drilled her dark brown eyes into me, as invested in the conversation as I was. "What are you...why... how are you?"

She laughed, so that meant that bad news wasn't pending, right? "Did I catch you off guard?"

"A little, but I guess in a good way. It's always nice hearing from you. What's going on?"

"A lot of things." The noise in the background sounded like she was outside, rustling wind and huffing when she spoke. "First things first, guess where I am?"

"I'm assuming not in Brooklyn." I paused to think, and if she wasn't where she lived, at least from the last I heard, there was only one other place she could be that was worthy of this call. "Are you in San Francisco?"

"Ding ding ding!"

My mouth dropped. Talia rounded her stare.

"Seriously?"

"Seriously. You know my brother lives out here, right?"

"Uh, no. When did this happen? Where does he live?"

"He moved right after Christmas. Working in Silicon Valley. Living in Santa Clara, which apparently is only an hour away from you, Google Maps tells me."

"Yeah, it's not too far. Geez, how long are you in town for?"

"Glad you asked. Jacob's getting married this weekend, can you believe it?"

I leaned back on the couch. "Wow. I guess that means we're not kids anymore?"

"Hey, speak for yourself. I don't have a house, a job, or a ring on my finger, so I'm still very youthful. But yeah, he's getting married this weekend, and I just landed, and you're the first person I called because obviously, I want to see you if we're in the same city."

My heart raced, practically leapt out of my chest the same way it did the last time I saw her, two summers ago after we finished up our junior year of college. We were both in Aspen Grove at the same time since high school. We met for dinner, which lasted the whole night, my heart never once taking a break from its sprint.

"I guess that's the rule now, huh?" I said, thinking back. "Any time we're in the same city we have to see each other?"

"Obviously. Unless you're too important since you'll be at the Olympics soon and all over the TV. Way too cool for me."

"I leave in a week and a half. It's pretty crazy, but I'm never too cool for you."

"You know how freakin' excited I am for you? You know how loud I screamed when I watched the trials and saw you qualify?"

I had an idea, but imagining it and hearing the excitement only made my smile grow. I loved that she watched me. After all this time, she still made time for it.

"Well, if you watched, then I guess you're still my good luck charm," I said, and my face burned. *Goddamn, you can't be blushing like this the next time you see her.*

"If that's the case, I think you need to see your good luck charm. You're not ready for Tokyo if you don't…if you're free, that is. I'm sure you're busy as hell."

"Busy doing nothing. It's tapering time."

"I don't know what that means, but you make it sound like a burden."

"It is a burden. I've been prescribed lots of rest, which means no going out, not even to the store down the street. But if minimal activity is involved, I might be able to squeeze you in."

"Really? Because I would really love to see you. It's been too long."

"A whole two years."

"I feel like that doesn't even count because it went by too fast."

I laughed. "The dinner lasted for four hours. We shut the restaurant down. It closed on us."

"And somehow, it still went by too fast. So can you squeeze me in? I want to treat you to a celebratory feast. I promise, minimal activity. A simple dinner and time to catch up."

"I can't say no to a celebratory feast. Let's do it."

"Yay! I'm so excited. I'll text you sometime when I get to Jacob's, and we'll go from there?"

"Yeah, that sounds good. I'm looking forward to it."

When we said our good-byes, I sunk into the couch and got lost in all the scenarios that could happen. Would it be anything like two years ago when we talked and laughed the whole time, not realizing four hours had sped by until the waitress told us they were closing? It felt like we'd had no time to catch up at all. And God, did we flirt. I thought our chemistry would have diluted a bit because of the time and distance since we broke up, but if that dinner proved anything, it was that our chemistry was more than alive and well, just like where it left off when we were eighteen...if not stronger. I thought about kissing her when I dropped her off. I wondered if she thought that too because she paused before opening the passenger door, as if giving me a silent invitation.

But like the idiot I was, I didn't do anything but tell her I'd had a nice time. Because apparently, while dedicating all my time to swimming and being alone with my thoughts, I'd forgotten how to make a move.

I thought back on our good-bye before the start of college, when we walked around my neighborhood, and I kissed her good-bye, a kiss I still thought about anytime she crossed my mind. We'd made a pact that night that we would try our relationship again after college if we crossed paths. Five years later, was this finally the moment I kept asking the gay gods for?

I told Talia that if I was going to be in a relationship with someone, I wanted to feel the spark. I hadn't felt it for a really long time. It was only after I hung up with Kennedy and got lost in the sixteen years' worth of memories that it dawned on me that the last girl to make me feel that way—the spark that I'd been searching for—was Kennedy Reed.

CHAPTER TWO

What the hell was this? Was this a date? A casual dinner between two ex-girlfriends?

What the hell did I even wear?

There had to be a happy medium between a "date" and a "casual dinner between two ex-girlfriends" outfit. I stared at my closest for fifteen minutes, tried on a few outfits, had Lillian and Talia yay and nay them, and ended up with a black short-sleeved button-down with a pineapple print, sleeves rolled up, skinny gray jeans that stopped at my ankles, and black Chelsea boots.

"Are you sure I look okay?" I asked and did a final spin as they stretched out on the couch.

"Are you seriously asking if you look okay when you're the fittest you've ever been and will ever be in your life?" Lillian said, holding a steaming bowl of chicken ramen. "Get out of here, clown."

I huffed. That wasn't the point. This was Kennedy Reed we were talking about. The bar so high that no girl had even come close to touching.

I tossed her a stern side-eye and then looked at Talia. She sat straight up and studied me. Hair, very little makeup, shirt, pants, shoes, and then back up for one last look.

"Hmm, can you French tuck your shirt?" Talia asked. "What would Tan from *Queer Eye* tell you?"

I tucked the front of my shirt into my pants. "He would tell me to French tuck it."

"Boom. There you go. Looks like you're going out on a nice, very gay date."

"That was the point…and also not to look like I'm trying too hard. Does it look like I'm trying too hard?"

They both observed me again. "No, not really. But are you going to try?" Lillian asked, wiggling her eyebrows.

"I'm going to see where the night takes us."

"Into your bed?"

"I'm not allowed to burn fifty calories going to the store. You think I'm allowed to have sex?"

"That's a wildly overdramatic rule if you ask me."

"Stop rubbing it in!" Talia hollered, and that garnered a bellowing laugh from Lillian, who'd been making it known that she broke her dry spell with Tinder Fireman the night before. "And do we need to keep tabs on your location?"

"I've known this girl since I was seven. Her go-to in Never Have I Ever is that she's never cheated on a test. I think it's safe to say that she's probably the one person you don't need a location for."

"I almost forgot what it was like for Quinn Hughes to go on a date," Lillian said, resting a hand over her heart. "My baby girl is growing up."

"We didn't get this whole outfit check before the last date," Talia said to Lillian.

"It's not a date."

"Okay," the two of them said with an eye roll.

This wasn't a date. It was a reunion dinner, or what Kennedy called a celebratory feast. It was just two people who had known each other for sixteen years meeting in a city three thousand miles away from home to have dinner.

Even though my heart and stomach fluttered as hard and fast as if it were a date. My brain needed to reassure all my organs jolting awake that this was definitely not a date.

I couldn't believe I had to Uber to the restaurant that was in the Castro District, one neighborhood over from my Mission house. At any other time, I would have walked the mile and a half so I could enjoy the cool fresh air, something other than stuffy chlorine air or stale sweaty air from the weight room. But nope, I had to be that person who spent ten dollars for a few blocks, leaving me with extra time to think, reflect, and worry. My heart thrummed in my chest as if I was already at the Olympics, ready to swim my first race.

The times I had used my dating app, I'd talked to quite a few women. It was how I'd met Alexis. But heading to the restaurant, my heart weighed more than it did on the way to my first blind date. This was much scarier than meeting a complete stranger. There were no expectations for those. The bar was basically set on the ground. No history complicated things. There was nothing to lose.

But now, I had expectations. This was the second time I would see Kennedy since high school and the first time after college. Throughout the past five years, I'd clung to this hope that Kennedy and I would find a way to be together again. But that ray of hope dimmed a little more each year with her on the East Coast and me on the West, and the texting that spaced out as time went on. We had so much history together, so much at stake, it fogged my mind until the Uber driver snapped me out of it to tell me we were here.

Then there was the waiting. I texted her when I grabbed a table that she'd have a drink waiting for her. I was so thirsty from all the worry and doubt that I needed lemon water ASAP. As for Kennedy's drink, I had no idea what to get. She'd been two months out from her twenty-first birthday back when we had our last dinner. Last I knew, she liked Captain Morgan. I went with a Captain and Coke. That was playing it safe, right?

My phone chirped on the table with a text from her. *Walking in!*

Holy crap. This was it. This was—

Kennedy stepped through the entrance, and my throat caught. The hostess gestured to me, and her eyes found me instantly. Her smile grew as she walked, and my legs melted into my seat. Her skin glowed with sun, and her ash brown hair curled in slight waves past her chest, the ends lighter than her roots. Her eyes were still a soft bright green that flipped my stomach upside down when they locked with mine. And that smile. I swear, the whole time she weaved around tables, my body thought it was getting ready for a workout from the rush of adrenaline and the sweat on the back of my neck.

She wore an olive green one-shoulder top that made her eyes pop and short jean shorts that instantly stole my attention. I stood to greet her, but the words died on my lips. "Hi," I said, but it felt as if the words carelessly spilled from my mouth. I tried not to let my stare linger, but my gaze went to her face, her exposed shoulder, and her legs, unabashedly skimming across every inch of exposed, sun-kissed skin.

"Oh my God, wow," were the first words she said before holding her arms out for a hug. When I accepted, I resisted the urge to sink into her embrace, but it was hard. Her hair didn't smell like flowers anymore. It smelled like high-end shampoo, maybe with argan oil. Her hug was so comforting. When she broke away, she held me in front of her so she could get a better look. As much as I wanted the embrace to last, I was thankful that it didn't because it would have been a shortcut to an instantaneous unraveling.

She scanned my face and then my body, a long and careful examination that sent a potent shiver down my spine. Her glance had a bit of hunger in it, almost as if I was being objectified, but since it came from Kennedy, I loved it. I wanted her to stare at me like that for the rest of the evening.

"Damn, you look amazing," she said as she took her seat. I followed. "You look like you're ready to kick some ass in Tokyo."

"Oh, I feel like it," I said, straightening my back and doing a facetious hair flip.

She continued to take me in. "Is there any fat on you?"

"I think all that kale made sure I had minimum fat. Could explain all the pizza cravings I've been having."

"I'll make sure I order the flatbread, then."

"You're awful."

She winked. "You like it."

I smiled "A little."

She noticed her drink and grinned. "Oh, you weren't lying when you said there was a drink waiting for me."

"Don't get too excited. I have no idea what you like these days."

She took a sip, then followed it with a wince. "Seriously, Quinn?"

After all this time, the power of her saying my name still did wonders to my insides. "What?"

"Out of all the drinks you could have ordered, you got me a Captain and Coke?" She shook her head, hiding a budding grin behind the rim of her glass as she took another sip.

"And in spite of all the advice I gave you, you still haven't ditched that satchel purse?" I gestured to the large handbag next to her feet. "It screams Captain and Coke girl to me. Like your red Jetta."

"Hey, I love this purse, and I loved that Jetta."

"Love it more than hooking up with women?"

Her cheeks turned a deep shade of pink. At least we were probably matching now. "It didn't ruin my chances by *that* much."

"Oh really?" I rested my chin on my palm and moved my eyebrows up and down. "Please go on."

She laughed and crossed her arms. "I'm sure you would love to know. Gotta loosen me up a little more to get that dirt out of me."

"Then let me get you another drink. Maybe a stronger one." I waved the drink menu. "They have a nice selection. All happy hour prices."

"That's not even fair since you're not drinking." She pointed to my lemon water. "You can't get me liquored up for juicy info when I can't do the same to you."

It was a very sad sight. I would have loved to order that delicious ten percent IPA that I'd only had twice in my life, but with a week out from leaving, I was in dry season, which meant zero alcohol, which also meant Lillian drank more to torture us.

"It's for a gold medal, Kennedy. Now tell me what you want."

Apparently, the right answer was a dry red wine. She let out a gasp and pointed to the menu as if I knew exactly what she was talking about when she said the restaurant had her favorite Petit Verdot, and she laughed when I told her I'd never heard of that wine before. Whatever the glass was, I forced her to order it.

"Are you a sommelier now?" I asked after the waitress took the order.

"Not in the slightest. When I studied abroad, I spent a long weekend down in southern France because my girlfriend's aunt had a place down there. We went to a few wineries, and this was the best I had."

Was it wrong of me to question if she meant girlfriend as a lover or a friend? Because I did.

I threw my hands up. "Oh, you went to southern France and acquired a taste for red wine. So fancy."

"Are you mocking me?"

"Of course. You set me up for it. Jetta owner Kennedy Reed, a French wine connoisseur."

"Quinn Hughes, a two-time Olympian. I guess a lot has changed since the last time we saw each other. What was it? Two years ago?"

"Yeah, I think so. The dinner back in Aspen Grove."

"Yeah, that dinner." She said it as if that moment in the car sprouted in her mind, and she too was imagining the kiss that never happened. She blinked rapidly as if to tear herself out of the memory. "And now you're traveling all the corners of the world."

"My entire devotion to swimming is solely based on frequent flyer miles. Who cares about gold medals?"

"I wouldn't. Those seat upgrades are key, especially for overnight flights. How many gold medals do you have now?"

"Thirteen gold. Eight silver. Two bronze. Only one Olympic medal." Rio was an interesting time. I tried out for the 200-meter and 400-meter free. I missed qualifying for the 200 by a literal hundredth of a second, which was much more devastating than missing the London Olympics by three. I qualified for the 400-free but ended up getting fourth, which added to my frustrations that I missed winning my first individual medal by a second. But I was on the 4x200-free relay that won gold, and I cherished that medal but was still bitter about my 200 and 400 performances. Rio brought me so much disappointment at the same time it gave me my first Olympic gold.

"Only one. Geez, the humanity," Kennedy said. "Let me make fun of you for that comment now since you're harping on my southern France story."

I laughed. "Okay, that's fair. I sounded a little ungrateful. I'm just upset I couldn't qualify for the 200-free, and I missed the bronze in the 400 by a second."

"Yeah, I bet that's disappointing, but since then, you've become a six-time world champion. Sounds like you're on a perfect path to winning gold in Tokyo."

"Oh wow. You've really kept up with my career."

"Of course I have," she said casually before taking another drink. "I've known you since I was seven. I dated you in high school. I was there when you decided that you wanted to go to the Olympics. Why the hell wouldn't I keep up with you?"

God, I was already in so much trouble. The exact feelings I'd told Talia I wanted to feel about a woman were already intoxicating me before we ordered our food. Everything was still there. Nothing had changed from high school. If anything, I felt a stronger pull. Besides my girlfriend Bethany, who was on my Berkeley swim team, no other girl had been interested or could keep up with my intense love for swimming. Alexis had found it boring. Other girls had found it too time consuming. And there was Kennedy, sitting back and cheering for me from the sidelines like always.

"I…I don't know," I said and shook my head. "It's a lot to keep up with."

"Not for me. I think it's amazing. You've grown so much since high school. Thirteen gold medals, six-time world champion. Now you have *five* events in the Olympics. You're moving up in the world, Quinn Charlotte Hughes. I'm so proud of you."

I waved off her comment as the warmth spread over my face and down my spine. My wide smile felt almost traitorous, ignoring the signals my brain let out. Despite being on good terms with Kennedy, I needed to have my guard up, knowing how much damage she could cause if something prompted a sharp twist in the night.

"But enough about me," I said. "Last time I saw you, you were applying to grad school. How's that going?"

Once we put in our order, she told me that she'd finished her first year of grad school at NYU, and she had one more semester before she graduated. I couldn't believe it. Studying news and documentary. I had to interrupt her because I was so proud. She tried waving it off as if it wasn't a big deal, but everyone knew how great a school NYU was, and the fact that she'd decided to continue her education was amazing. She tried to diffuse the accomplishment by saying that a local TV network had offered her a summer internship that was seventy percent coffee orders and thirty percent editing scripts, nothing special. And when she wasn't interning, she was taking a summer class. I reminded her that she was officially Hermione from *Harry Potter*, and she threw her napkin at me.

"That's not an insult," I said and tossed it back. When we were kids and ODed on all the movies and books, we'd always said how annoying Hermione was when she was being all studious because what kid would spend all their time studying when they had magical powers and Hogwarts to explore? But now Kennedy was the one who volunteered for another few years of school. That was the most Hermione thing ever. "Look at Hermione now, she's a freakin' babe. If anything, you should take it as a compliment."

She rolled her eyes but squeaked out one last giggle. "Don't even try to play that card right now."

"What? Why?"

"You know why."

"I don't. Please elaborate."

"You're making this all so easy."

"What's so easy?"

She bit her lip and flashed me this look as if I should know exactly what she was implying, and my thoughts went straight to the sizzling connection fusing us together. Ever since she'd sat down, I'd forgotten that it'd been five years since we were something because it felt as if no time had passed at all.

But before she could continue, the waitress brought our food. Kennedy got the flatbread, and if Lillian and Talia had been there, they would have choked on their laughter knowing how much I was craving greasy bread and cheese. It looked amazing. My thirteen-dollar arugula salad was nothing compared to it. As excited as I was to compete in the Olympics, I was also excited for the week after the games so I could revel in the marvelous forbidden foods diet, consisting of cheese, pizza, nachos, a bag of kettle-cooked salt and vinegar chips with ranch sour cream dip, and fried boneless chicken wings. The forbidden foods diet added to the Tokyo excitement.

"Okay, you remember back when we were eleven? The Beijing Olympics?" she asked as she swallowed a bite.

Did I remember? So much happened that summer. I remember sitting cross-legged, inches from my TV, sharing a big bowl of popcorn with Kennedy in my basement as I fixated on swimming, explaining everything she needed to know about the sport. I remember the two of us screaming and jumping when the U.S. men's 4x100-free relay beat France after the drama of France's smack talking. To this day, it was one of the best swimming races ever at the Olympics. We screamed again during Michael Phelps's 100-butterfly when he went from seventh place to first in a matter of fifty meters and won gold by a millisecond. And the race to top all of that off was when forty-year-old Dara Torres made a comeback at her final Olympics, and even though I was only eleven, I knew that as a forty-year-old swimming against women twenty years younger, the odds were against her. But she won a silver in the 50-meter free, and I was in awe. It was when I decided I wanted to be an Olympian. Dara Torres, Natalie Coughlin, Michael Phelps, all inspired me to go for it. I told my parents the following week that I wanted to try out for London in four years, and they gave me this look like I was crazy. But with enough harping on the subject and constantly blowing my competition out of the water, they knew I was serious and that I might actually have a shot with the right coaching.

Insert all the swim camps they invested in to hone my technique, finding the right age group club team to challenge me and propel me toward the Olympic trials. That Olympics, I'd told Kennedy that one day, I would swim for Team USA, and she was the only person who didn't laugh or doubt my ability. Instead, she'd smiled, held my hands, and said that *when* I made it, she would be in the front row, wearing a T-shirt with my face on it with text that said "My best friend."

So, yes, I did remember the Beijing Olympics. All too well.

"I remember," I said and took another sip of lemon water.

"And how I told you I would wear a shirt with your face on it?"

There was a tug in my chest. She remembered too. God, I'd wanted so much for that to happen. During the trials for London, we hadn't been talking. At Rio, when I swam in the relay, she had sent me texts, and although they were sweet and made me smile ear to ear, it wasn't the same as the shirt in the front row. I wondered if she would accept a plane ticket to Tokyo. Would that be too much given the fact we hadn't seen each other in two years? Would that distract me too much? Would that set me up for getting my heart broken if she didn't feel the same way about keeping the pact we made? Because wasn't this dinner—post-college, in the city I'd been living in for five years—a sign of our paths crossing and that we were destined to be together?

I nervously stirred the straw around until a small current formed in the glass. "Of course I remember. What about it?"

"I should have a shirt made and wear it during your races. Since I'm your good luck charm and all. Imagine all the powers I'd have."

"I'm sure it would do wonders."

"Golden wonders." She moved her eyebrows up and down with an impish smile.

"If you really want to wear it, I'm not going to stop you," I said. "I need all the luck I can get."

She wiped her hands on her napkin and flipped over her phone.

I furrowed my eyebrows. "What are you doing?" I asked.

A satisfied smile grew as if she found whatever she was looking for. "Ah, found it."

"Found what?"

"A place to make custom shirts. According to this place, I can have it ready before I leave."

"Are you serious?"

She lowered her phone and gave me a deadpan expression. "More serious than you are. I want you to have a gold medal."

"I want that too, hence this lame salad and lemon water."

"You've been saying I was your good luck charm since we were seniors. I need to take that extra leap and get the damn shirt." Her eyes fell back to her phone as she tapped against the screen.

"Now what are you doing?"

"Facebook stalking you. I need to find a picture to put on the shirt."

I laughed. She was really serious. "Kennedy—"

"Oh look!" She turned the phone around to show me an old photo of me and Alexis.

It was one of our more romantic nights together, spending my twenty-second birthday at the gay club for lesbian night and having all the drag queens lift me for the perfect picture. A dinner out to our favorite Mexican place or watching Netflix would have sufficed, but no, Alexis had spoiled me with a loud, stuffy, crowded club, with alcohol running wild, when I'd limited myself to three drinks that night. Lucky me.

"I remember tattoo girl," Kennedy said with a curious tone that begged for more information.

"Ex-girlfriend."

"Oh, I'm well aware."

Kennedy and I had stellar communication our freshman year of college. But the further into college we'd gotten, the busier we'd become, and the less we'd texted each other. Before her call to plan this dinner, our last messages were when she'd wished me a happy birthday in April. When Alexis and I dated, my conversations with Kennedy had dwindled to sparse texts for things like birthdays, Christmas, wishing me luck during international swim competitions, and when something reminded us of each other, usually when our Beyoncé song, "XO," popped up on shuffle, or when we shared theories about our favorite singers secretly dating. Then we freaked out when leaked texts proved the theories true. Blair Bennett and Reagan Moore were really celesbians, and the confirmation had us talking the most since freshman year of college. But we never talked about our love lives. I didn't know why she didn't bring it up, but if it was anything like my reasons, it was too hard to talk about when all I wanted to do—still—was be with her. It was easier to pretend there was nothing there.

"I never saw you as a tattoo type of gal," she said as her fingers continued swiping.

"Everyone has an exception."

"And what made her yours?"

Apparently, we were at the point when two glasses of wine loosened Kennedy up so we could get the answers to all our burning questions. The real question was: Without having a drop to brace myself for the worst, was I ready to hear the updates of Kennedy Reed's love life?

I guess we were about to find out.

I exhaled as I tried figuring out what the hell drew me to Alexis besides her skills in bed and her ability to make me have a painful belly laugh. There was no doubt she was attractive, and now that I thought about it, maybe the fact that she was distant, difficult to read, and anything but supportive made her a challenge. Any person who dedicated their whole life to competing in a sport at the highest level loved the thrill of a challenge. Maybe I also found her convenient since she didn't beg for time and attention that I couldn't give, and she was totally happy being my number two in life. We got what we both wanted from each other, someone to fill the void.

I shrugged. "I don't know. She was just different. Not too needy, which was awesome for me since swimming is very time consuming. She's hot, hilarious—" I wanted to say a really good lay, but that might have been crossing the line.

Kennedy slowly nodded, and it felt as if she didn't buy anything I said. "Interesting. And how long did that last?"

"Nine months."

"Oh. Okay."

I buzzed my lips and went for another drink. "Yeah. Swimming has been a nice roadblock in my love life. Too busy to maintain a relationship." I paused. Her curious stare felt as if she was trying getting a glimpse into my mind. "I feel like you're judging me."

She threw her free hand up. "I'm not judging at all. Why would I judge?"

"Because my longest relationship has been nine months."

"Why would I care?"

"What's your longest relationship, since we're on the topic?"

She went for her first sip of the third glass of wine, but that didn't tame the pink in her cheeks. "I don't know. Like a year? A little more?"

I definitely didn't expect that answer. "A year? A little more? Geez. I feel like I get nothing out of being your Facebook friend. I would have never known."

"That's the point. I don't want to be one of those people who throws her relationships out in the open. That signs you up for nosy people asking about them when they don't work out."

Kennedy hardly did much on social media, which really sucked for me, the high school ex-girlfriend who found her insanely beautiful and still clung to the hope that we would get back together. I really could have used some photo evidence right about then so I could have gauged where I stood with her.

"Okay, who was the girl? Come on, spill."

My teasing smile washed away when Kennedy's loosened. To fill the silence, she went for a long gulp of wine.

I could feel our playful banter shift like tectonic plates, and the next words out of her mouth would be the earthquake.

"Well," she began and paused as if she was trying to find the right words. "I met her in my study abroad program." She scratched the back of her head. "So, yeah."

I tried to figure out why the mood changed. Our dinner two years ago was a few months before she left to spend her senior year in France. If she'd dated this girl for "a year or a little more," that would have made the relationship a pretty recent one, depending on when it all started. Halfway through the year meant they broke up a few months ago. If they started dating in the spring of her senior year, then that would make them still together.

An uneasy burn started in my stomach. "What happened?"

She nervously chuckled. "We broke up about three weeks ago."

"What? Three weeks?" She nodded. "Wow. What happened? How are you doing? You want to talk about it?"

I really felt for her. Dating someone for more than a year, and they'd just broken up? Even though my body buzzed with optimism, underneath my selfish feelings, I really did hope she was doing okay.

"Yeah, I'm doing okay, thanks for asking. It was kind of inevitable. She lives in Boston doing law school. I'm in the city doing grad school. Long distance is really hard."

"I bet. I've never done it and really have no intention of ever doing it."

"Yeah, it's not recommended. She asked me to move to Boston and was shocked when I said I couldn't."

"Of course you couldn't. You're in grad school."

"Exactly. There was a lot more to it, but in the end, I broke up with her. There was a lot of crying. She said some pretty hurtful things that I'm still trying to shake off."

"What did she say?"

"That I wasted the last year because I didn't want to move in together," she said, and I could hear her rising anger. "That I never made time for her. How she put so much into the relationship and I didn't. I don't even know what that was about. Ever since we got back from France, I went up there every time. She came to Brooklyn once. She acted like her education was far superior to mine and made it seem like she couldn't be bothered coming to me because of it."

I frowned, officially not liking this girl. Kennedy always incited something protective in me, the kid version wanting to protect her from mean kids in the neighborhood or at school. She was one of the sweetest, most caring people I'd ever met, and I hated knowing that people took advantage of that.

"She sounds like a pretentious asshole," I said through my bitterness.

"Maybe that's what Harvard Law does to a person. Anyway, she's been a pain in my ass because we still have a few things that belong to each other. So now we're in this weird limbo of trying to organize an exchange, but on top of all the things she said to me when we broke up, she called me drunk the night before I left to come out here to tell me she slept with someone else. She's been single for three weeks and already found a rebound. And I'm sure she told me to make me feel like shit, like I should be guilty that I broke up with her. So that's cool. Ugh, God, if I keep talking about it, I'm going to get angry. I'm sorry."

"No, it's fine. I'm sorry you're going through that. This girl sounds like she doesn't deserve you at all, and it's her loss. Not yours."

Her eyes softened. "Thanks, Quinn. I appreciate that."

"I don't like her."

She laughed. "Of course you don't."

"Seriously, she's an ass."

She nodded and shrugged. "Yeah, a little bit. I'm just glad I'm here, doing some soul searching in a different city, on another coast. It's nice to take a break for a little bit after a tumultuous month or so. I don't want her sucking up any more of my time."

I raised my water glass. "Well, fuck her, and let's enjoy the night."

She smiled and clinked her glass against mine. "Cheers to that."

The rest of dinner was light. She asked me questions about preparing for the Olympics. I told her everything, from all the schedules I had with NBC producers to film the bio that would air before my races, my practices getting easier, my diet becoming harder, to not being able to walk to the grocery store, drink alcohol, or have sex, and of course her eyes widened at that, but I assured her that my busy schedule and the lack of shaving repelled the women.

"I doubt it," she said in a low, flirtatious voice.

"You can feel my legs if you want. I haven't shaved in a week, and I can't until the night before the Olympics."

"Yeah, your body and face are pretty perfect, so I think you need to try harder to scare women away than with some hairy legs."

I paused, feeling the air thicken around us. It was like our dinner two years ago when the flirting came so easily that it would feel unnatural to try to hold it back. I didn't want this night to end. I wanted it to keep going until the perfect moment found its way between us, and I would actually kiss her this time because who knew when the next opportunity would be or if there would be another? My mind hadn't stopped spinning with the idea that this was the moment we'd based our pact around when we were eighteen.

The check came, and we bickered about it for a few minutes. Kennedy insisted she pay and that she wanted to treat me to a pre-Olympic dinner, but I didn't want her to because the French wine was expensive, and I knew she'd already spent a bunch of money traveling, paying for the bridesmaid dress, and everything else that came with being in a wedding. But she wouldn't let it go. At one point, her fingers brushed mine as she fought for the check, and my insides flared in an arousing warmth that involuntarily surrendered the check. Kennedy stuck her credit card down and smiled victoriously.

"I don't know why you can't let me pay for it," I said, angry that I had to accept defeat.

She flagged the waitress to hand her the check. "Because I wanted to do this for you. Just accept it."

"I don't want to."

"Well, too late. You lost. Don't be a sore loser."

"I'm not really used to it," I said jokingly and offered a wink.

"You're cocky. I need to humble you."

Whatever that entailed, I was all for it.

I stared intently as she signed the check. As she looked skyward with the pen hovering over the tip line, our eyes met, and something passed through us. It was crazy how much my lips begged for hers just at the tingling memory.

How couldn't this be something? Right before I left to compete in the biggest game of my career, one of the people I cared the most about reentered my life. I couldn't remember the last time my chest fluttered this quickly over a girl, a fluttering that wasn't fueled solely by lust. I had to see her again before we both parted ways.

"Quinn—"

"Do you think—"

We both laughed as we spoke over each other when we stepped outside. I guess both of us wondered what would happen now, and I hoped she saw this as something bigger, like I did.

"You go first," I said, feeling warmth consume my face.

She gave me a shy smile and tucked a strand of hair behind her ear. "I know you're probably really busy until you leave, but I would really like to see you again."

A relieved sigh slipped out of me. "Yeah, I would like that."

"The rehearsal dinner is tomorrow, wedding on Saturday, family stuff Sunday, then I'm spending a night with one of my best friends from college in Yosemite, which only leaves us two days before you leave. Does that leave any time for us to see each other again?"

"My roommates and I are having a going-away party next Wednesday. You should come. I have the whole day free after my last morning practice."

She smiled. "Okay, let's do that. If you have the whole day free, I want to spend it all with you."

"I've already penciled it in."

After a tight hug good-bye that filled me with buzzing warmth, we went our separate ways. She Ubered back to Santa Clara, and I went back home. I didn't realize that I'd been smiling the whole time until I was a few blocks away from the house, when I snapped out of my daydream and felt my face muscles still working to form a grin.

I'd crossed paths with the one who got away. I'd promised her in high school I wouldn't ever forget about the pact. I hope she hadn't forgotten either.

CHAPTER THREE

I couldn't resist texting her.

I'd been thinking about her nonstop since our dinner, and even though I knew she was preoccupied with her brother's wedding, I couldn't let go of the anticipation of seeing her or the curiosity of what she was doing, what she looked like in her bridesmaid dress, if she was also wondering about me.

Part of tapering was being well rested, and on top of easier practices and swimming less, that also meant proper sleep. David wanted us in bed by nine p.m., but by that time on Saturday, I found myself lost in the picture she sent me of her and Jacob. Him in his fitted black tux with a white flower pinned to his collar, looking like a twenty-five-year-old version of the teenage face that lived in my memory. Kennedy had her arm around him, wearing a dusty rose dress that brought out the color of her eyes and summer tanned skin. They had the same close-set, almond-shaped green eyes, bright, welcoming smile, and ash brown hair. You could tell they were siblings and inherited their parents' best physical traits.

I got lost in the picture, using my fingers to zoom in on Kennedy's face and get a closer look of her perfect eyes and smile.

I typed back, *This picture is really making it hard to go to sleep at 9 p.m. You're gorgeous.*

But then I thought about what sending that text would result in. I would stay awake, waiting for Kennedy to text something flirtatious. Then I would spend more time dwelling on it, imagining her face, imagining us kissing, all sorts of thoughts that would spiral out of control and unlock the mentality I'd built up in preparation for Tokyo.

Despite what I wanted to say, I followed my gut and erased what I typed for something new.

The Reeds are looking really good. Tell Jacob I said congrats, and say hi to your parents for me.

The lamest text.

In the days following the wedding, she asked me how my hairy legs and pizza cravings were doing. I asked her how sightseeing was, and she sent me pictures of her adventures in Yosemite: El Capitan with her in tight yoga pants and a tank top in front of a sequoia tree, and I found myself zooming in to check out her beautiful face and toned arms and legs.

I checked my phone during the free time I had in the NBC interviews. The crew followed us to the pool to film us practicing and interviewed Coach David. It felt like being a part of a reality show for two days as they gathered footage. They came into our home to interview us. Lillian and I hid in the downstairs hallway and listened as they asked Talia tons of questions about growing up in Kauai and how her family taught her how to swim at two. They asked about competing at Stanford against Lillian and me and how she survived living with two Golden Bears since our colleges were ultimate rivals.

When it was my turn on the second day, the same female interviewer asked me what life was like living with fellow Olympians Talia Papani and Lillian Verkler. I tried to lay on the charm and wit, discussing how Lillian and I were always trying to pull pranks, and ever since the International Swimming League formed a year back, and the three of us signed up for the San Francisco–based team, the Cali Condors, Lillian and I got the ultimate revenge for Stanford stealing the Pac 12 and NCAA championships: All of Talia's swimming was done in the Berkeley pool.

Then she asked what inspired me to be an Olympian, and I reflected on those pivotal moments during Beijing and thought about Kennedy. Every moment, she'd been by my side.

My agent, Lucy Ehlmann, sat behind the camera as the interviewer segued into my personal life. She'd put me through media training in preparation for the biggest stage in swimming. All of Team USA had to know how to respond professionally, divert any questions looking for dirt, and suppress negative emotions. Plus a bunch of other rules, like how we had to sing the national anthem and put our hands over our hearts because people would criticize us, our patriotism, and our spot on the American team if we didn't do those things. The NBC interview was my first true test.

Part of it was learning how to answer personal questions, and I'd get more of those than my teammates because I was the only out swimmer on Team USA. She asked me what it was like being an out athlete in an industry that had a history of not being accepting. I told her I was very privileged. I had a supportive family, supportive friends, a supportive college. I discussed how my sport was more accepting than a lot of others. When the International Swimming League started last fall, they agreed that all men and women would be paid the same, and that set how progressive the sport was compared to others. I'd never felt pressured by my teammates to stay in the closet. But I recognized my privilege. Football still faced homophobia. Soccer still faced a large pay gap and fans shouting homophobic slurs at games. We didn't see that in swimming.

"Hungary's Amira Kőszegi is the number one swimmer in the world, favored to win all her races in Tokyo, and she's also out." The interviewer just had to remind me of the biggest thorn in my side, someone I'd done a good job compartmentalizing about until I landed in Tokyo. "How have you been preparing to go against the reigning Olympic gold medalist?"

I gulped. I could only imagine Talia and Lillian listening, and I could picture them hiding their laughter behind their tightly cupped hands. All the races Amira Kőszegi qualified for were mine: the 200, 400, and 800-meter free. Plus the two free relays. I'd only beaten her twice out of a handful of races. I also might or might not have slept with her in South Korea the summer before at the world champs. Oops. But with that small tidbit aside, the interviewer was right, she was one of the few out athletes in the swimming world. Sure, she'd never had a grandioso outing, but she'd dated a British actress, and in all her interviews, she'd made it no secret that she was into women.

I thought a lot of things about Amira. I envied her because she was so fast. I was jealous that she caused an upset in the free events in Rio and snatched them from the Americans. But then, I also thought she was a class act. I admired how she didn't care about what people thought of her or her sexuality, and I loved how she was a leader for the LGBTQ+ movement in Europe.

And I thought she was an amazing lay. But I couldn't tell the interviewer the last part. I told her everything else.

Lucy gave me an A in my first media training test.

❖

"Earth to Quinn," Talia called from the next lane.

We were on our second to last practice before leaving. We'd gone from swimming nine miles a day to two. David had us doing easy kick sets using the kickboards. We loved them because it meant we could talk during practice.

"She's been in a daze lately," Lillian called across the lanes.

"Must be the girl," Talia said.

I rolled my eyes. "I'm sorry I tuned out while you guys were discussing Tinder Fireman for a good ten minutes. You know my brain can only handle about two minutes of heterosexuality."

Except I wasn't sorry. Tuning them out while they discussed boys wasn't new. Plus, while they rambled about Lillian going on a second date with Tinder Fireman, I thought about all the things that could happen when Kennedy and I spent the day together. She wanted to sightsee the next day, and I agreed to take her around as long as we did it via Uber or electric scooter since I wasn't allowed to walk. A whole day with her sparked so many thoughts. If the perfect moment to kiss her sprang up, would I react? If I kissed her, would I be thinking about it too much during the Olympics? If the opportunity happened, would I be able to ignore it until after my races?

"You're thinking about your high school sweetheart and your date tomorrow," Talia said in a teasing tone.

"Maybe I am."

"You gonna kiss her?" Lillian asked.

Talia fought back. "Lil, you don't have an overthinker kiss an ex-girlfriend right before the Olympics."

"She clearly wants to kiss her. Make up for that other date two years ago."

They knew our whole story. I'd retold them while we analyzed the dinner. Lillian and Talia assumed their usual roles. Lillian was the risk taker; obvious, as evidenced by her ACL injury. She told me to pursue Kennedy. If the moment was there, I needed to act on it because I'd been thinking about her since high school, hadn't found a girl who came close to her, and was still upset with myself for not kissing her two years ago.

Talia, on the other hand, was the cautious one. She didn't get off on adrenaline, evidenced by her need to keep an eye on her friends' locations during dates. Like me, she liked everything planned to a T. No surprises. Had Plan B, C, D all the way to Z laid out for any possible scenario. Talia said that kissing a girl who'd been on my mind for the last five years would unwind all my mental training. I had to be freed from stress so it wouldn't ruin my races. She'd said I waited this long, waiting another few weeks to sort out my feelings wouldn't be a huge struggle. Plus, after Tokyo, I was scheduled to have a few interviews in New York City if I did well, so I could always try to see her—and kiss her—then. Talia had also said the lack of sex was skyrocketing my libido, and I had to think with my brain, not my vagina.

But that was easier said than done since I was ten months into my dry spell.

My brain told me Talia was right. Occasionally, I liked to do what I wasn't supposed to do. A small amount of thrill did intrigue me. Especially when it came to kissing a beautiful woman. I'd spent two years living a life constructed by coaches and my agent, with no room for error. All the obedience made it even more enticing to break the tiniest little rule.

"It's one kiss," Lillian said from my left. "That doesn't mean sex."

Talia kicked a little faster on my right, pulling ahead to flash Lillian a sharp side-eye. "When you haven't had sex in months, yes, kissing does lead to sex."

"Guys, I haven't even kissed her yet," I said, feeling torn between the angel and devil on each side of me.

"And you won't kiss her tomorrow," Talia demanded. "Say it out loud."

"Do I have to?"

"Yes. I know how your brain works. It wanders and overanalyzes. You want those individual golds, or you want to lose them to Amira Kőszegi again? Because you better believe she isn't dwelling on that British actress. She's dwelling on beating you."

"That's a low blow," I said, knowing I needed the tough love.

"It's the truth," Talia said. "Now, Lil, stop peer pressuring, or we'll make you go get groceries that we don't need."

Throughout college and Team USA swim camps, in order to fine-tune techniques that extended beyond the water, we'd met with many specialists: nutritionists, physical therapists, weight training coaches, and sports psychologists for mind training. Yes, that last one was a thing and played a huge role in our training. If our bodies were the accelerators, our minds were our brakes. We wouldn't drive a car if one of them wasn't working properly. Bad brakes allowed a person to drive out of control, and cars needed something to steady them. During college and training at my club team, we devoted forty-five-minute sessions once a week to learning how to set attainable goals, relaxation and concentration techniques, how to manage our self-talk, and how to use visualization. After my first session my freshman year at Berkeley, I'd wished I had those skills when I was younger. Maybe then I would have calmed my anxiety enough to make it to the London Olympics, medaled in my 400-free, or qualified for the 200-free in Rio.

My anxiety always seemed to get the best of me when it was go time. I couldn't afford to miss another opportunity to medal because of anxiety or distractions. The swimming season was four years long, and the end goal was the Olympics, our Super Bowl. Swimmers got one week every four years to win gold, the very thing that determined success in the sport—like championship rings, World Cup titles, and green Masters jackets. But unlike most sports, next season was four years away...or never again. If we were talented and lucky, we could squeeze three Olympics into our careers. By the time we hit thirty, we were senior citizens. Tokyo was my only time to shine as bright as I ever could. My next season would be Paris. I'd be twenty-seven years old and past my peak. I'd either still have it, or I'd sink. It wasn't worth the gamble.

Tokyo was my Olympics, and I couldn't let anything take away from it.

Since Rio, my mental techniques had become stronger. I saw results in the world championships and Pan Pacific Games. I'd won six golds in the world championships. My path to Tokyo was everything I'd hoped and worked so hard for. I needed to use those same mental techniques with Kennedy. I needed to visualize how the night would go just like I'd been trained to visualize my races. In mental training, visualization enhanced motivation, confidence, and self-efficacy. If I kept visualizing the same scenario, I was more likely to go through with it.

She'd come over, I'd think "holy crap, she's so beautiful," we would modestly flirt, have a good time, and then as the night ended, she'd wish me good luck. I'd tell her I was so glad that we'd been able to see each other, and how I wanted to see her when I came to New York for my post-game interviews. The night would end with a hug. *Just* a hug. As much as I wanted to kiss her, I trusted my gut. I knew how I would spiral if I kissed her. I wanted the Olympic gold more than I'd ever wanted anything.

I had to repeat this visualization over and over so my heart didn't take control. I'd spent four years crafting my mind and body to be like a tight Jenga set, and here came Kennedy Reed, threatening to pull out one of the bottom blocks.

The second I saw her standing outside my building the next morning, my chest fell to my stomach. She wore jean shorts that accentuated her sun-kissed sexy legs and a plum tank top that dipped to the top of her breasts. She clutched two iced coffees and flashed me that perfect smile when she extended a cup.

"You're still allowed to have coffee, right?" she asked.

I accepted it. "If I wasn't allowed, I would have given up swimming a long time ago."

"Good. I got you an iced with almond milk because protein, and I'm sure your diet wants that. And I asked for no sugar. Is it close to being right? I can buy you another one if you can't have it."

I pulled a sip through the straw and grinned because I thought it was cute how nervous she seemed about giving me anything bad, as if I'd break out in an allergic reaction. "Mmm, it's delicious, and the order is perfect. Thank you."

"I'm not sure how to feed an Olympian."

"We're basically spending the whole day together, so maybe after today, you'll know how."

With our coffees in hand and caffeine running through our veins, we Ubered around the city to take in all the sights San Francisco had to offer. We started at the sharp twists and turns of Lombard Street, then went across the bridge to the hills of Battery Spencer for the perfect view of the Golden Gate Bridge. I volunteered to be her photographer for the perfect Instagram picture. She wanted to visit Alcatraz, but unfortunately, without electric scooters, all the walking and standing would be too much. I offered to buy her lunch to make up for being a really bad tour guide.

We scootered down Fisherman's Wharf to look at the shops and sea lions and to get some lunch. Since I was used to eating about thirty-five hundred calories a day, by the time we sat down at the restaurant overlooking the bay, my stomach growled at me for not giving it its early afternoon snack.

She didn't hesitate to order a piña colada and had no remorse for rubbing it in my face as I sipped my lemon water.

"Thanks for this," she said as she dipped her straw in and out of the frozen drink. "Coming out with me. Enjoying another day together. I couldn't go back home after seeing you only once."

I focused on the goal: no distractions. I could already feel my stomach flying to my mouth. The goal was to enjoy the day without dwelling on any regrets that could taint my Olympic goals.

"Yeah, I feel the same way," I said.

"I can't believe we're here together. Thousands of miles from home. Sure, I'm here because of Jacob getting married, but he could have picked any city in the country to work in, could have had his wedding back home, which we're still surprised he didn't, but he says California is more scenic and beautiful than New York. It's crazy that it all sort of fell into place."

I knew exactly how she felt.

I attempted a joke. "Dinner date every two years?"

"Or you could stay an extra few days during Christmas, so we'd actually have time to see each other."

"The world champs are right before Christmas, and I planned on taking a month off. I feel like a break is overdue. So that might actually be a possibility. Dinner date then?"

"Yeah, maybe." She paused to drink. "Our dinner date seems like forever ago. I don't want to do something every two years. We need to see each other more."

I wanted to tell her that it sucked for me as much as it sucked for her. Maybe this sudden reunion was what we needed to realize how much we needed each other in our lives, and our texting would resume as frequently as it did the first year of college. I had no idea what our relationship would look like. It was one thing to talk a few times a week, knowing nothing was going to happen. We did a decent job keeping it platonic. We avoided our dating lives, probably because our wounds were still healing from our breakup. But this was different. At eighteen, we'd been on different trajectories. We'd wanted to experience college, meet all sorts of people, date those people, and get a better sense of what we wanted out of life. But at twenty-three, our trajectories had slowed. We had accumulated some life experience.

And if she was anything like me, the more I attempted to fit dating into my schedule, the more I got sick of it. I hated the blind dates from apps. I hated getting my hopes up on the first date only for there to be zero chemistry. I hated the games that came with it. I wanted to find someone who would be in it for the long haul, but out of the handful of girls I'd dated over the years, no one really stole all my thoughts. Not like Kennedy did.

"I agree," I said and played with the water droplets on the side of my glass. "We should make sure life doesn't get in the way again."

Her eyebrows furrowed as she studied me closely. "Can I ask you something?"

Her tone was low, and her gaze was pleading. I noticed how the dusting of pink on her cheeks enhanced the green of those eyes that seemed to search for something in me. What was she searching for? I didn't know. But I would tell her anything. She didn't have to look that hard.

"What?" I said.

"Our dinner two years ago. Did you…did you feel it?"

"Feel what?"

She broke her stare and let it fall to her half-drunk cocktail. She cleared her throat and resumed stabbing her straw. "Us? Did you feel us?"

Another stomach flip. Forget about swimming. My stomach had mastered the art of dives and flips so well in just a week that I was pretty sure that together, we could have medaled at the ten-meter platform dive.

This wasn't the time to play games. We had a few hours left before we separated. I had to assume that today was the only day to let her know how I felt, so maybe after the games, I could kiss her the way I'd been thinking about since we broke up.

"Anytime I'm with you, I feel us," I said.

The pause between us piled on all the things I wanted to ask her. Did she think about me during all those years? What did she feel now? Was her stomach flipping like mine had been consistently since she called me? Did she see a future with me? Did she want to kiss me? Did she want me to kiss her? What did she want to come out of this whole day we were spending with each other?

"You know, I kinda thought that night would end with—well—I don't know." The redness from her cheeks consumed her face and neck, and it seemed like she wrestled with whether she should continue. I was on the edge of my seat, hoping she would tell me at least one thought, just the smallest glimpse of what was going on in her head. "I…um…I thought that, you know, that maybe the night would end with us…I don't know…kissing or something."

Now it was my turn to feel the sun color my face. I couldn't even look her in the eye, I was that nervous. Instead, I focused on the lemon slice floating in my cup and used my straw to stab it. My nerves had to escape somehow, so I'd abuse some fruit. *When life gives you lemons during your conversation with your high school sweetheart, stab the lemon so you don't have to look her in the eye and let her know how easily you melt around her.*

"Honestly, I thought about it the whole night," I said through my arid throat.

"Really?"

I nodded. "I know there was a moment in the car when I dropped you off, and you waited a second before opening the door. I knew what you were waiting for."

"Then why didn't you do it?" Her tone seemed irritated, and I couldn't blame her. I was irritated too. "You think I would have said no?"

When I glanced up, her eyes were back on me, still searching. I shrugged. "I don't know," I muttered as the shame stacked in me again. "I was dumb and scared. We would have kissed and then what? I fly back here?"

That question still applied if we found ourselves encapsulated by another moment tonight.

Just then, the waitress brought our food. Kennedy had ordered a crab cake sandwich with a pile of fries, and my wedge salad with vinaigrette looked like the depression it was. I was so sick of salad; every salad for the rest of my life would send me into a depression. Only two more weeks until the forbidden foods diet started.

"Your meal looks really sad," she said, shoving a fry in her mouth.

"I know. I think I just started having an existential crisis."

She dangled a fry in my face. "Look at this? Doesn't it look delicious?"

"You're being mean, and you're going to hell."

"Of course I'm going to hell. Mike Pence has a special seat saved for both of us. Do you want to wash your salad down with this amazing piña colada? It has the perfect balance of coconut and rum. My stomach is so happy right now. Is yours?"

"No," I whined. "And I really hate you right now."

"No, you don't. Quite the opposite."

All the talk about dinner two years ago never came back up, even though during every shift in conversation, I hoped it would. But even if it never found its way back to the table, that didn't mean that we weren't reminded of all the history we had. After she allowed me to pay for lunch, since I begged for the check, we watched the sea lions barking as they soaked up the sun. She squeezed my arm when trying to get my attention about a sea lion being extra adorable.

We found electric scooters and zoomed down the remaining shops at Fisherman's Wharf. Sometimes she'd stop to window shop, and I would circle her on my scooter and ruin her view. Or when I stopped and viewed the window display, she touched my arm or brushed her hand on my back to get my attention.

Our last stop was at a high-end jewelry store on the last block. A ring in the window caught her eye as we weaved around the crowd. After looking for a few seconds, she parked the scooter and said she had to go in. I followed.

"Oh my God, this is the most beautiful ring I've ever seen," she said, looking longingly at the glass display.

I'd never really noticed rings before because I didn't wear jewelry. I spent the majority of my day in the pool, and wearing jewelry during a meet meant instant disqualification. But when I spotted the ring, I found myself entranced. She was right. It was stunning, platinum with a pear-shaped dark blue gemstone and round diamonds along the side of the band.

"Would you like to try it on?" the cashier asked. Her name tag said Carol, and she had dollar bills flashing in her eyes. Her smile was nice and wide.

"Yes, please!" Kennedy put it on her left ring finger and showed it off like someone who'd just got engaged. If it wasn't for the teasing during lunch or all the arm squeezing and back brushing, I would have studied her hand and pretended I was equally interested. But all of those things had happened, and it tangled my thoughts into feelings burning low and deep in my gut. I think what did it for me was the fact that she showed off her left finger, sending my mind into this trance that the ring symbolized our engagement. Without even thinking, I caved in to the unknown force billowing between us and held her hand to take a better look. She relaxed her fingers. They were so soft, and I couldn't help but let my thumb rub her hand as I pretended to study the ring when really, I was watching our hands together.

"It's really pretty," I said.

"Right?" Her voice was breathy and light. "I love blue topaz. It's my favorite gemstone."

The enthused smile loosened to a neutral gaze, as if she felt the same dull burn in the pit of her stomach. I attempted to flatten all the things I wanted to tell her, muting how much I loved the flecks of olive in her eyes, how great the ring looked on her, how great she always looked. I attempted to pull my stare away from her so it wouldn't linger too long, but as I gave in to the temptation to look at her, her stare flicked to mine and held. Our connection sizzled as the moment strung us back to that lost moment at lunch.

"It's a platinum band, London blue topaz, heirloom stone, three point eight carats," said Carol, snapping us out of the hypnosis. I dropped Kennedy's hand as if I was doing something wrong. Carol's grin grew with her eyes. "Are we shopping for a special occasion today?" Her eyebrows wiggled.

Kennedy and I exchanged an awkward look as we both fumbled "uhs" and "ums." When I finally found the words, I said, "Oh no. We're not together."

"Oh, you're not?" She appeared surprised. "Oh, I'm so sorry. I thought—"

I waved my hand in a flat line to shut down her next words. "Nope. We're just...um...just friends."

"I saw this ring and wanted to see it up close," Kennedy added, her voice low and soft. "Just out of curiosity, how much is it?"

"Forty-five hundred."

I muted the cough in my throat.

"Oh, wow," Kennedy said and slipped the ring off. Neither of us were worthy to hold a forty-five-hundred-dollar ring. "I guess I should start saving, then."

"We do offer a payment plan."

"That sounds very tempting. I'll have to think about it and come back after we shop around some more."

Nice girl code for "Hell no, I'm not buying that."

"Sure. We're open until eight. The ring will be waiting in case you change your mind."

I hope you don't hold your breath on that, Carol.

When we stepped out of the shop, Kennedy let out her laughter. "Holy crap, that's, like, the most expensive thing that I've ever had in my hand."

"You know you led Carol on," I said. "She's gonna be waiting for you now."

"Like hell I would spend four thousand dollars on a ring. That's two plane tickets to Australia."

"About nine round trips to France. Maybe even ten."

She threw her hands over her chest as if I'd mentioned her weakness. "Oh my God, you're right. Nope, not worth it. And that's saying a lot because it's my favorite gemstone. My mom bought me this blue topaz ring for my sixteenth birthday, and you want to know what happened? I lost it."

"You lost it?"

She nodded with her lips pressed thin, and I bellowed with laughter. "God, I cried so hard. I was dumb enough to wear it tubing down a river. My mom claimed that it was only seventy-five dollars, but to a sixteen-year-old, that's so much money. And the gift was so sweet, and I lost it."

"That's so awful that it's funny."

"It kind of is now. At the time, I was really upset. Ever since, I've really wanted another one."

"Maybe it's a good thing the price of this one scared you away. Could you imagine losing a four-thousand-dollar ring?"

She shuddered at the thought. "I'm getting anxiety just thinking about it."

After we hopped back on our scooters, Kennedy noticed a San Francisco souvenir shop. "Oh hey, let's go in there. I can get a cheaper souvenir."

Chapter Four

We Ubered back to my apartment and decided we needed a nap because if we didn't, we wouldn't be able to make it through the party in a few hours. It wasn't until we got there that I realized a nap was more complicated because we had to address who was sleeping where.

As I kicked off my Vans in my room, Kennedy plopped on my bed and spread out like a starfish, letting out a long, tired grunt.

"Okay, princess. Would you like some clothes to sleep in?" I said.

She lifted her head. "If you're willing to donate some for an hour, I'll gladly accept."

I fished out a shirt and sweatpants from my dresser and tossed them on her face. She held them in front of her nose for a second. The mood in the room shifted, just like at the jewelry store, just like at lunch, just like it always seemed to do.

"You smell the same," she said softly, then lowered my clothes.

I wondered if she smelled the same, and I wanted so badly to be reacquainted with the scent that permeated her clothes and skin. The memory of her smell almost reached my nose, but the lost five years prevented it from sweeping me up.

When she changed in the bathroom, I breathed out the heavy exhale I'd been holding. I really needed to lie down on the couch in the living room, practice some deep breathing to loosen the knots in my stomach, and rest.

When Kennedy came out, I was jealous of my clothes that got to touch her while my hands and lips couldn't. She set her folded clothes beside the bed and glanced at me as if waiting for me to guide her.

"You can take my bed," I said and gestured for her to lie down.

"No, you take it. I'll take the couch."

"No, seriously. You're my guest. I'm taking the couch."

"Or we can both lie on the bed."

There was that tense tandem silence again. A deafening silence. My chest plummeted, and I braced myself for rejecting her proposal. Could we really share a bed with our past stifling us? I didn't know if I could do it.

"I don't know—"

"Just a nap."

"Okay," I acquiesced, and she gave me the smallest grin. Following her, I lifted the covers to gesture her under. Both of us situated ourselves on the farthest ends of each side of the bed. A part of me was relieved she was thinking the same as me: Nothing could happen.

"I need, like, an hour to refresh, and then I'll be good," she said and set an alarm on her phone. "Good night. See you in an hour."

She flipped over, facing away from me. I lay there, stiff and straight like a pencil, hands stuck to my sides, watching the ceiling fan spin on the lowest setting. Her presence was intoxicating as much as it was suffocating. How could she jump into my bed, curl up in a fetal position, and snuggle her arm underneath the pillow while I could barely bend my elbows? Her soft hair pooled over the pillow, and I couldn't wait until I went to bed so I could smell the remnants of her hair lingering on the cover.

Even though she looked so innocent when she slept, that sweet face had the power to break my heart all over again.

And that was when it hit me, a very delayed reaction. Lying in bed with her wasn't part of the visualization. If I stuck to the script, I could easily get back on track.

I leapt out of bed and went downstairs, trying to gain control of my visualization. It was best to retreat to a safe space, a whole floor separating us.

In the kitchen, Talia assisted Lillian in putting groceries away. When they saw me, both flashed smug smirks, and the heat reached the tops of my ears.

"Where's the wife?" Lillian said as she collected the items that needed to go in the fridge.

"In my bed."

They gasped, Lillian as if to celebrate us rekindling our love, and Talia to tell me I was a dumbass.

"Cool it," I said before they could say anything. "She's taking a nap."

"And you were with her?" Talia asked.

"She insisted we share the bed, but I felt like I was trapped in cement. She was right there next to me."

"Quinn," Talia deadpanned. "Come on."

"I'm trying!"

"Not hard enough."

Talia collected the paper bags and shoved them under the kitchen sink. Lillian wasted no time opening a beer and leaning over the kitchen bar to collect more gossip, her eyebrows high and her stare begging for more.

"So? Did anything happen today?" she pried.

I grunted and took a seat at the bar. "If you're talking about many sexual-tension-filled moments, then yes. It was the whole day."

She squealed. "Ah! Tell me."

"For starters, she brought up our dinner two years ago and asked me if I felt it."

"Felt what?"

"I don't know. Feelings? Tension? And then she said she thought I was going to kiss her."

"Oh my God."

"Oh no," Talia said as she joined us.

"We went to this jewelry store, and she showed me this beautiful ring, and I found myself holding her hand."

"Intentionally?" Talia asked.

"Of course, intentionally. And now she's up there, and I have to deal with it for the rest of the night."

"Sounds so awful," Lillian said facetiously.

"It is when I know nothing can happen. I can't be thinking about this in Tokyo. Make sure nothing happens."

"Well, at least you *know* nothing can happen," Talia said. "There's still some sane in you."

"You know that the more we try to help, the more you run away," Lillian said.

"And you need to chase me. She's dangerous."

"Will you listen to us when we pull you away?" Talia asked sternly, like the overprotective mom she was. I nodded. "Good. Now help me make some hummus."

After I helped whip up some hummus and guac, I snuck past the sleeping Kennedy and hopped in the shower. My shower radio played, steam hung like San Francisco fog, and I realized as I stood there, the hot water hitting my back, that I'd shampooed my hair but hadn't rinsed it. I got lost in thoughts about the day, what had transpired over the past week, what had transpired over the past ten years. I had a few more hours with her, and I was already dreading letting her go. I'd built this moment up in my head after all this time—our paths finally crossing. I didn't want this day to end because that meant tomorrow would be filled with uncertainty and things left unsaid. Not the safe words I'd practiced in my visualization, like how great a time I'd had, how I wanted to see her in New York, how we should grab dinner during Christmas.

I wanted to tell her the truth. But I knew I couldn't. Not before Tokyo.

By the time I finally emerged—showered, changed, and ready to go—Kennedy was awake, out of my clothes, and back in hers. She stood in front of my full-length mirror, smoothing her shirt until she noticed me watching. Her eyes fell on my stomach below my black crop top.

"Oh wow," she muttered, and I couldn't tell if she meant to say that out loud, or if it slipped; it sounded like she had no control over her words. "I...uh...I really like your shirt. Damn, do you eat anything unhealthy?"

I patted my stomach. "Not anymore. My girlfriend's named Spinach."

"I can tell. Your abs are just...all right there."

"Yeah? Are they going to distract you? Should I put on a real shirt?"

The sunburn on her cheeks darkened. "No, uh, no. It's a good sight. You don't ever want to get rid of a good sight."

"Well, I mean, if you're gonna be looking there instead of my eyes, maybe I should put on another shirt. I don't want to feel like a piece of meat."

She gave me a side-eye as if she knew I was full of it. "Okay. I'm pretty sure you wore that shirt so I can look at you like a piece of meat."

She was half-right.

"Hey, it's just a top. It's not my fault you can't control your eyes. Now I'm going to whip myself up some dinner. Want some?"

"Yes, I'm starving."

"Just to warn you, it's going to be healthy as fuck. Strict diet, remember?"

"Lucky for you, I'm not a picky eater. I should probably eat more spinach."

Lillian and Talia were already dressed and sitting on the couch, catching up on episodes of *The Bachelorette*. Talia nursed a large lemon water and Lillian the same beer as before. When we came downstairs, their eyes followed us into the kitchen. I introduced all three, they exchanged pleasantries, and Lillian offered Kennedy any alcohol she wanted in the fridge.

I opened a bottle of IPA and gave it to her as she took a seat at the bar. She asked if I needed help, but I declined. She was my guest, and I wanted to impress her with the cooking skills I'd gained from my strict diet. Sitting on the barstool and nursing her beer, she went back and forth, watching *The Bachelorette* and adding her two cents about the episode to Lillian and Talia. She told me how I needed to watch *Bachelor in Paradise* for the two girls who fell in love. I had no idea that was a thing but added it to the mental list of all the shows I needed to catch up on. Major emphasis on anything gay. Everything else was inferior.

At one point, she snuck behind me. I almost dropped the spatula when her chin rested on my shoulder.

"It smells delicious," she said, and her words tickled my earlobe.

This was absolute torture. I wanted her chin to stay on my shoulder. I wanted any part of her to touch me. I wanted her arms to hug me and her chin to cozy into the nape of my neck. But luckily, the chin only touched my shoulder for a few seconds before she pulled away and grabbed two beers. One for Lillian. The other for herself.

I cleared my throat. "Dinner's almost ready," I said and forced a smile.

We ate at the kitchen table, and she marveled over the pan-seared salmon with a squeeze of lemon juice, salt, pepper, and olive oil, a monstrous spring mix salad topped with chickpeas, edamame, strawberries, green apples, and avocado, with a homemade red wine vinaigrette. Exactly what my dinner plan asked for in terms of the macros I needed to plug into my app. Kennedy told me I needed to audition for one of her favorite shows, *Home Kitchen Masters*, where amateur cooks competed in knockout eliminations for a cash prize. I said maybe, if they had an athlete edition, but I wasn't that amazing a cook. I just followed recipes. I was amazing at following directions. My whole life was basically recipes for success: swim sets, weightlifting sets, a meal schedule, recipes for the meal schedule. Give me directions, and I would always ace it. Tell me to improvise, I probably would stand there, looking doe-eyed.

Once I cleaned up, my roommates snatched her up on the couch, seeking embarrassing childhood stories about me. I sat next to her on the sectional, leaving a pretty generous space between us as she told them how I got the scar underneath my chin: flying off my bike. I told them how she bought me a teddy bear from the hospital because apparently, she already liked me at the age of eleven. That got her blushing. She told them about the one crush I had on a boy and how I wrote his name in her *Harry Potter* closet at her old house, a tiny space underneath her basement stairs. In exchange, Lillian told embarrassing college stories about me too.

"This one time, our swim team went to this bar," Lillian said, a smirk covering her face. "Quinn was talking to this hot girl all night. They were all over each other. And right as they reached the dorm, the girl hurled all over her foot."

Kennedy and Talia laughed. Lillian had a tipsy blush dusting her cheeks, so I knew the stories were going to continue to run freely. Hopefully, nothing too traumatizing.

"Needless to say, I didn't bring her to my room, but I did call her an Uber," I informed them. "You know, she texted me the next morning and thanked me for the ride? She asked me out after that."

"Seriously?" Kennedy said with a full belly laugh.

"Obviously, I said no. I still had her barf on my Vans. Had to throw them out. I was pissed."

"One time, this guy flirted with me," Kennedy said, "and he reached into his pocket to get his wallet to buy me a drink, and a condom fell out and landed on my foot."

"Both are equally disturbing," I said.

"Yeah. I took the drink, then ran."

Lillian put a hand over her heart. "Oh my gosh, I'm so proud. You don't need no man."

I held my lemon water up in agreement. "I second that."

"But," Kennedy announced and turned to Lillian again. "I have a story that trumps all the stories you have on her," she said, smiling behind her beer bottle.

I gave her a curious look, and she stared me down as if trying to tell me what she was thinking. Then it hit me. The most embarrassing moment of high school. Still the most mortifying moment of my life.

"No," I said, mortified. "Don't you dare say it. It's too soon."

Lillian bounced in her seat. "What? Oh my God, tell me. Spill the tea!"

My freak out burned my face and made Kennedy's laugh more vicious. "But it's funny now," she said.

"Is it? It still gives me nightmares," I said.

"You do realize you're not helping this sound less appealing," Talia said. "Please resume, Kennedy."

"It's as embarrassing for me as it is for you," Kennedy said. "No, he's not your brother."

"Oh my gosh," Lillian squealed. "Did your brother walk in on you guys?"

I buried my face in my hands as the room filled with laughter. Kennedy comforted me with a hand on my back. I pretended to be mortified a few moments longer just so she had an excuse to rub.

"Sounds like you have a lot of bad hook-up stories," Lillian said.

I was done acting and shot up to glare at her. Competitive side activated. Kennedy retrieved her hand. "World champs last year," I said. "I'd say that was pretty successful."

"Oh yeah," Talia said, scowling. "South Korea. When we roomed together, and you sexiled me."

"What? You sexiled her?" Kennedy said with eagerness in her tone.

"Can I tell her?" Lillian said.

"That depends on if she can handle a hook-up story," I replied.

Kennedy rolled her eyes. "Don't flatter yourself so much." She turned back to Lillian. "We're drinking buddies right now. Drinking buddies don't keep secrets from each other, especially when they have to do with Quinn."

I sipped my water and leaned back, fulling taking in Kennedy trying to pry info out of Lillian. If she didn't care about my sex life, would she have yanked for information from my roommate? No, she wouldn't have.

"Quinn slept with her archrival last year at the world champs," Lillian said. "It happened in their hotel room. Poor Talia got booted."

"Amira Kőszegi is drop dead gorgeous," Talia said, her eyes zoning out as if picturing the beauty. Amira had that effect even on straight women. "If she came on to me, I would say, fuck us hating her for being so good, let's go to bed."

"Wow, Talia. Ruby Rose and Amira Kőszegi are the two girls to convert you?" I asked.

"I mean, everyone is a little gay. I've appreciated beautiful women in the past."

I lowered my water. This was new information. "Have you?"

"Once or twice. I follow Amira Kőszegi on Instagram. She posts really sexy modeling pictures. She's a huge model in Hungary, you know."

"Oh, I'm well aware."

I wanted to tell them she was even more gorgeous when she was below you, but I fought the urge to say it. For Kennedy's sake.

"I still can't believe you slept with your competition," Lillian said, shaking her head. "I'm not sure if I should be impressed or feel betrayed that you slept with the enemy."

"Probably a little bit of both," Kennedy said quietly, but I could read the dulled smile on her face, almost as if she forced herself to give a half grin to show the story didn't bother her.

Speaking of Amira, the conversation segued into Lillian and Talia telling me that I had to be the one to prevent her from upsetting Team USA for the second time. Kennedy drank her beer in silence, and I felt bad for bragging about my hookup in front of her. I didn't want the weirdness to linger for the rest of the night. We only had a few hours left before it ended. As much as it killed me to know that we were in the middle of walking cautiously around our feelings, it was a little comforting to know that I wasn't the only one feeling this way.

Hoping to get us back to the mood from before my Amira story, I offered to get her another drink.

The weight of the story hung in the air until guests started arriving, mostly college swim friends who'd stayed in the city after graduation. After introducing Kennedy to everyone who came through the door, she held her own for a little bit while I mingled, but then she migrated back to Talia and me when the two of us were discussing Olympic ring tattoos.

"Promise me you'll let me know when you're getting it," Talia said. "Because I want to come with. I think this is very overdue."

"I don't think I deserved the tattoo when I only medaled in the relay."

"I think you're selling yourself short. You swam the 400-free."

"And took fourth."

"You're getting a tattoo?" Kennedy said from behind me, squeezing into the conversation.

"After the Olympics," I said. "It's basically a badge of honor. All the swimmers have one."

"Except for this one," Talia said and hooked a thumb at me, "who refused to get one after Rio because she didn't have her own events."

Kennedy rolled her eyes. "Sounds like Quinn."

"Never giving herself enough credit?"

"Exactly! Talia, where's your tattoo?"

She rolled up her shirt sleeve on her right arm to show the rings on her bicep. Lillian got hers on her left shoulder blade. Both of them got their rings after Rio, where they won their first gold medals.

"Where are you going to get this tattoo?" Kennedy asked.

"I have no idea. Any suggestions?"

"Hmm." She tapped her bottle against her lips. She looked at my face, then my neck, then my arms, then spent quite a bit of time on my stomach. She practically stripped my clothes off, and during the long look, heat crawled up my spine and the back of my neck. "Your hips," she said. "Right there." With her pointer and middle finger, she drew a circle on my bare hip, and the touch of her most important fingers on my sensitive waistline spread a dull throb to my center. She could rub her fingers in circles there as long as she wanted.

"Is that a good spot for a tattoo?" I asked. She bit her lip and nodded. "All right. I'll think about it."

The party stopped for a moment when Lillian called for everyone's attention for a toast. Everyone else had a shot in hand while Talia and I clasped glasses of water. While Lillian spoke, the gravity of Kennedy standing on the other side of the living room kept pulling my gaze. No matter how hard I tried fighting it, my stare kept landing on her. The words Lillian spilled from her heart didn't stand a chance with Kennedy in the same room. We kept stealing glimpses, and the further into the speech Lillian got, the more we stopped trying to be secretive.

"To Quinn and Talia," Lillian said as she raised her shot. "May you bring home ten medals, or you're dead to all of us. Cheers."

The group tossed back their drinks, and our eye contact broke. Once we downed our shots, Talia grabbed my wrist and Lillian's and tugged us into the nearest corner.

"Okay, spill," she said with a light punch to my arm.

My eyebrows folded. "About what?"

"Kennedy. You've been eye fucking each other all night."

"No, we haven't," I said with an eye roll.

"Oh my God, I felt like the third wheel in your eye fuck during the toast."

Lillian laughed. "More than the sexiling in South Korea?"

"About the same. She's totally eye fucking you right now, for the record," Talia said and nodded to the back of the apartment.

Kennedy was talking to two girls who'd lived on our dorm floor freshman year, but her eyes were on me and flittered back to the two girls when she noticed me watching.

"We have chemistry—"

"You have more than just chemistry," Talia said.

"I've been with you most of the night, and I give one toast, and you two are eye fucking," Lillian said.

"She eye fucked me."

"You know, this apartment has been stuffy with your sexual tension all day. I need to breathe, and I bet you do too."

"Nothing can happen, guys. It's already messing with me."

"Okay, then as your guardians, let's go where you can't see her and dance." Talia grabbed both of our hands and twirled us around.

She was right. Dancing was a good distraction. We stayed in the corner of the kitchen dancing, with the occasional friend passing by to grab more alcohol. But a few songs later, "Drunk in Love" by Beyoncé came on, and I searched for Kennedy, thinking back to when I deemed "XO" our song, and anytime Beyoncé came up on my music, I thought of her.

Turns out it did the same thing to her. I found her maneuvering through the crowd with a crooked grin. She awkwardly danced over to me, as if trying to be funny, and when she reached me, she held out her hand.

I felt trapped between Talia, Lillian, and Kennedy's extended hand.

"It's our girl," she said over the music. "So now you have to dance with me."

"Oh, is that a rule? Must dance with Kennedy when Beyoncé plays?"

"There are a lot of rules to Beyoncé songs," she said, and the weight of the memory found its way to us. I told her back when we dated that the rule when listening to "XO" was that she had to kiss me every time Beyoncé demanded it.

"Dance with me?" she asked.

Dancing was innocent, right? Especially when it was next to Lillian and Talia, who knew nothing could happen. Their presence would hold me accountable. I accepted her extended hand and spun her around.

It could have been the tequila shot for her, maybe it was Lillian's comments for me, but as the song progressed, Kennedy's dancing grew freer. Midway through the song, she was inches in front of me. Her hand slipped behind my back and pulled me into her. Before I knew it, the two of us were grinding in the middle of my living room. Her butt moved against the part of me that burned with desperation and controlled my body as if my mind had decided to take a quick break because it'd been working overtime the past couple weeks.

She twisted so we could face each other again, hips still glued together, swaying loosely. I positioned my hands on her waist as I forgot all responsibility. I couldn't have my hands on her hips without sliding them up her shirt to graze her skin. That was all I'd allow myself to do to dilute the desire to touch her. I would only allow my fingertips, almost as if it were an accident.

At my touch, she extended her hand over my neck and pulled my face into the side of hers. Our sweaty cheeks stuck together as the song changed. The new song didn't help end the grinding. If anything, it was even stronger than the Jose Cuervo she'd consumed, and I realized my brain was going to remain on vacation for as long as she was attached to me. The sensations beneath my underwear and the burning in my gut triggered me to move my hands up her sides and reacquaint my palms with the soft skin of her back. She leaned in and brushed her lips against my ear. Her teeth clasped my earlobe, sending sharp shocks down my arms.

"Take me to your room," she whispered and followed it with another nibble.

A nibble to the ear sent my body into a storm of fervor. With barely any common sense left, I used the last remaining bit to pull away to see if I heard her correctly. She looked at me with purpose, and her eyebrows were set and determined, her stare direct and hungry.

"What?"

"Take me to your room," she ordered.

My mind drained. No thoughts. No words. No worries. No conscience. No ability to determine rights and wrongs. It was an empty space looking for a pilot to lead it, and that pilot was Kennedy.

"Okay."

I barely registered Lillian and Talia's wide eyes, both of them tightening their jaws as if telepathically telling me not to do it. But when it happened, the only thing that clicked was that they were in front of me, not that they were trying to stop it. My brain wasn't able to function when my libido was in control.

Kennedy had me completely under her spell. I grabbed her hand and pulled her around the people, up the stairs, and into my room. The second I closed the door and pushed in the lock, she tossed me on the bed and forced her thigh in between mine. She applied pressure at the right spot for me to catch a moan in my throat. My heart hammered with adrenaline, knowing that her hovering over me was this dangerous and exciting thing that shook up a life so dulled with mundane schedules. Everything was a schedule. Everything was a roadmap to something. My day-to-day for the last four years had been literally written out, factoring in no time for adventure, spontaneity, or risks.

I was desperate for that jolt to awaken me, so I could be reminded what it was to finally live, to have free will, the power to choose something that hadn't been chosen for me.

I hooked my fingers through her belt loop and yanked her down until her lips landed on me. They were so hungry; there was no time for the acquainting peck. My mouth fell open and welcomed the passion and urgency of her kiss. She sucked in my bottom lip and pulled a moan from me, and I dug my fingers into her back to hold her in place. She tasted like fresh tequila, and that made me suck on her lips. Somehow, I always remembered the drinks she tasted like. Root beer, chocolate malts, and now tequila. Jose Cuervo was by far my favorite Kennedy taste. Maybe because I knew it was dangerous, just like her kiss.

I skimmed up the warm skin of her back until I reached her bra, and I held her close so the pressure of her thigh pressing between my legs wouldn't leave. Her shirt bunched around her stomach, and because of the beauty that was my crop top, our bare midriffs stuck to each other, only intensifying our kiss. While she held herself up with one hand, the other ran over my stomach, feeling each ab before grazing my sides and down to the top of my skinny jeans. My pulse twitched faster, goose bumps broke out on my arms, and my chest tightened in a buzzing fervor. When was the last time my whole body experienced these kinds of sensations? I hadn't been touched by a girl in months, and even then, they weren't able to make every sense as heightened as if I'd ingested some magical drug.

Our passion had been a sleeping bear. Once it awoke, it came in the form of hands wandering. I took in each curve and detail of her skin, relishing in the faint noises fleeing from her, the way her tongue explored mine, feeling my lips reddening and swelling from the immense desire I had. As the kiss progressed, I started remembering the way her lips used to dance. She still kissed the same, ravenous and needy but gentle and reverent, and it was the latter that sent me soaring, feeling the indelible emotions she still seemed to have, but with a few acquired techniques, like nibbling on my bottom lip and sucking on my tongue, which created another wave of warmth running through me. And the way she held my cheek, and her thumb twitched in a soft graze on my neck, then stopped, almost as if she became conscious of the intimacy and thought it might be too much. But I wanted that intimacy as much as I wanted her passionate aggression. I wanted all of it with her.

Her hips started to undulate, and her movements lit me up in an amazing intoxicating feeling. Just when I thought I couldn't feel enough, she latched on to the button of my pants. She flung it open, pulling away from my mouth and watching me as she slowly unzipped. Staring at me as if asking permission, she grazed underneath my underwear, skimmed the top of my center. Her touch elicited a murmur that I tried to hold back, but that steady eye contact and the determination in her stare made it so hard. She slipped her fingers inside me with ease, and I buried my head in the pillow. This time, I wasn't able to mute my noises. An unbridled cry bellowed out that only encouraged her to move in insistent strokes.

Having the touch of another person fogged any sort of clarity I'd been focusing on the past few days. The feelings were so overwhelming. In my heart. On my center. The faster she moved inside me, the more securely I held my comforter, twisting the fabric with each jolt she sent through me.

"Holy fuck," I said, completely defeated.

I was paralyzed, in complete darkness, with Kennedy firing tingling warmth all through my body while she kissed my neck and collarbone. The more I relaxed, the faster and more calculated her technique became. I dug my fingernails into her back, and her breathing against my ear grew heavier and ragged. The way I felt when she touched me was different than the girls I'd hooked up with. There was something more than the sexual pleasure. I didn't feel a simmer in my gut when another girl looked at me, or a buzz on my lips when they kissed me, this gravitational pull when our eyes met, or the burning in the pit of my stomach from the immense desire. The only girl who made me feel like that was Kennedy.

Who was drunk.

Who just broke up with her girlfriend.

Who was going to disappear to the East Coast in a few hours.

Shit, what the hell were we doing?

This wasn't right at all. This wasn't part of the visualization.

"Kennedy," I said, barely able to squeak out her name from the pleasure so close to claiming me. She continued faster, and I had to collect the gasp that danced on the tip of my tongue which would only encourage her to continue.

I grabbed her wrist and held it steady. Her smile blended into the darkness.

"Ken, you're drunk."

"Yeah, but I'm coherent." Her tone still had hope that she could finish me, and I didn't doubt that she could in sixty seconds or less.

"I don't want to do it. Not like this."

ALL THE PATHS TO YOU

"What do you mean?"

"You're drunk. I'm sober. That's not how I want this to happen." I should have saved all this talk until she was out of me, but when my mind went on vacation, it later scurried back to its post chaotically to make up for its incompetence. Kennedy retrieved her hand and planted herself on the edge of my bed, her back to me, staring out the window at the streetlamp.

"Ken," I said, feeling guilty for ruining the moment, for ruining the whole day. But as hard as it was feeling the weight of ten years of romantic history collapse on top of me, I knew it was the right thing to do. For her and for myself.

"Are we really something that just spontaneously happens on your trip out here?" I asked softly. I wasn't mad, and I didn't want her to think so. I was trying to help her see the error of what we'd allowed to happen. "Am I really a casual hookup? A drunken rebound?"

There was a heavy pause. Her head tilted to the ground for a moment. "It's not a casual hookup," she muttered, her tone defensive yet one hundred percent sure.

"Then what the hell is this?"

She paused for a moment and ran her hands down her face as if what happened finally hit her. "I don't know, Quinn."

"I don't want to be your rebound."

She shot me a glare that pierced the darkness. "You really think you're some rebound?"

I shrugged. At that moment, yes, I did. "What's the plan? We fuck, and you go back to New York, and I go to the Olympics, and that's that?"

"No!"

Through the locked door, the bass of the Bluetooth still thumped against the walls over the chattering of multiple conversations. One of them no doubt Lillian and Talia wondering what the hell was going on in my room. But the two of us sat on the edge of the bed, taming our beating hearts, and for me, the arousal that still ignited my center. The air between us had never felt thicker. I had no idea how to come back around to where we'd been most of the day, to end the night on the positive note we wanted. I'd rather dance around the giant crater that was our relationship than be stranded at the bottom of the crater like we were right now.

She jumped off the bed and faced the door. "I need to get some air."

I hopped off the bed, buttoned my jeans, and fixed my hair, making sure that when we walked downstairs, I drew less attention. "Okay, I'll go with you."

She kept a steady sprint to the front door, and I trailed her until we reached the stoop. The warm night air greeted us when we took up spots on the cement steps. We sat in silence at first, listening to the car horns and sirens in the distance. The bay breeze ruffled my hair, and it helped calm my short, ragged breaths.

"Say something," I said, hearing the desperation in my voice, trying to salvage the little grip we still had. "Anything."

She shook her head and dropped it to her fingers tapping against her bouncing knee. "I can't believe you think I'm using you as a rebound."

"Kennedy, how can you not see that this is a horrible time? You're drunk, and I'm not going to sleep with you for the first time in years while you're drunk, and I'm stone-cold sober—"

"I'm really not that drunk."

She was. It colored her cheeks, blurred her eyes, strung her words slightly together. I'd watched her consume beer and tequila. But I wasn't going to use the time to argue with her about that. There were other factors at play.

"I'm leaving tomorrow," I said quietly and tried to remain as calm as possible despite her defensive tone that was only because she was embarrassed and drunk. "I'm not going to sleep with you for the hell of it and then wonder when the hell I'm going to see you next."

"Christmas. We said Christmas," she said, wiping her face.

"We said Christmas before this happened. There's too much between us for this to be some random hookup."

She played with her fingers, refusing to look me in the eye. The longer I waited for her to look at me, the bigger the ball in my throat grew. I wanted to tell her that I cared about her too much to meaninglessly fuck her. Without even kissing her and spending the whole day with her, I knew that I'd be going to Tokyo with so much weight on my mind, and the last thing I needed was mental drag. I wanted to tell her that I compared all the girls to her, still after all this time. I wanted her to know how open and vulnerable I felt around her, especially today. I wanted to tell her how terrified I was about losing her.

But admitting anything more would add to the emotional sludge.

"You should be at your going away party," she muttered and reached for her phone tucked in her purse. "I should go. I'll call Jacob and see if he or Ava can come pick me up. Or I'll call an Uber."

"Is that what you really want?"

She exhaled. "No. But it's what I need."

I needed to know what all of this meant. I needed to know what to expect when I got back. Where did we stand?

She opened her Uber app, and I sat there with a stuttering pulse as she ordered one. I wanted to fight for her to stay so we could resolve this, but I felt as lost as she did. I had no idea where to even begin with all the hurdles in our way.

My throat tightened around my words. I couldn't muster up anything but defeat. "Um, okay," I said. "Can I at least sit here with you until it comes?"

She looked at me with an expression so wounded that I wondered how I was supposed to heal after seeing it. She nodded, then quickly looked back at the ground. I wasn't sure how I was going to hold in my sobs until the Uber came and whisked her away.

When it arrived, she gave me a tight hug and buried her face in my neck. I inhaled the smell of her hair and shampoo and imagined I was breathing her in, so the memory could stay longer, so I could keep a part of her after I let her go.

Again.

Why am I always letting her go?

As I pulled away, she tugged me back, not finished with the hug. "Good luck in Tokyo," she said softly in my ear. "I know you're going to do great. I'll be watching. And remember that I'm so proud of you. No matter what happens, I'll always be proud of you."

The reminder of the Olympics should have flicked a spark of excitement in me like it'd been doing for the past few weeks, but it didn't. It didn't fill me with anything except more regret that I was leaving her with things unanswered, unsaid, and unresolved.

All I could do was nod as she pulled away to get one last look. She gave me a thin smile that didn't reach her eyes. My throat balled with emotions as she closed the door. Everything I'd been holding in started leaking out.

I held up my hand to give her one last wave, and she did the same before the Uber started down the street. I didn't go back inside until the warm July air relaxed all my muscles, and I fully cried all my emotions into my palms.

I beelined to my room and locked the door. That was when I found the pile of clothes I'd lent her for her nap folded neatly on my nightstand. A part of her still lingered. Hovering over the clothes, I debated whether I should smell them or toss them in the laundry where the dirty scent of my sweat from dryland would taint the fabric. But I couldn't bring myself to do it. I held my blue Berkeley shirt, brought it up to my nose, and searched for the answer to my question. I wanted to remember. I wanted to relive those days when we were us. I closed my eyes and inhaled a long breath that filled me up with the smell of her. My heart dropped.

She still smelled the same.

CHAPTER FIVE

The Olympics was a magnifying glass. Everything, even the smallest things, was bigger than life. Every triumph—like winning a circular slab of gold pinned to a ribbon—was considered the Holy Grail. Every misstep—like taking fourth in an event or losing by a millisecond—was magnified as a complete failure. The number of medals determined your worth and your prowess. Medals and success were currency in the Olympic Village. The games created two weeks of a fantasy land, and the athletes were at the heart of it all.

Team USA had been in Tokyo for a week, squeezing in last-minute taper sessions, mental training, team exercises, and adjusting to the huge time difference. Seventeen hours for Talia, me, and the other West Coasters. Thirteen hours for American prime time on the East Coast.

I livestreamed our walk into the stadium, hidden in the sea of over five hundred athletes that comprised Team USA, wearing designer navy blazers, red and white striped long-sleeved shirts, white slacks, and boat shoes. Hundreds of thousands of people were packed into the stands. All the athletes wore their country's opening ceremony uniform. Right in the middle of the USA parade, we followed the billowing flag and spent the remaining hour watching dancing, music, and storytelling, followed by the lighting of the torch that signaled the start of the two-week fantasy. The ceremonies magnified our senses, our adrenaline, our excitement, and our nerves.

When I got back to the apartment I shared with Talia, we tore off our opening ceremony uniforms, put on cheap practice suits, and started the shave down. After three weeks, I finally got to cover my body in shaving cream. My armpits, my legs, and yes, even my arms. The men shaved everything too, and I imagined all of the hair congealing in the Tokyo pipes and was grateful not to be a plumber. After the shave, I felt so light. I had an extra spring in my step from having silky smooth limbs, pent-up energy from tapering, and adrenaline, and I was ready to fly through the water.

As I plopped on my twin bed, not being able to control marveling at the smoothness of my legs, I checked my phone, and a wave of text messages from friends and family lit up the screen, probably in response to my Instagram. But the first person I went to was Kennedy. We hadn't spoken in the eight days since my party. Honestly, it didn't seem as long since the second I'd landed, I'd been so busy doing last-minute training and preparations that by the time all of that was over, everyone had stormed back to our apartments, mingled with athletes from other countries, kind of like the first week of college, and passed out. But now that her name appeared on my phone, I felt eight days of unresolved issues suffuse the room.

Saw your Instagram story. Can't wait to try to spot you when they air it tomorrow night. Good luck on your relay heat tomorrow. I'll be watching.

She ended the text with a smiley face.

My heart soared. She was thinking about me.

I responded, *Thank you! It was definitely an experience. Still can't get over it. We're antsy right now and just want to get in the pool.*

Once my text was delivered, the typing bubble appeared. I sank in my bed, feeling a smile, and thanking God Talia was finishing her shave, or she would have been lecturing me. She'd said back home wasn't anything I needed to focus on. It was another world. The only things I should allow myself to think about were my races and hook-up leads for after the events. During our first week, Talia had met two Italian rowers. I'd met a Peruvian surfer who flirted with me for a good twenty minutes, and what was so exotic about her was that surfing had made its debut at the games. Plus, Team Peru was a floor below us, so the convenience was pretty spectacular.

But the surfer seemed less appealing when I had Kennedy texting me.

She said, *I bet. I can't wait to start watching. Time zones are weird. I can't believe you're thirteen hours ahead. This is putting my patience to the test. I have to avoid spoilers online. Or should I avoid the time delay? I have no idea.*

I support any decision you make. Might be more fun if you watch it on prime time. Then you can see my athlete bio.

I added a winky face.

I definitely want to see your athlete bio. Your goggles and cap kind of ruin the beautiful face you have going on.

Yup, her text had me blushing in time for Talia to flick off the bathroom lights. "Oh my God, I feel like a dolphin...why are you smiling?" She stopped in the bathroom entrance and scowled at me.

I lowered my phone and slipped it under the covers. She watched, but I didn't care. Kennedy had called me beautiful and said she couldn't wait to watch me, and no one was going to take that moment away from me. Not even Talia and the detailed scowl she'd nailed.

"Tell me more about feeling like a dolphin," I said in my most convincing tone.

She directed her pointer finger at me. "No. I will throw your phone in the pool. Just joking. The diving well. I'll throw it in the diving well, so I can watch you struggle to swim down sixteen feet, and the probability of the water pressure breaking it will be very high."

"Wow. That's pretty evil."

"It's calculated. We have a relay together, and I want you to win a fucking individual gold."

"I want that too."

"Then stop texting her, or your phone will meet the bottom of the diving well."

When Talia went to the bathroom right before bed, I snuck in the blushing smiley emoji and called it a night.

❖

On Sunday morning, I woke up with my stomach in knots. It was the second day of the games and the day of my first final at the morning session and my 400-free heat at the night session. The top eight swimmers in the 400-free would advance to the finals.

On our walk to the natatorium, we all blasted pump-up music in our headphones. I set mine to noise canceling to block out everything that could puncture the zone. I kept them on as I struggled into my tech suit, which felt like squeezing into jeans I'd not worn since I was fourteen. It took around ten to fifteen minutes. The purpose of tech suits was to maintain optimal body position and make us swim faster by assisting our muscles. The first time I put one on, I was fourteen, at my first national meet, and it took forty minutes. I started crying around the twenty-minute mark, and the veteran national team girls swarmed me, comforted me, and told me as they helped me that it was normal to struggle. I qualified for the London Olympic trials right after that. In high school, since we weren't allowed to wear tech suits for dual meets, my coach made us wear suits four sizes smaller than our practice suits, making them tight enough to do almost the same job.

The locker room was silent. The smell of chlorine was strong. I looked at myself in the mirror, at Team USA's swimsuit hugging me so tightly that my muscles popped around the edges, making it look extra awkward. But it didn't matter how I looked. My body and mind felt amazing. I wore the colors of my country proudly. The navy-blue suit had red stripes crawling up from the front of my waist to my shoulders, with white stars on the side.

Wearing it was the greatest honor of my life.

I was ready to win Olympic gold.

As I pulled myself out of the pool after warm-ups, I saw her.

The goddess of the chlorine sea. My number one rival whom I would have to swim against in every race. The person who could snatch gold by as little as one hundredth of a second. She was the reason I was seeded second in my individual events. She was the best swimmer in the world.

Amira Kőszegi.

Her nickname was "A sellő," which translated to "the Mermaid" in Hungarian. She had a large following on social media because she looked like an actual goddess, was one of the most famous female athletes in Hungary, and was a staunch LGBTQ+ advocate. She'd graced the cover of *Sports Illustrated*—the swimsuit edition after Rio—and *Maxim*—ranked in the top fifty for the past four years—and even had a modeling contract with a high-end European designer.

Her life outside of the pool was everything I hoped I could be to the queer community. I planned on sneaking in some pride flags and my pride Speedo shirt while on my walk to the natatorium one day, hoping the press would capture it and throw it up on the internet. Amira inspired me that way and was a role model for all aspiring athletes still in the closet or athletes who had just come out.

But now, I tossed her admirable advocacy aside. She was my competition. My nemesis. And I hated so much that I had no idea how to feel about her. Intimidated? Threatened? Turned on? Maybe all of the above?

All six feet of her in her dark red competition suit headed straight toward me; her curly chestnut hair was tossed in a bun and dripping water down the column of her neck, and her black cap and goggles were tucked into the shoulder straps of her suit. I could tell by her smirk and confident saunter that the memories of our sleepover played behind her sapphire eyes.

I gulped.

"Oh, hey there, Yankee," she said, bumping her butt into mine. Her accent was thick but so sexy.

She had an unfair height advantage, which meant she didn't have to take as many strokes as I did. My five-nine self looked like a small child in the swimming world, so I had to work a bit harder to steal the medal, but man, her deep blue eyes and wavy brown hair did things to me. And everyone else in Europe.

"Amira, hey," I said, way too nervously right before we were about to race. My voice needed to be stern and confident. But God, did she make competitive swimwear sexy. And it was the least sexy thing in the whole world.

"I just wanted to say hi and good luck in this relay," she said. "Try not to stare too much at my butt when it's a body length in front of you, all right? The whole world will be watching you drool."

My mouth parted. Here I thought she was going to act as if last summer didn't happen. Except for a few hi's during the first final of the International Swimming League in November, we hadn't talked. Not once did we address our hookup.

Until forty-five minutes before we fought over Olympic gold.

I swear to God, as she walked to catch up to her teammates, she purposely pulled the tie out of her messy bun and shook her hair so it fell past her shoulders.

The Mermaid played dirty, and two could play that game.

Forty-five minutes later, the eight relay teams were assigned to their lanes. We claimed lane five, which was for the number one seed; Australia claimed lane four, for the number two seed; and Hungary claimed lane six, the number three seed.

Four short blows of the whistle echoed on the pool deck, a signal to the fifteen thousand people packed into the sold-out natatorium that they needed to quiet so the race could start. And then a drawn-out whistle prompted the starters to take the blocks. Talia was our lead, followed by Chelsea, Sydney, and me as the anchor.

Once the beep went off and all eight women dove into the water, my mind went from being on Earth to a galaxy far away. Nothing else existed except lane five. No other lanes. Not my parents and brother watching in the stands. No city outside and definitely no girl watching in Brooklyn. It was only lane five and my three teammates. I'd gotten pretty good at mental training. I think my psychology degree helped, and it was half the reason why I wanted to major in it, to understand how the brain worked and how to use techniques to minimize anxiety and distractions because they were always looming over Olympians' heads.

A 100-meter swim never went as fast as this one. Before I knew it, Talia was patting me on the shoulders for good luck, and Sydney was doing her flip turn fifty meters away.

When Sydney was halfway to me, I stepped on the block. My heart pounded. My body was ready to explode from all the pent-up adrenaline. I took one last deep breath, exhaled through my mouth, and then sprang into the water when Sydney touched the wall.

Diving into the cool water and releasing all that adrenaline I'd saved up for weeks was the best feeling in the world. With zero hair on my body, I really did feel like a dolphin zipping through the water. I wanted to send Amira a message that just because she dominated Rio and was favored to win gold here, Tokyo wasn't going to kiss the ground she walked on. I wanted to be a part of the relay that brought home the first gold medal for Team USA swimming. For that to happen, I needed to deplete all my energy and oxygen so my three teammates would have to hoist me out of the pool. That's how people won gold. The race had to pump all the oxygen out of us.

When I smashed my hand against the timer, the wave from my

race thrashed me into the wall. I gasped in the biggest inhale of my life and spun to the scoreboard on the other end of the pool. I couldn't take my eyes off the number one in front of lane five. My team jumped ecstatically behind the block, and my heart showed no signs of slowing. American flags danced throughout the natatorium as the crowd roared. Our relay had beaten the American, Olympic, and world record by a second. I almost sank to the bottom of the eight-foot pool when I tried wrapping my head around the knowledge. As I tried catching my breath and processing the three records we'd barely beaten, I drifted over to the lane line we shared with the Hungarian team. Amira met me with a handshake and a one-arm hug.

"Congratulations, Yankee," she said, as out of breath as I was. I could hear the disappointment in her tone, but I wasn't even sorry. All that panting was because she was trying to catch me. I was glad I'd given her a workout.

"You too." I leaned in close. "Looks like your butt doesn't distract me anymore."

Then I pulled myself out of the pool. Two could definitely play this game.

After the medal ceremony, I spent the rest of the afternoon resting, which helped me advance to the finals in my 400-meter free. After the night session, Team USA celebrated the medals we'd won on our apartment floor with loud music, the medals around our necks, and bottles of water that we pretended were champagne.

Right when I was about to change the song blasting through the Bluetooth speaker, I noticed Kennedy had sent a text twenty minutes before. I smiled wider than I had all night.

OMG. YOU WON A GOLD MEDAL AND GOT ALL THESE NEW RECORDS! THIS IS THE COOLEST THING EVER! I'm SO incredibly proud of you.

My smile was already big. Her text made it reach capacity. I quickly snapped a selfie of the medal around my neck and sent it to her.

It's crazy! We're celebrating right now. Also, you read the spoilers.

She responded. *I couldn't help it. I've been thinking about you all day, and I had to know. I'll try to avoid them so I can be surprised for your 400 final.*

Or maybe you should watch it live. You're my good luck charm, remember? Help me win my first individual gold.

All right, maybe I will.

❖

The nerves in my stomach felt like a spinning whirlpool when I woke up on Monday, the day of my first individual race. My stomach pain and adrenaline were ready to bust through my skin, a feeling I loved because once I hit the water, it turned into energy like a chemical reaction.

I stood behind lane four with Amira in lane five, and stripped off my warm-ups and jiggled my legs and arms. I took in the sights to make sure I remembered this moment for the rest of my life: All the people packed into the seats. The rounded ends of the cameras pointing at me and seven other women. I skimmed the stands until I found my family in the first row against the railing, sporting their homemade T-shirts: "Quinn's mom," "Quinn's dad," and "Quinn's awesome twin brother."

I wish you were here, Ken. I allowed that one thought and shut off my brain.

The official blew the whistle, signaling the crowd to hush. The event couldn't start until you could hear a pin drop. Swimmers were trained to jump into the pool from the start sound, and any little movement could result in a false start, which meant all those years of hard work—blood, sweat, and tears—would result in disqualification. I had nightmares about that so many times during training. It was a horrible thing to witness live, and if I, the top American swimmer, got disqualified from a false start, I would forever be known as a complete laughingstock to my country and my sport.

Once the pool deck became dead quiet, the official told us to take our mark. As I leaned over and gripped the block, I inhaled a deep breath and exhaled from my nose.

Buzz.

We flew into the pool, kicking as fast as we could to get as much distance underwater since we were faster there than at the surface. The first half of the race, I had to give eighty percent of my energy. Even then, I couldn't shake Amira. She was almost a full body length ahead, and I blamed her height.

Stop looking at her. Swim your own race.

The second half of my races were always my strongest. I cranked my energy up to one hundred. No, more like a hundred and ten. I wanted to finish and have the timers drag me out of the pool because I'd used every bit of energy to snatch the gold from the favorite. Each length, I inched up to her. Slowly but surely. But if she and her coaches had done their research, they would know that my superpower was that final flip turn that tossed me forward. At that last flip, I kicked as hard as I could and popped up right at Amira's head. We were neck and neck. I could hear the crowd whistling, chanting, and yelling a thunderous roar. I could see my coach jumping up and down, using all his energy to wave me to the wall. I could see the crowd on their feet. American and Hungarian flags rippled in the stands. I could imagine Kennedy livestreaming it in her Brooklyn apartment. I could hear her screaming. My heart pumped out of my chest.

Breathing felt like sucking in and expelling cement in that last hundred meters. With the last twenty-five, I couldn't afford to breathe every stroke. I didn't need oxygen for the last twenty seconds. Breathing only slowed me down. *Twenty seconds. No breath. Go.*

I slammed my hand against the wall and breathed in all the oxygen I'd starved myself of the last twenty seconds. When I popped out of the water, the sounds from the crowd reached the highest I'd ever heard. With barely any energy, I huffed and puffed as I checked the scoreboard. There, lane four had the number one followed by a WR.

I'd beaten Amira by a full second. I'd gotten my first ever world record. I'd won my first individual gold.

If I'd had the energy to cry, I would have. Some swimmers flipped out in their lane when they won gold or broke a record, and I always thought that was tacky. We were professional athletes and had to be good winners just as much as we had to be good losers. But even if I'd wanted to freak out, I couldn't. I literally couldn't move or breathe. I was so shell-shocked and exhausted that I just floated, gasping for breath and looking at the board, wondering if I'd dreamt the whole race because I—some average girl from an average upstate New York town—couldn't possibly have won Olympic gold along with a new world record. It couldn't be.

Amira slid over to the lane line and woke me out of my daze. I floated over, and half her body fell on top of me. Although she'd wanted the gold like we all did, she wasn't a poor loser. She flashed me a smile mixed with genuine happiness and disappointment.

"You did it, Yankee," she barely said, as out of breath as I was.

"You deserve it. Good job."

"I think you killed me."

"That's what it feels like to win a gold medal, my friend. Welcome to the club."

She patted me on the back and lifted herself out of the pool.

Twenty minutes later, at the medal ceremony, I was still collecting my breath when the presenter draped gold around my neck. The fifteen thousand people, including my parents and brother, stood in the stands, whistling and cheering. Like I was taught in media training, I gave the crowd a smile and a wave. The cameraman moved right in front of me, about to capture the moment the national anthem echoed in the natatorium. It hadn't even begun, and the stinging hit my eyes and flared my nostrils, and emotions collected in my throat. I wanted to know if Kennedy saw it, if she was watching, if she was proud of me.

"Please stand for the national anthem of the United States of America," the announcer said, his deep voice ringing throughout the natatorium.

Just hearing my country's name gave me goose bumps and started the tears.

Put your hand over your heart. You'll get criticized if you don't, Lucy's voice reminded me in my head.

I placed my right hand over my heart, and "The Star-Spangled Banner" started playing to all fifteen thousand spectators and everyone watching all over the world. The Hungarian, American, and Chinese flags slowly rose, and at the sight of the American flag in the middle broke the tears. I'd heard the anthem hundreds of times before, but it never sounded as sweet as it did when echoing at the Olympics. It was the greatest honor of my life having that song played and the flag displayed because of my race. I tried holding in as much emotion as I could while singing along—*you need to sing along or at least mouth the words so everyone knows that you know your country's national anthem*, Lucy's voice reminded me—but I completely failed. When the rockets started glaring red and the bombs started bursting in air, tears fell freely. That was when I realized that this wasn't some dream. It was a childhood dream turned into reality because I could feel the moisture on my cheeks, the ball in my throat, and the stinging in my eyes from the chlorine mixing with my emotions. All the feelings indicated this was very much real and not just a daydream anymore.

I'd missed the London Olympics. I'd missed the podium in Rio. But four years later, my country's flag rose high in the natatorium, and my country's national anthem played on every TV in the world on the largest sports stage. The biggest accomplishment of my life dangled around my neck. My family witnessed all their time, energy, and support paying off right in front of them. Hopefully, the girl who'd been my number one fan since the Beijing Games watched it all back home.

This very moment was worth all the wait and the heartbreak.

I had never been prouder of myself.

Tokyo was my Olympics.

CHAPTER SIX

On Tuesday, after qualifying for the final of the 200-meter free, on my way back to the Olympic Village, I spotted Amira. Her red, white, and green duffel bag hung across her tall, skinny body, and soundproof headphones hid her ears. It was the perfect opportunity to psych out my competition. She had swum her 200-free race a second faster than me, and if she could use her sexuality to distract me, I thought it was fair that I could use fear to distract her. No one was safe in the Olympic Village.

Unless you stayed inside or used condoms.

I ran up behind her and grabbed her shoulders, and she sprang forward, yelling something in Hungarian that I assumed were swear words. When she saw me cackling, she calmed down, lowered her headphones around her neck, and forced a smile.

"You scared the shit out of me."

"Good. I need to fuck with you until about nine o'clock tomorrow morning."

"I didn't know you were such a dirty player."

"You started this on Sunday."

She gave me a smirk. "What did I do on Sunday?"

"You…" I paused and thought about it as her sneer widened. It was a trap, and I fell right into it.

"I what?"

I scoffed. "You know what you did."

"I don't. I think you should remind me."

I continued on the sidewalk that led back to the village without letting myself get tangled in the trap. Amira snickered and scurried up to continue heckling. "Are you frustrated, Yankee? You seem frustrated for just having won a medal."

"You make me frustrated."

She feigned shock. "I wouldn't ever do such a thing."

Various country flags hung over the balconies of the apartment buildings. Tourists stood on the sidewalks, snapping pictures of the buildings and the Olympics statues and paraphernalia scattered around the premises, and I even caught a few tourists snapping pictures of Amira.

"I have to admit that beating you for a second time will be the highlight of my swimming career," I said to divert the conversation, trying to probe her inner trash talker, a way to get in her head and flirt with her at the same time. "The gold medals are kind of the consolation prize."

"I think it's cute that an Olympic rookie is trash talking a third-time Olympian. American arrogance is alive and well."

"I might be an 'Olympic rookie,' but I'm also a six-time world champ. I've earned my stripes to trash talk."

"I guess we'll see tomorrow morning. Just know, I have a record for upsetting Americans. It was the most wonderful sight I'd seen in all my twenty-five years on Earth."

"That was when you were twenty-five. Do you still have what it takes to beat the young'uns at twenty-nine? I mean, you're basically ancient now."

Her full lips dropped in shock but still curved into a grin. "And yet I'm still seeded first in the two hundred."

Okay, she had me there. I tightened my jaw and looked away. She laughed victoriously. She might have won the trash talk, but she wasn't going to win the 200-free.

She insisted we take a picture in front of a sculpture of the Olympic rings outside the village gates. I went along with it, suspecting she was posting it on her Instagram to hype up the 200-free. Whatever I could do to help draw ratings for swimming, I would do. If that meant taking a picture with my frenemy, sure, sign me up. Plus, that meant that when she took the selfie, she wrapped an arm around me, and I was surprised by how her touch sparked that sharp lust brewing inside me.

It wasn't until I reached my apartment that I got the notification that Amira had tagged me in the photo. The caption read, "Reunion with this lovely American, @QuinnCHughes. Can't wait to greet her at the finish line tomorrow for the 200m free final #Tokyo2020." She'd added a winky emoji and a heart at the end of her caption.

That picture prompted my phone to blow up with her fandom's comments. And she had quite the fandom in Europe.

"@TheRealMermaidAmira Gold medalist in trash talking," I responded.

Once my head hit the pillow for my afternoon nap, I checked my phone. I had so many unanswered congratulatory texts about my 400-free that had just played on American prime time. I thought, why not catch up on some while I had the rest of the day off. But amid the friends and family waiting for a reply, I searched for the name I wanted to see the most. Even though Talia didn't want me to acknowledge anything that wasn't happening in Tokyo, it was really hard when I had four pending messages from Kennedy. Any time my brain had a break from shielding unnecessary stress, the thoughts of the girl back home came rushing to the forefront.

OMG! YOU WON A GOLD MEDAL! OMG!

Excuse me while I sob during your medal ceremony.

Okay, I definitely cried during the medal ceremony. I'm so, so, so proud of you, Quinn. You have no idea. You're truly amazing.

Also, that little athlete bio that they showed before your final was super adorable. Might have gotten teary eyed during that too. You looked super pretty.

Those texts pumped potent excitement in me powerful enough to win another gold if that meant I could have a series of texts like those.

I responded, *Stop making me blush. And I'm surprised you waited to watch.*

She texted back a few minutes later. Since it was eleven p.m. Monday for her, I wasn't expecting her to text back right away when I was sure she had to wake up early for the last few days of her summer internship. But she texted anyways. *I just miss your face and wanted to see it.*

I replied with a smiley face, and then let the phone fall front first on my chest, my smile still reaching my ears.

❖

Tuesday night in Tokyo was when the media found their hook for the rest of the swimming events.

Talia woke me up from my nap and told me about all the articles circulating online. When I sat in the Team USA section with my team and family during the night session, Liam and my parents also told me what they'd seen on the internet: Articles comprised of screenshots of Amira's Instagram picture and my comment back to her. Pictures captured by the tourists who snuck photos of the two of us innocently walking around the Olympic Village.

By Wednesday morning, article headlines had already built up our 200-free final. Every article mentioned how both Amira and I were lesbians. Half of those articles mentioned how Queer Twitter hoped we had a thing. I'm sure plenty of them were Amira's fans.

"Two Fastest Swimmers in the World Go Head-to-Head in 200m Free Final."

"Will Quinn Hughes Upset Defending Gold Medalist Amira Kőszegi Again?"

"Fans Are Shipping Out Swimmers American Quinn Hughes and Hungarian Amira Kőszegi Despite Their Duel for Another Gold."

"The Biggest Rivalry at the Tokyo Games Could Result in a New Heroine of the Pool."

"Quinn Hughes and Amira Kőszegi: Friends or Foes?"

I rolled my eyes and shoved my phone in my duffel bag. Another example of how the Olympics magnified everything. An innocent rivalry between two people who mutually respected and liked each other blown up to fit the narrative of two nemesis with seething resentment facing each other in front of the world.

As the eight finalists for the 200-free lined up in the back room, waiting to be called, I stood in front of Amira, forcing my mind into the perfect zone it was in two days prior when I won the gold. I could feel the weight of the headlines suffusing the room, humming between Amira and me. This race already felt different than the 400. Once we stepped out on the pool deck, all the eyes and cameras would be on us. The magnifying glass would hover over us to find one gesture of intense attraction.

"You ready for a chase, Yankee?" Amira asked, and I could hear the crooked grin.

Physically, I still felt as if I could slice through water thanks to the tapering, the drag, and newly shaved legs. And my mind felt good coming off a huge victory, bolstering my confidence. "Let's just give them a good show, all right?" I said and glanced over my shoulder, watching her smirk grow even more impish.

"That I can do. I can't let an American be the new heroine of the pool."

"You might need a new nickname after these games. *Sellő* isn't going to do it anymore."

"Perfect pronunciation. How many times did you practice that line, huh?"

Quite a bit. But I wasn't going to tell her that.

Once we were all on the deck, the natatorium became quiet when the officials blew the whistle. I took one last deep breath and ignored the cameras and eyes zeroing in on the two of us.

Then the officials sent us off.

Unlike the 400, the 200 was a sprint. A very long sprint. I had to give it one hundred and ten percent for all four laps. I was half a body length behind Amira the whole time, and it really pissed me off. Maybe the fifteen seconds we devoted to trash talking ripped me out of the zone that could have pushed me into the lead. I couldn't let her win. A "rookie" had to beat the vet, the reigning champ, the heroine, the best female swimmer in the world, the *sellő*. That was the narrative I wanted the media to write about.

On the final hundred, I squeezed out the very little energy I had left. This was when all the tapering came into play and the hidden energy I saved up from lying in bed, not drinking, not having sex, scootering around San Francisco, and forcing Lillian to get my food, all came out.

I took advantage of my strength during the final flip turn and was able to propel myself right up to Amira. For the last length, I couldn't tell who was winning. I couldn't shake Amira. My legs were made of rubber, but I couldn't give up. Every time I breathed, I saw glimpses of the crowd on their feet, mouths open, the roar muffled by my quick breaths and water splashing in my ears. Taking in one last breath, I sprinted to the wall. No more checking on Amira. Eyes on the line below me, using every bit of energy left.

I slammed my hand against the wall and pulled my head up to

breathe. The crowd roared as my body filled with oxygen. I would have sworn that Amira had beaten me. Her red-suited mass never trailed. She was so tall too. Too fast. Too determined.

But when I turned, I saw a one next to lane five, a two next to lane four, and ten hundredths of a second separating our times. My mouth fell open, and my heart raced chaotically as the crowd burst into cheers and applause.

I'd won my second individual gold. By ten hundredths of a second. God, did we give everyone a good race.

The medal ceremony was less leaky than my 400. My heart sprang at the possibility that my nail-biting race and brand-new gold would warrant another text from Kennedy. But after celebrating with my team, I didn't get anything. I figured she didn't want to spoil prime time for herself by keeping up with the news on the internet.

Three gold medals cradled me into a deep slumber. I woke up Thursday morning feeling adrenaline pump through my limbs by just thinking about winning another gold in a few hours in the 4x200 meter free relay. I turned off my alarm that was set to go off in ten minutes. But there was still no text from Kennedy.

It's only six p.m. back home. Prime time hasn't happened. She'll text you after the morning session.

Our relay finished in first, another gold for my collection. By the time I was dressed and out the door, walking back to the village after the morning session, it was ten thirty at night on the East Coast. A slew of text messages invaded my phone, signaling my 200-free had already aired. My heart raced at the anticipation of finding Kennedy's name buried in the pending messages. I kept scrolling until I reached those I'd already opened. Her name was right underneath Liam's, the last message was my smiley face Tuesday afternoon.

Why the hell didn't she message me? Where was the congratulation text for my second gold?

Maybe she got busy. Maybe she had a happy hour with friends. Maybe she had a bad day. Don't worry about it.

❖

By the time I had my final event on Saturday morning—the 800-meter free against Amira—the week got weird. That magnifying glass never strayed off us. The media buildup for the 800-free was off the charts. They fed into our relationship like a starving pride of lions on a dead antelope carcass. She liked messing with them and told me to wear something gay on our walk to the natatorium Thursday night for our 800-free heat, one last hurrah. We had to go out with a bang, she said. So I wore my pride Speedo shirt, each lane a different color of the rainbow, and Amira wore her swimwear sponsor's pride shirt. The magnifying glass intensified once again. Something as little as a shirt underneath our warm-ups or a congratulatory pat on the back after our races blew up to feed the narrative.

"Amira Kőszegi and Quinn Hughes Make Gay Pride Statement Ahead of Their Final Race."

"Swimmer Amira Kőszegi, Darling of the Rio Olympics, Attempts One Last Chance for Gold."

"Amira Kőszegi and Quinn Hughes Races Draw Astronomical Ratings."

"Fans Want Star Swimmers to Date after Their Battle in the Pool."

"Quinn Hughes's Rise and the Downfall of Amira Kőszegi."

Once I swept up my fifth and final gold in the 800, I could see the disappointment on Amira's face. I almost felt bad for her, but I'd swept gold in all my events, claimed Tokyo as my games, and dethroned the fastest swimmer in the world, which meant what? That I was the fastest swimmer in the world? That couldn't be. I felt anything but. I could feel how fast Amira was; it squeezed my lungs like a stress ball, my breaths short and shallow. And the 400-free was really anyone's race if ten hundredths of a second separated first and second.

But the weirdest thing to come out of the week was that by Saturday night—when the swimmers finally went out and celebrated with alcohol and sex—the girl who kept painting smiles on my face earlier in the week hadn't texted me since Tuesday. And that was when I knew something was going on. As much as I wanted to celebrate and float in the clouds for reaching my dreams, I couldn't help but feel confusion and anger as to why I hadn't heard from Kennedy. Was this intentional? Was I creating problems now that the Olympics were over for me, and I could finally worry about the things I'd been ignoring? Was I even allowed to be upset?

"You look *so happy* that you won five gold medals," Talia said in our apartment as she did my makeup. She'd insisted, and since I hardly ever wore it, and we needed to soak up the last bit of fantasy, I allowed it.

"I'm confused," I said with a deep exhale.

"That's definitely not the emotion I expected to hear. Look up." She dunked the mascara brush in the tube and proceeded to smooth it on my eyelashes.

"Kennedy hasn't texted since Tuesday morning."

"That's probably a good thing, right?"

"No. Something's up. You don't go from texting every day, saying how much you miss me and how pretty I am, and then ghost me."

"That does seem odd. Did you text her?"

"Well...no."

"Couldn't you?"

"Yeah but...she's been texting me constantly, and now it's been four days of silence."

"How about you text her? Do you wear lipstick?" She pulled a dark red tube out of her bag.

I frowned. "No. It makes me look like a clown."

"Is that a no?"

I pulled out my phone and stared at my text thread with Kennedy. I had no idea what to say. Like, "Hey, are you still alive? Hey, do you have power? Did you see my races?"

Did it really matter what I said? If something was going on and she was ignoring me, she would continue no matter what. If she wasn't ignoring me, she'd respond to anything.

Talia wants to put lipstick on me. I think it will make me look like a clown. Yay or nay? Help.

It was the lamest text to send after four days of silence, but I had nothing left to lose. "There, I texted."

"Good. Now wait. It's still early for them. Don't let this ruin your night. You deserve to celebrate. You are the newly crowned fastest swimmer in the world. You dethroned the Mermaid, and you have a Peruvian surfer making eyes at you. Live in the moment."

"But—"

She put her finger to my lips. "No buts. We deserve tonight. Nothing is going to get in the way. If she's not going to text you for four days after you've won three more golds, you deal with it after tonight. Have fun. Let loose. Go hook up. Who are the contenders for tonight?"

My mind went to Kennedy and how I wished she could have been a contender. But Talia had a point. I didn't work my ass off for four years just to mope at the Olympics after winning five medals, setting two world records, and dethroning my biggest competition. If Kennedy wanted to ignore me, fine. I'd worry about it when I flew to New York in a few days. Until then, I had no reason to hold back.

"We need to pick contenders," I said with new determination flowing inside me. "I need a distraction."

She shook my shoulders. "There we go. That's the spirit. You gonna text the surfer? She got silver, right?"

"Yeah, but I don't know—"

"Why not? You have another prospect?"

"Maybe. We'll see if they fall for the bait."

"The bait?" Talia tossed her head back and laughed, then pulled out some skin-colored liquid. Concealer? Foundation? I had no idea, but I allowed her to put it on my face.

"What about you?" I asked. "The Italian rowers?"

She grunted. "Ew, no. They were hitting on every single woman. I'm way over them."

"The Spanish diver? The South African IM-er?"

"*Psh*, I did a Spaniard in Rio. I've moved on from that country," she said and winked.

I played along and put my hands up. "Oh, sorry to have missed that memo."

"My eyes are on the South African IM-er."

"Sticking to swimming, eh?"

"Yeah, and he's sexy. Ripped body. He could hoist me up and—"

I raised a hand. "I love you, but I don't want to picture it. Sorry. I'm sure Lillian will want all the straight details."

Since non-Olympians weren't allowed inside the village, Liam met us outside the premises, already drunk. I guess he and my parents had taken a few shots of cold sake before he ditched them to barhop with us because like all of us, he wanted to hook up.

"I got you something," he chanted, alcohol stinking up his breath. He reached for something in his back pocket and presented me a flask. "Happy five gold medals, my favorite twin."

He pulled me in for a half hug and kissed the top of my head. I opened the flask, sniffed, and shuddered. It smelled awful, very much like Liam, but hey, I wanted to enjoy the fantasy. I would celebrate with all the alcohol I had been "strongly discouraged" from drinking for the past few months. I tossed the encouragement fuel back, and it tasted as awful as it smelled.

"Jesus, what is this?" I said choking. "Rubbing alcohol?"

He chuckled. "No, it's sake. Drink it. Catch up. Get on my level so the Hughes twins can take Tokyo."

Liam and I never got drunk with each other, except for the time he flew out to San Francisco to celebrate our twenty-first birthday. That night had been a blast. We'd gotten drunk together for the first time…and really the only time. Sure, we'd had a few beers and wine during the holidays, but most of the time, I was training or didn't feel like swimming off my hangover the next morning. I thought back to how much fun it had been on our twenty-first birthday, exploring the city, taking him to my favorite bars, and how the night consisted of us laughing, making fun of each other, being each other's wingmen, and saying how much we loved and missed each other.

I wanted another night like that one. I really missed my brother.

Sometimes. Most of the time.

I hadn't had a drink in months. I hadn't been drunk in…well…a year? Maybe longer? I'd lost track. But now that my brutal training had earned me five beautiful medals, all the alcohol was at my fingertips. We barhopped as if it was our twenty-first birthday. Liam flirted too hard with my teammates, and the only one who fell into his charming trap was Talia, much to my surprise. Gorgeous Talia, who could have had the South African IM-er, the Spanish diver, or the two Italian rowers, but for whatever reason, she decided to flirt with Liam. I mean, he'd aged well, sure, but if Talia wanted ripped bodies and muscles, Liam couldn't match Olympian standards. He was just my twin who worked out a few times a week but spent more time on cardio than weights. And sure, he had a good smile and charm, but…he was *Liam*. I had no idea how he consistently got beautiful women or how his idea of flirting like a seventeen-year-old got six-time Olympic gold medalist Talia Papani to pay attention to him.

The Olympian diet hadn't prepared me for barhopping. We were lightweights wanting to buy out all the alcohol. As I was about to order a beer at the third bar, Talia pulled me into the bathroom and asked if she could hook up with my brother. I noticed the glaze in her eyes, her flushed cheeks, and an extra spring in her tone. The girl was happy and drunk…just like the rest of us.

"Really? Liam over the South African diver?" I said and heard the slurring in my own voice.

She waved off my comment. "I haven't seen Rosco tonight, and he has my number so…he snoozes, he loses."

"You sure you want to settle for Liam?"

"Ugh, I know he's your brother, and my asking you this is totally weird, but he's got a cute smile and he's really funny—"

I raised my hand. "Tal, if you want to hook up with my brother, then do it. On one condition."

"What's that?"

"Share zero details with me. Nada. You can either give me a thumbs up that it happened or a thumbs down, but save all the details for Lillian and never tell me."

She saluted. "Yes, boss."

The bar was crowded with swimmers. The Australians. The Swedish. The Japanese. I lost Talia and Liam to the corner where they made out like two drunk twentysomethings who hadn't gotten laid in a long time. I could either continue chatting with the guys and check out women with them, or I could throw myself out there and have as much fun as Talia and Liam. It'd been so long. I wanted something meaningless. And I didn't want to have to wait for it. The alcohol and the success of my week pumped more confidence in me as I whipped my phone out and noticed I still had zero texts from Kennedy, despite it being a normal time of the morning back home.

So I typed in the name of my distraction.

Where are the Hungarians drinking tonight? I think we should run into each other since we've been doing that a lot this week.

Amira was quick to respond. *The Hungarians are looking for the Americans. Or at least, one Hungarian is.*

I responded. *I'm not giving you your gold medals back if that's what you want.*

You're so conceited. I think I need to put you in your place.

And where is that exactly?

Twenty minutes later, Team Hungary walked through the doors, and my jaw plummeted. All that confidence I'd exerted throughout the night? Yup, completely drained right out of me when Amira strutted in, showing me how a million universes out of my league she was. She wore a white cocktail dress that perfectly sculpted her body and stopped halfway between her waist and knees, rounding out her toned butt and contrasting with her summer tan. The dress was so tight that her abs created faint outlines in the fabric. I'd only ever seen her in a competitive swimsuit or warm-ups...or that one time I saw her naked. Seeing her dressed for the real world made her a beautiful stranger.

Her gaze never flinched as she sauntered over as if she'd come with one mission. I could see determination darkening her smoky eyes, and she did something right because she didn't have to walk the whole length of the bar to reach me. I floated over to her as if under hypnosis.

"And I thought you looked good in a Fastskin," I said over the loud music. "God damn."

"Oh, you mean this?" She twirled like the brat she was. And her wavy hair fell perfectly into place. It needed to stop looking perfect. I could help with that. "I rolled out of bed. And you make Americans look good. I never thought I would say that, but I guess there's an exception to everything, right?"

I put my hands on my chest. "That is the best compliment anyone has ever given me."

"I know. I'm quite the charmer."

I leaned into her ear, and the corners of her dark red lips pulled into a smirk. She had perfume that smelled like pure elegance, and it made me want to pull her hair back to nibble at the smooth column of her neck. "The real question is: When are we going to consummate this Quamira thing? I feel like we should give the internet what they want."

When I pulled back to see her reaction, her wide eyes told me she hadn't expected that. And I guess I hadn't either, but I liked the surprise and thrill of anticipation roiling in my stomach as I waited for her answer.

"We can make it happen right now if you want."

I slipped my fingers into hers. "Let's go."

It was a hookup waiting to happen...again. There was sexual tension and hateful tension all balled into one. All those tensions needed to be released, and we finally made Quamira official in her apartment. It was closer than mine, and after taming ourselves for a whole week, we couldn't wait the extra quarter mile walk to mine.

It was even better than our adventure the summer before.

My flight back to the States was on Tuesday, so that meant I had three days to sightsee with my family, catch a few Olympic events like track and field, soccer, and diving...while squeezing in a few steamy sessions with Amira.

Each time deserved a gold medal for performance. Sleeping with an Olympian...well, I strongly recommended it after that. Their strength, their bodies, their endurance. God. No wonder it happened six times in three days. All the position changing. All the standing. All the roughness. All the hair yanking. Amira did an amazing job making me forget what I was about to fly back to.

But once I strapped into my plane seat, ready for the fourteen-hour flight to JFK, I set my music on shuffle, and the first song brought back all the memories I'd suppressed. The six sessions with Amira drained away, and the song swept me back to everything I'd forgotten I'd lost.

It was "XO" by Beyoncé, and tears claimed my eyes.

CHAPTER SEVEN

Everything felt different as I lay in my NYC hotel bed, like the heavy feeling of the last night of summer before school started. I couldn't believe the Olympics were over, those two weeks that came every four years that we'd been counting down to the same way kids counted down to Christmas.

Lying alone, with no rare and dramatic spectacle on the other side of the wall, life became dull and ordinary in the snap of a finger, a flickering of a torch, a plane ride over the Pacific. And now I had to deal with the very thing I'd been pushing to the back of my mind. It was right in front of me, a hurdle I had to leap over if I ever wanted to get home to the bed that I missed and the R&R that waited for me the second I landed in San Francisco.

But not until I faced this issue and all the questions that came with it.

I'd had all this time to analyze what the hell had happened between me and Kennedy. Why she'd stopped texting. She didn't even respond to my lipstick question, which informed me something was going on. The only thing I could think of was the Quamira coverage. She'd stopped texting when it all blew up.

But she studied journalism. She should have known that was dramatized.

The only way to settle this was to text her, but this overwhelming fear rushed through me; once I texted, we would figure out if this was going somewhere or not. There was so much to lose right after I'd won so much. I'd already whacked Olympic failure at the other end of the field, but my love life was next at bat. Once Kennedy and I talked about what had happened in San Francisco, we would find out if our paths really crossed, or if our time before Tokyo was a simple wave as we carried on straying paths.

The thought scared me to the point where I almost didn't want to text her. But I was only going to be in the city for three days. I had to muster the courage and fight for us. If there was still something worth fighting for.

Hey, I'm in the city right now until Saturday. I was hoping we could meet up and talk if you're free.

The next thing I knew, it was twelve hours later, and my phone bellowed the most obnoxious siren, alerting me that it was six o'clock in the morning and time to wake up for a day of interviews. I was so tired from the plane that even though I'd slept like a baby, the lingering tiredness weighed heavily on my eyes. When I turned off my alarm, I saw a text from Kennedy, waiting for my reply.

She'd responded five hours after I sent my text message. *I'm free every day after six.*

Still half-asleep, I typed, *Can we meet up tonight? Eight p.m.?*

And then I waited some more.

Lucy had scheduled interviews for *The Today Show*, *The Tonight Show*, the local NYC news, and a full feature and photoshoot for *Sports Illustrated*. She even squeezed in the first pitch for a Yankees game when they asked. All in three days. At least I got a free jersey out of it with "Hughes" and the number five, for my gold medals, on my back.

For my *Today Show* interview, I threw on my wide smile, my five medals around my neck and strategically styled them the way all Olympians do on their media tour. I answered questions about swimming against Amira and our friendship, but the interviewer said it with a tone that hinted like it was something more. I said that we competed against each other at least once a year, so we had a civil friendship that was mutual respect for one another as well as fun banter.

And then I quickly shut down any rumors about us being more than friendly competitors. In case Kennedy was watching.

After my morning interview, all I wanted to do was sleep before *The Tonight Show* taping in the late afternoon. I could barely keep my eyes open as I headed into the hotel lobby and up the elevator. I could feel my irritability. I thought I could nap it off so I wouldn't be cranky for my first late night appearance...or for when I talked to Kennedy right after. And the hour-long nap helped a little bit to keep me peppy. The interview was a fun distraction from the most dreadful thing I had scheduled for the day: Kennedy. Then I spent my whole Uber ride from Rockefeller Center to Brooklyn wiping my perspiring, jittery hands against my skinny jeans and feeling my chest tighten the closer we got to her apartment.

Right as the Uber dropped me off, I inhaled until it landed at the bottom of my lungs while glancing up at Kennedy's four-story building. I exhaled as I walked up the stoop and buzzed her apartment. Seconds ticked by slowly as my brain kicked on anxious gears that hadn't been in use since before the Olympics, when I pulled the plug and refused them from operating. But ever since I'd landed in NYC, I could feel the gears moving and producing all these thoughts that made it hard for me to take a much-needed afternoon nap or stop my hands from sweating. It wouldn't shut off.

When she buzzed me in, I took my time climbing to the second floor, trying to buy more time to settle my tremulous pulse. I knocked on her second-floor apartment, and she opened the door dressed in an oversized purple NYU sweatshirt and short gray Soffe shorts. My gaze fell to her legs, remembering how toned and perfect they were, and then my mind reminded me that I couldn't react to her beauty or our chemistry until we settled the unsettled.

"Hey, come in," she said with a cordial smile that seemed to hold back a lot.

Her apartment was bigger than I expected a Brooklyn apartment to be, but then again, she lived with three roommates, sharing two bedrooms, more people to pay for space. Light wooden floors. Tall windows that brightened the apartment. And even though the kitchen was practically a corner, the cabinets were modern, with full fridge and stove. Cute furniture and decorations really made it feel like home. She gestured me to the couch across from a white brick fireplace that had a TV mounted to the wall above it. Textbooks littered the couch and floor, prompting me to move an open notebook from the couch to the coffee table.

She offered me a glass of pinot noir, and of course, I accepted. I was going to need alcohol to get through this conversation. She sat on the farthest end of the couch and took a large gulp. That gave me a clear indication of how uncomfortable she was.

"What are you studying for?" I asked to make small talk and also procrastinate about getting to the questions. I bought myself time by taking liberal sips of wine to ease my anxiety, hoping it would stop my hands from shaking.

Kennedy glanced at her collection of books. "Long-form editing."

"I have no idea what that means."

She offered a quick and thin smile, a sign that she had a lot of thoughts swirling in her mind. "Different editing techniques and how to apply them to the documentary we have to make. Nothing remotely exciting."

"Is it hard?"

She shook her head. "Not really. Just time consuming. How are you? Still jet lagged?"

"A little bit. Haven't really had time to rest since I've gotten back. I have all these interviews."

"I saw you on *The Today Show* this morning."

That perked me up. That meant she saw me deny any claims that Amira and I were a thing.

"Oh yeah? And I just finished *The Tonight Show* taping."

Her eyes enlarged. "Wow. That's pretty big."

"It was terrifying. All the interviews are terrifying. I have to do this photoshoot on Friday that I'm absolutely dreading."

She let out a modest chuckle. "Why?"

"I don't know how to pose. I'm not a model."

"They'll tell you what they want from you."

I sighed. "Where are the roommates?"

"Out at the bar. They wanted to give us time alone."

Oh great. What did they know?

Apparently, it was enough to scare them out to a bar.

"Oh, I got you something." She went into the small kitchen and came back with a newspaper and plopped it on my lap. It was the front page of the sports section of *The New York Times*, and there, taking up the majority of space above the fold, was a picture of me on the medal podium after my 800-free, a gold medal around my neck with the headline, "Quinn Hughes Earns Fifth Gold, Becomes Most Decorated Athlete at Tokyo Games."

"I thought I'd save you a copy," she said softly. "It's not every day you're on the front page of *The New York Times* sports section or the most decorated athlete at a Summer Olympics."

The butterflies awoke in my stomach. I closed my eyes, latching on to this moment that had to mean something. The fact she saved the newspaper meant something to me. It meant she still cared.

"Thank you," I said and stared at the paper for a moment. "But I have to ask you a question." When I glanced up, I noticed the shaking in my hands from the ends of the newspaper moving. I dropped it on my lap so it wouldn't give any indication as to how nervous I was for this conversation. "This was after my 800-free."

"Yeah, I know."

"Four days after I last heard from you. Why did you stop texting?"

Her eyes rounded as if I'd caught her in the act. "I, um, I was busy, Quinn. Grad school and—"

"Don't lie to me, Ken. Come on." Anger simmered in me. Did she really just try using her classes as an excuse? Did she think I was going to buy that?

She started playing with her fingers, and as the air thickened in the room, I downed the rest of my wine. The hesitant silence really got to me. I looked at her after setting my glass on her coffee table. She still stared at her hands. She was allowing the air to congeal and heat the more she sat there with nothing. I was too drained to play this game. Either we figured out what the hell was going on, or I would leave, and we would never have any closure.

"Kennedy?" I pressed. "What did I do? What's going on? Why did you ghost me?"

I noticed her swallow and her jaw clench. "Did you sleep with her?" she asked.

"What?"

"Did you sleep with her? The Hungarian swimmer?"

She asked so quietly, I feared this whole conversation would be her talking in that decibel, causing my crankiness to seem more severe than it was. And the fact that she asked about Amira—confirming that all of this was because of something as insignificant as that—heated up my anger to a boil.

"Amira? Why does it matter?"

"Because it matters," she said flatly.

I sat there, pinned to my spot. My mouth opened and closed, picking up and discarding all the responses running to the front. I had to choose my words carefully, even though my mental filter was drained by how tired I was...of everything.

"That's not answering the question," I said. "Actually, it has nothing to do with my question. Why did you ghost me?"

"So that's a yes?"

"Kennedy, answer the question!"

My voice seemed to take her aback; her mouth parted, and she rapidly blinked as she studied me. I wanted to apologize since I didn't mean for it to rise that assertively, but I couldn't say any words with her silence choking me. My throat closed around the apology.

"I..." she began, hesitated and then tried again. "I wanted to leave you alone."

"What does that even mean?"

"The whole world was shipping you two. One day we're texting, the next morning, any coverage about you is also about her and how they want you two to date because you're both gay swimmers, and it was...too much. They weren't rooting for us to be together. They were rooting for you two. It broke my heart."

Her voice rattled, and she wiped her eyes before sniffing back another round. A dull ache tugged in my chest as I pictured her getting lost in the media storm that magnified all the littlest things that came from the games, my relationship with Amira being one of them. Clearly, by how scared she was telling me the truth, how it made her cry and act so insecure, she actually thought Amira was a better catch than her. As if Amira erased all the history Kennedy and I had. It irritated me that she actually questioned her worth. If only she knew how hard it had been trying to forget about what happened or how many nights I'd spent since high school hoping and wishing we'd find a way to beat all odds and be together again.

But clearly, she had no idea.

"That's why you ignored me?" I said, and now I was irritated at myself for not masking my frustrations better. "Because of some stupid speculation?"

"Well, was it speculation?"

"Why does it matter, Ken? I'm single, and some silly speculation over something as little as a hook-up shouldn't warrant being ghosted. That's not even fair."

"So you fuck your competition but not me?"

"You ghosted me out of nowhere. You spend the first few days telling me how much you missed me? How beautiful I am? How you were thinking of me? And then, bam, silence until literally last night? You don't get to do that and then also be upset about me being single and having fun. I didn't do anything wrong. We aren't together."

"Thanks for the reminder, Quinn. I think I know that."

She wiped her eyes with her sleeve and pounded back the rest of her wine as if it was hard liquor. Then she got off the couch, snatched up her glass, and headed into the kitchen where I heard her pour herself more. I buried my face in shaky hands, wishing I could get more wine and wishing that Kennedy realized she was the exact opposite of Amira. I was so delicate with Kennedy because she meant everything to me.

"Kennedy, please come back," I pleaded and inhaled a deep sigh.

It took her a few moments, as if she needed an extra second to collect herself and brace for the rest of the dreaded conversation. When she came back, I pulled my face from my hands and watched her set her glass on the coffee table, tuck her knees into her chest, and stare at nothing. While the deafening silence hung heavy in the air, I familiarized myself with breathing techniques I'd learned in yoga and mental training exercises to put anxiety and negative emotions at bay until one of us knew what to say.

When I checked on her, at our sudden eye contact, she flitted her focus back to her knees.

"Say something," I said.

"Do you, um, did it mean something? What happened at your place? With us?"

"Did it mean something to you?"

My tone sounded too defensive, but she shot me a creased brow that prevented me from reeling the tone back in. "Why are you being so hostile right now?" she said.

"Because I feel like you're playing a game."

"A game?"

"I have to yank every single thing out of you. Clearly, you have a lot of thoughts, so just say them. I'm right here."

"I'm asking if it meant something to you—"

"I already told you that you're not meaningless to me. That's why we didn't sleep together. Because I'm not going to sleep with you only to be separated by distance again, and I'm not going to sleep with you when you're super drunk, and I'm stone-cold sober. Like, you really thought we'd be okay with hooking up for a night and then saying, 'Okay bye, have a nice life'? Are you fucking kidding me?"

She shifted so her whole body squared mine as if committing herself to this argument. "You think I was using you?"

"I don't know what was going on, but whatever it was, it wasn't a good idea. If we'd slept together, I would have been opening myself up to be vulnerable to you, and once I do that, I'm allowing you to break my heart all over again, and it fucking terrifies me. I've still never felt as low as I did after we broke up. It's the most heartbroken anyone has ever made me."

Her nostrils flared, and streams rolled down her cheek. This time, she didn't try to stop them. I watched them become thicker and fall, and it pained me with this uncomfortable burning sensation I didn't think I could shake. I had to look away because the longer I watched, the stronger the burning that balled in my throat.

She sniffed and scrunched the end of her sweatshirt sleeve to dab her face. "You know that my ex-girlfriend came into town a few days ago?" she muttered. Now she had my undivided attention. A surge of jealousy rumbled through me at the same moment the tears brimmed in my eyes. "Brielle. To finally swap items. She begged me to take her back." As my mouth dropped, she was quick to finish, "But I said no. I told her that I had feelings for someone else."

"Really?"

"Really. What happened at your place meant something to me. You weren't a rebound, and yeah, I was drunk, but that doesn't make my feelings for you any less real. I kissed you because I wanted to, and I thought you wanted to too."

"I did, but the timing was—"

"I know it wasn't right, and I'm sorry. But that's not the point I'm trying to make. The point is that I want you, Quinn, no one else."

We were silent for what seemed like forever. It was a puzzle neither of us could solve. She lived in Brooklyn, and I had one full day packed with a photoshoot before hopping on a plane back to California.

How the hell did someone manage to be with the only person they'd ever cared about, who lived on the opposite end of the country, while managing such a demanding sport?

"Ken," I said and exhaled from the pit of my stomach. "Of course I wanted to kiss you. I spent all day trying to fight back the urge to kiss you or cuddle you when you were napping. I wished so much that the circumstances were different so I didn't have to stop you in my room. I wanted to hug you until you stopped crying before you got into your Uber and felt like I lost so much when you drove away. I cried for the rest of the night because all I wanted was you."

"Quinn, I'm so sorry—"

"I've been thinking about you since high school. I've been waiting for this moment to happen ever since we made our pact. Amira means nothing to me, and you shouldn't compare yourself to her because you're, like, five universes beyond her."

She choked back a cry and swiped the corner of her eye. I wanted to scoop her up in my arms and kiss her all over, but instead, I stayed in my spot.

"Yes, the kiss meant something to me," I continued. "Everything that happens between us means something to me. I don't want anyone else either. Every girl I meet comes nowhere close to you or all the feelings I felt with you…or still feel."

She ran her hands down her tearstained face before looking up. A pang ran through me when I saw her watery red eyes filled with so many questions.

"Say something," I said.

She shook her head. "I…I want this so much, Quinn. I just want this to work. I want to be with you. I want to stick to the pact and try again. This is the time to do it."

"But how do we make it work?" I asked. "Didn't you break up with your girlfriend because of long distance?"

"I mean, it was way more than that."

"Like what?"

"Like she wasn't the one, and she was kind of an asshole, I'm starting to realize in hindsight. But I'd try long distance if it meant I got to be with you."

I rubbed my aching temples. "But I'm going to be training for the world champs. You're in grad school. We have schedules *and* distance."

"I graduate in December. Your world champs are in December. My classes and your training aren't permanent things."

I paused to figure out the puzzle. I needed some liquid encouragement. "Do you mind if I have some more wine?"

She went to the kitchen and refilled both of our glasses with a liberal amount. Either to finish off the bottle or because she knew we would need it in order to trudge through this conversation. We both reached for our glasses and gulped through the silence. I tried to make sense of all of this.

"I want this to work more than anything," she said softly and insecurely. "I'd rather get heartbroken for trying everything I could than get heartbroken for not trying anything at all."

I rubbed my fingers against the stem of the glass, easing some pressure accumulating in my hands. I agreed with everything she said, but a broken heart was terrifying. It had been debilitating when I was eighteen. I couldn't even imagine how those same feelings would translate being older and opening my heart more for her. Heartbreak wasn't an option.

I let out a long grunt and tossed my head back against the top of the couch. "Long distance. The thing that ended your last relationship and the thing you told me to never do."

"I know it's not ideal, but Jacob lives an hour away from you. I'm sure I can squeeze in a few trips out there to see you. We can see how we do at this long-distance thing, and if it works, then we're meant to be together."

"But how long does this last?"

She rubbed her forehead. "Maybe I could move out there after I graduate."

I lifted my head back up and saw the seriousness in her eyes. "What?"

"I graduate in December. Maybe after the holidays, I move out to San Francisco."

"That's a huge move."

"Yeah, but the only thing holding me here is school. After that, I need a job, and I can apply anywhere I want, and I'm okay with that, especially if that means you." She paused for a moment. "I feel like I'm convincing you to be with me."

I saw the hurt reflected in her eyes, so I sat up and rested my hand on her leg. Like every time I touched her, a jolt went right through me, straight for the spot in my gut that was burning a few moments ago. It was the last sign to tell me that even if I was terrified to lose her, I had to do it. She was the only girl who was able to send jolts through me from a simple touch of her leg.

"I'm scared of losing you again," I said. "I want this to work, but I'm terrified of losing so much if it doesn't."

"You don't have to lose me. I'm right here."

She slipped her fingers into mine, and feeling her grip made my heart settle in my chest. She finally gave me a smile that wasn't empty. It was a smile than meant so much, that we were doing something right.

"We can take this really slow if you want," she said. "And then see where we are in December?"

A silence fell. We stared at our laps, and I wondered if this was something I could really do. My schedule was crazy. Her schedule was crazy. Plus, the three-hour time difference. As complicated as it sounded, I knew one thing: The days without her in my life where nowhere near as bright as the days she was in my life. I'd done some pretty exciting things, but none of them compared to the excitement I felt knowing I had Kennedy to look forward to. Although the technicalities of our relationship were complicated, I'd rather give it a chance then spend the rest of my life wondering "what if."

"Okay," I said and pulled her hand up so I could kiss the back. She relaxed in my grip. "Let's do this."

She gave me an unsure yet hopeful grin. "What? Really?"

Seeing that gorgeous grin was contagious. It amazed me that a woman gave that kind of smile at the thought of being with me. I wanted to frame it and remind myself that I had a woman who looked at me like that. God, I was lucky.

"Really," I assured her, feeling my lips match her smile. "It's scary but feels right. I mean, this is what we promised back in high school, right?"

Her smile grew. "Right." She kissed the back of my hand before resting her head on my shoulder. "It's time to put that pact into action."

"Only been wanting that for five years."

CHAPTER EIGHT

H ow's the tattoo, Kat Von D?"
 I pulled down my sweatpants to reveal the newly inked skin scabbing behind the clear tattoo bandage on my right hip.

"It's sore," I said and focused my phone on the rings.

Ever since I last saw Kennedy, we'd been FaceTiming daily. I called her when I came home from afternoon practice, and as I whipped up some food—or waited for Lillian or Talia to whip up food if it was their night to cook—I'd finally get to see her beautiful face take over my screen. She was usually in bed, finishing up studying or doing some kind of schoolwork, and we would talk for about two hours until she had to go to bed. Those were the tame nights. On the not-so-tame nights, we would talk longer, usually on the weekends, when she didn't have to hang up around midnight her time. Our first FaceTime, when I got back home, we talked for six hours. It amazed me how much time flew during our nightly calls. If time didn't exist, we could have kept going because the conversation never slowed down.

I'd just told her the story about going to Alexis to get my tattoo because she hadn't stopped texting me about it since the Olympics were over. Kennedy and I got a good laugh when I told her about Alexis coming on to me while she tatted my skin, suggesting that I shouldn't wear any underwear for a few days to prevent it from irritating my artwork. I knew she was serious, but she made me question it with that smug smirk of hers. And then a couple of minutes later, she asked me out to get drinks.

Kennedy's eyes darkened as she looked at my tattoo, and my

stomach did a flip when she licked her bottom lip. "It's pretty hot," she said salaciously.

"Oh yeah?"

She bit her lip and nodded. "Tattoo ex-girlfriend did a good job. You put it in the spot I recommended."

"I did." I winced when I let my pants fall back in place a little too forcefully against the sore skin. Alexis had made a good suggestion about not wearing underwear. Even the pants irritated it. I positioned the camera back on my face. "You said it was a good spot."

"I can't wait to see it in person."

I straightened my back against my headboard. "That's funny you say that because I got an idea at practice today."

Her eyebrows arched. "Oh really?"

I nodded. "The International Swimming League starts up in two weeks. We have our first meet in Italy on the second weekend in October—"

She grunted through her laugh. "Oh, a meet in Italy. You say that so casually."

"Because I'll be in a pool instead of a winery. Zero time to sightsee. But anyway, I was thinking of making a pit stop in New York on my way back. Maybe for a week? Until I have to fly to Indianapolis the following week for another meet."

"Really? A whole week? What about practice?"

"I can afford a week off," I said.

It was a partial lie. If I took a week off, David wouldn't be happy about it, but I really didn't care. It was one meet, and coming off the Olympics, I wanted a break from the pool and schedules and diets and everything that came with the sport. All I wanted to do was relax, sleep in, eat whatever I wanted, and have many days dedicated to watching Netflix.

"What do you think?" I asked. "We could get a hotel room, have our own space. One in Manhattan close to campus, so that's less time you have to commute to your classes. Escape your three roommates for a few days and live with me instead?"

"Oh my God, yes! I'm so freakin' excited!"

"Me too. And remember senior year when you asked me to take you to dinner?"

"And we broke up instead? Yeah, that was a really good time," she deadpanned.

"I'm thinking about making up for it and finally having that date."

"Oh yeah? Are you asking me out?"

I cleared my throat and got into character: the nervous, awkward person asking someone out for the first time. "Kennedy, do you maybe want to go out sometime?" I even added puppy dog eyes and a nervous scratch on the back of my head.

"I feel bad for all the girls you've used that line on."

I rolled my eyes but laughed at how she continued to troll me when I was trying to do something cute. "Kennedy Renee Reed, I want to take you out on a date."

"When you say it so demanding like that, how can I resist? Now, answer this: Do you kiss on the first date?"

She laughed when she saw my grin dwindle. I took it as a jab about our dinner two years ago and the last time I saw her, when I left her apartment without kissing her. Why didn't I kiss her? Because I was an idiot. She'd suggested we take it slow, and I guess I really ran with that idea. In my defense, I felt weird arguing with her one moment, making up the next, and then kissing her good night. Plus, after what happened at my going-away party, I really wanted our next kiss to be something special, not a swift peck while our argument still lingered in her apartment. I didn't want to rush anything. We had to get to know each other all over again. If I wanted our relationship to last and develop into something deeper, I had to do it the right way.

"It depends on if the moment is right," I responded.

"You sure about that? I think the moment was right two years ago."

"You're never going to let me live that down, are you?"

"Nope. But I'm really excited about this date. We've only been waiting five years."

"I'll make sure it's worth the wait. Trust me."

❖

God, that Italy meet was awful. So awful.

My times were appalling. They were on another planet than my

Tokyo times. The woman who beat me in both the 200 and 400-free was a Stanford swimmer on the DC team who hadn't made the Olympic cut. Even she looked at the scoreboard as if it had glitched and given her the wrong time and place. But nope, she beat me fair and square by a good two seconds.

Talia and Lillian could see the disappointment and confusion on my face. They asked me what the hell had happened. Was it really the forbidden foods diet that caused me to sink? Was it because I was so tired? Was it because this was my karma for questioning if I should take a break? Was it a combination of a lot of things?

The media was quick to start questioning the results too, and one article with the headline, "Is Quinn Hughes a One-Hit Wonder?" really got to me more than it should have, but as I waited for my flight to take off, I wondered if the headline bothered me so much because it was a question I kept asking myself.

Was I a one-hit wonder? Was Tokyo my only time to shine? Ever since coming back, all I wanted to do was stay at home. Chill out. Catch up on some shows. Sleep in. Do anything besides getting in the water. Maybe this was a sign, a big slap in the face that I really did need a break.

With a ten-hour flight ahead of me, I had plenty of time to suppress my disappointment and anger. I refused to let that columnist and *one* meet dampen an amazing week with Kennedy. That was what we swimmers did perfectly, right? As well as conditioning our bodies to swim long distances and eat a lot of calories, we also conditioned our brains to shove any sort of crap we didn't want to deal with in a box, seal it up tightly, and shove it way back to the dusty part of our brains for another time.

I made a promise to myself that once I landed at JFK, I would forget about the Naples meet.

❖

The Manhattan skyline sparkled below, and knowing Kennedy was somewhere in that glowing concrete jungle elicited a flicker of excitement in my stomach. The great perk about flying first class was that I was one of the first people off the plane, and man, did I take advantage of that. I sprinted to baggage claim, cheered when my bag was the first on the belt thanks to the priority tag, and briskly walked to where Kennedy said she'd be waiting for me with a cab.

The crisp fall air greeted me when I stepped outside, and it only took a few seconds of scanning to hear a familiar shriek. That was when I found Kennedy bundled up in her purple NYU sweatshirt like the studious grad student she was, bouncing up and down as she waved for my attention. I ran over and dropped my heavy duffel bag on the ground, and she jumped on me. Catching her by her hamstrings, I could smell the peppermint gum that made her mouth more desirable, adding to that elated smile.

"God, I missed you," I said, twirling her around before placing her back on the ground. "And you're so warm. Let's go to the hotel and cuddle."

"With some tea or hot chocolate?"

"Yes please."

"Gah! I can't believe you're finally here," she said and squeezed me again as if we didn't already do that a second before, but I wasn't about to complain. I hugged her back. "I've been counting down the days since you told me about it."

"Me too. I never thought this day would get here. I swear that flight was the longest flight of my life."

"Well, it's finally over, and you get to be with me for a whole week. I'm sure by the end of it, you'll be eager to leave."

"I highly doubt that. I've never been sick of you. Not even in the summers when we were little, and we were with each other every single second of daylight."

"We have a whole week of sleepovers ahead of us. Do you know what that means?" She waggled her eyebrows up and down.

I looked skyward as my grin grew. "Lots of cuddles. Pillow talk."

"Wine chats. Oh, please tell me we can make pizza rolls like old times?"

She clasped her hands in front of her chest, pleading. I laughed. It wasn't a good idea for me to indulge too much during my stay, given the fact I was still pissed at myself for my Naples performance, and with the Indianapolis meet a week away, I had to prove to myself and the stupid media that I wasn't a one-hit wonder. I was already planning on practicing at the NYU pool while Kennedy was at class, using the workouts David emailed me.

But for the time being, I could indulge in a night of pizza rolls and worry about it later.

"Sure, one night, though. I can't get too crazy."

She hopped and cheered. "Yes! Ah, I can't wait. Let's go."

After I showered the ten-hour flight stink off me, I hopped in our king bed with Kennedy already sprawled across it in her pjs. She let out a pleasured sigh as she cozied into me, head right on my boob and an arm slung over my stomach. After all that traveling and the restless sleep the night before, being in the city with her, in a king-sized bed, would serve as a remedy to the disappointment hanging heavily on me.

"God, I barely remembered how comfortable you are," she said, burying her face into the fabric of my sweatshirt.

I gripped my arm around her shoulders. "We only had a few cuddling sessions way back when. I think we need to make up for lost time."

"A lot of lost time. We can fully enjoy being free and adults and not having to worry about our parents walking in. No open door policy."

"Thank God. It's the best part of adulthood."

"So how was Naples?" she asked.

I bit my lip as I glanced at the popcorn ceiling. Half of me was so comfortable with Kennedy in my arms, but the other part of me still wrestled with how poorly I did and what the stupid sports columnist had to say. A con of having a professional swim league was that it offered another window for criticism, and I was starting to believe that I wasn't ready for that.

"I don't want to talk about it," I answered and tried as hard as I could to keep the sound of my stress at bay.

But she shifted to get a better look at me. Her eyebrows puckered. "What happened?"

I opened my mouth and then closed it, running my tongue along my sucked-in lip as I tried to find the best words to describe how much of a failure it was. "It was…I…I don't know. It just wasn't a good meet for me."

She rubbed my arms, causing me to close my eyes and relax. "Everyone has a bad day once in a while."

"Yeah but…this is right after Tokyo. I shouldn't be swimming like this. You know there was an article with the headline 'Is Quinn Hughes a One-Hit Wonder?'" Her frown became more detailed. "Yeah, there was. The guy spent the whole article talking about how he thinks I'm going to be like a lot of swimmers, amazing for one Olympics and then failing for the rest of my career."

"He's saying that after one meet? I mean, you've been going nonstop for how many months? With no time to rest? You're probably exhausted. You'll do better next weekend."

"I am fucking exhausted. I…" I exhaled a heavy breath and looked down at her while her fingertips grazed my arm and tamed the anger. I tucked a strand of hair behind her ear and caressed her cheek with my thumb. "I want to forget about it. I just want to enjoy this whole week with you."

She gave me a soft smile. "We can do that."

Kennedy was done with classes around two p.m. on Tuesdays and Wednesdays. While she was in class both days, I went to the campus pool and did workouts, hoping that swimming during my week in the city would put me on the right path for the Indianapolis meet. Afterward, I showered at the hotel and lay around until it was time to meet Kennedy outside her lecture hall so we could spend the rest of the day together. She wanted to show me the apartment her family had lived in for the two years in between eighth and tenth grade. I had no idea that they'd lived in a three-bedroom apartment in Midtown East, blocks from Rockefeller Center, the Met, Grand Central Station, Radio City Music Hall, Studio 54, and southern Central Park.

"We were on the sixteenth floor," she said, pointing up.

"Ken, this is a prime location," I said and marveled at the eighteen-story building towering above us. "I had no idea that you lived in the heart of Manhattan."

"You would have known if I kept our promise and wrote to you, right?" She smiled and elbowed my arm.

That pulled the smallest smile from me. At least we could somewhat laugh about that now that we were in each other's lives again, but during eighth and ninth grade, when my best friend had broken her promise to stay in touch, it broke my heart. Guess we'd come a really long way.

She pointed north and said to get to their prep school, she and

Jacob walked to the 57th Street subway stop right on the corner of their block, took the F train, then the 4, 5, or 6 train up to Carnegie Hill, about a twenty-minute ride. But it was such an insignificant blip in her life that it wasn't worth paying a visit. I trusted her judgment. Instead, we walked around Central Park and took in the beautiful sights of the red, orange, and yellow trees. She continued to tell me about her forgotten two years in Manhattan, the years that turned us from best friends to strangers.

She took me to Cop Cot, a famous Central Park landmark that was a gazebo made from logs, sheltered by trees that intruded inside the structure. I had no idea it existed until Kennedy showed it to me. It was absolutely gorgeous. We stepped inside, and I took a seat on one of the benches and glanced up to admire the architecture. She reminisced about how she'd gone on a date with this boy in her science class freshman year. He'd disguised it as a run around the park because he was on the boys' soccer team and she was on the girls' team, so he'd suggested that they both needed a running partner. On one run, they'd stumbled into Cop Cot and decided to catch their breath on one of the benches. After talking for some time about the upcoming homecoming dance, he'd kissed her.

"Did you kiss him back?"

"Yeah. We kissed for a couple of minutes."

"Oh damn."

"But the thing was, I didn't kiss him because I liked him. I mean, okay, he was cute. But can I confess something?" I nodded, and she took a step forward and leaned into me. Her breath tickled my ear, and the hairs on my neck rose. "I spent the whole time pretending he was you."

Just as she pulled away, my heart fluttered as I remembered our very first kiss on her patio. I dropped my gaze to her lips, her beautiful, full lips that shined from a quick swipe of her tongue.

"You did?" I said breathlessly because my heart wouldn't stop sprinting.

She bit her lip and nodded. "Probably why I kissed him for a few minutes. I couldn't stop thinking about it. Not until we kissed in the Swensons parking lot, and I had a new memory to replace that one with."

I swallowed nonexistent saliva, and the need for her turned into an ache. "I still think about that kiss," I admitted. "Both of them, actually." *Do I kiss her now? Is the moment right? Can I kiss her and bring her daydream to life?* I wanted to so badly. She gave me that emboldened eye contact again, and I could feel myself becoming undone. My stare landed on her lips, and the desire sent a constant throb to my center. Her eyes flitted between mine and my lips, and I enjoyed the moment the thrilling anticipation created. A rush of energy hummed through me, and my heart quickened. As I slowly leaned into the connection, two small children shrieked with laughter and stumbled inside the gazebo. Kennedy and I jolted back and directed our attention to the kids, who had to have been about seven and five, chasing each other around the benches. Their parents ran over, and their dad grabbed both of their hands to pull them away, offering us an apologetic smile.

"We're so sorry about that," the mom said, her face colored with embarrassment.

Kennedy nervously scratched the back of her head and took a step back. I stood to try to undo the scene.

"It's, um, it's fine," Kennedy said and attempted a friendly smile.

And just like that, the moment vanished. When the family of four walked out of the gazebo, we looked at each other, and the lost moment that hung between us.

Kennedy sighed. "Wanna get some pizza? There's this amazing place I used to go to all the time down the street."

I painted on a smile. "Let's do it."

She'd mastered the art of scheduling classes, which meant she didn't have any on Friday. Thursday afternoon was the start of her weekend, and since I had to fly out early Saturday morning for Indianapolis, we had two nights remaining to fully enjoy being together. While she spent Thursday morning and early afternoon on campus, I ran out and got her a bouquet of flowers and a bottle of champagne. Just a few things to kick off our date night. We'd never gotten a chance to go on a date, so this one, our first one, had to be perfect.

I showered, straightened my hair, put on skinny black slacks that stopped at my ankles and a long white T-shirt underneath a fitted black blazer. After I finished putting on makeup, I poured champagne into the hotel glasses as the door opened.

"Oh my God, Quinn," Kennedy said as she tossed her book bag on the bed. She spotted the champagne next to the bouquet of red roses and white lilies. "Are those for me?"

"Oh shoot, no, they were for the other girl I was expecting," I said, and she playfully pushed my arm.

She smelled the flowers, and I handed her a glass. "These are beautiful. And so are you." She stepped back to absorb the sight of me in my date attire. "Damn, my date is hot."

I did a twirl for her. "Oh, thank you. Now drink up and get ready. We've got reservations at six."

"Reservations? Sounds really fancy."

"It is. You're a sommelier now, so I have to try to reach your very high standards."

She waved a hand. "Occasionally, I like to treat myself to a nice glass of wine, but I'm a broke grad student and usually buy Barefoot. For the record."

"Sure," I said and made a doubtful face. "Now go get ready. I want to pregame with you and this bottle before we leave."

"You always boss your dates around?"

"Only the ones who can handle it."

She winked and clinked my glass before taking a sip. "Oh God, this is some serious champagne."

"Well, yeah. I'm not buying the cheap kind."

She threw her hand over her heart. "Aw, because I deserve quality champagne?"

"No, because *I* deserve quality champagne."

She smacked my arm again but hid her growing smile behind her glass.

"Who's the one with high standards now?" she asked. I proudly raised my hand. "I'm taking this in the shower with me."

"If I knew you were going to shower, I would have waited. You know, to save water."

"Sorry. I only allow people who kiss me in the shower with me."

She laughed when my mouth opened. I wanted to defend myself by saying how I was trying to kiss her in Cop Cot before those pesky kids ruined it but decided to save that bit of knowledge for myself. Although we'd agreed to take it slow and let our chemistry flow naturally, she wasn't going to stop teasing me until I finally kissed her.

When she emerged from the bathroom a half hour later, that urge to kiss her buzzed on my lips again. She wore a knee-length violet dress that hugged every inch of her body. It revealed enough cleavage and skin to reel me in, yet it withheld enough for my mind to wander about everything underneath. Her straight hair shined in the light, and her makeup highlighted the most gorgeous features of her face. She had me completely stunned. As she observed my shocked expression, she poured herself another glass of champagne, and a wave of freshly spritzed perfume wrapped me up in another hypnotic spell.

"What?" she said as her lips curved upward, and her cheeks turned pink.

"Nothing," I said softly, taking in the color of her soft eyes. "You're just really beautiful."

"Oh yeah? You're not too bad yourself."

"Let's finish this champagne and go feast. I want to show you off."

When we stepped outside, the tense humidity greeted us. Gray clouds warned of precipitation, and I prayed to the weather gods that any rain would hold until we got to the restaurant. We looked too good to have the rain ruin the hard work we put into priming. I ordered the Uber before we left the hotel, and we only waited a minute until a black Escalade rolled up in front of us. Kennedy's eyebrows drew together when the driver, wearing a black suit and tie, came around, opened the door, and gestured us in.

"Did you seriously order an Uber Black?"

"Um, of course I did. We've waited five years for this date. Why not have fun with it?"

"Did you suddenly become bougie? Fancy champagne, roses, Uber Black?"

"It's about to get even bougier. Now get in the Escalade."

I've never used Uber Black but thought the gesture would add a fun element to the date. We were about to embark to the fanciest restaurant I had ever been to, and I didn't feel right rolling up to a high-end restaurant in a Toyota Camry. The mood needed to be set, and champagne, roses, and a black Escalade set it perfectly.

I loved how close she sat next to me during the ride. She made conversation with the driver, something she no doubt always did because Kennedy Reed had been a social butterfly from a young age. Apparently, our driver had just moved to Brooklyn the weekend before from a small town in Mississippi, and Kennedy's face lit up at all the recommendations and insider scoop he wanted from her. As she helped my Uber rating go up to a solid five, I reveled in her leg pressing against mine. I wasn't sure if she did it on purpose or if her body naturally wanted to relax into me. But either way, I wanted more. I wanted to bask in the thrill of sneaking in a secret moment in the back of the car. I moved my hand on top of hers, and my midsection fluttered when she didn't hesitate to grip me back. She didn't stop talking to the driver or take her eyes off the rearview mirror. I studied our hands as her touch sent a buzz through me. Hers were smaller than mine, her fingers slender, and she started rubbing the soft part between my thumb and forefinger. I rested my head against the back of my seat and held her tighter, not caring that the traffic going uptown to Midtown was bumper to bumper or that the ETA for our arrival was ten minutes after our reservation time. I was holding her hand for the first time since high school, and it was even better than I remembered.

I could have sat like that forever, honestly.

When there was a lull in their conversation, Kennedy turned to me, noticed our hands still intertwined, and her eyes darkened, with a soft smile touching her lips.

"What?" I asked quietly.

She smiled as she looked at my lips. "Nothing," she said, squeezing a little harder.

The restaurant was in Midtown, on the forty-eighth floor. I waited to see how long it would take Kennedy to realize where we were, but instead of picking up on it, she seemed too fascinated by her ears popping while the elevator propelled us upward. When the double doors opened, we were greeted by a sign that said Axis. Her mouth dropped open.

"Seriously, Quinn?" she said, grabbing my wrists.

I couldn't help but laugh; she was like a child being told they were going to Disney World. "Yes, seriously," I said and pulled my arm to get her to move.

"But this is Axis." Her voice fell to a whisper. "This is a Serena DeLuca restaurant."

"You don't have to whisper," I whispered. "We're allowed to go in. That's where the food is."

She still held my hand as we approached the hostess, and two women in black jackets, black slacks, and black ties greeted us, and one of them led us to our table.

"You know this restaurant moves," Kennedy whispered.

"I figured that based on the name."

"It's one of two restaurants in the city that spins a full three hundred and sixty degrees."

Our table was right next to the window, offering us a perfect view of Midtown, the lights from Times Square bouncing off the skyscraper windows. The table was adorned with a white tablecloth and a glass candle flickering against the soft lighting.

"Quinn, this place is absolutely beautiful," she said as she took her seat. "You know I've had this restaurant on my NYC bucket list for a year now? I never thought I would actually get the chance to come here. This is, like, a two-star Michelin restaurant."

"I have no idea what that means."

"It means it's fancy as fuck. And equally delicious."

"When did you become so high class?"

"My one year in France," she joked in an impersonation of a thick French accent. "But seriously, you didn't have to take me to a two-star Michelin restaurant."

"I know I didn't have to, but I wanted to. We've waited a long time for this."

Apparently, Serena DeLuca specialized in Italian food. I had no idea until I opened the menu and saw a bunch of words I couldn't read. The only Italian I'd been exposed to was in Olive Garden or the one authentic meal I had in Naples, but I stuck to the ravioli. This restaurant was so eclectic, I didn't even know where to start. I told Kennedy to pick a bottle of wine, and it took about five minutes to convince her to stop looking at the prices and enjoy a place she'd wanted to go to for a year.

"Quinn, the wine is so much."

"Kennedy, I knew what I was getting myself into. Live a little."

"But—"

"If you complain, we're leaving," I joked. "It's called gold medal compensation, and the girl I've wanted to take out on a date for five plus years. Now, pick out the wine, damn it."

Her features went soft after that. "Okay, boss," she muttered and accepted defeat.

She finally settled for a Burgundy pinot noir. Once our waitress poured our first glass and set the bottle next to the candle, she took our order. An assortment of meat, cheeses, bruschetta, and olives for an appetizer. Kennedy ordered baked salmon that wasn't called baked salmon on the menu. And she laughed when I attempted to pronounce the Italian name of my dish that was supposed to mean double cut pork chops with a vegetable I'd never heard of.

"That was difficult," I said, feeling my warm face once the waitress took our menus away. "I'm not this fancy. I think you might be out of my league."

She sipped her wine and tilted her head back in pleasure. "Uh, this wine is definitely out of my league. Try it."

"I don't even know what good wine is."

"This. This is good wine."

I imitated the wine snobs of the world by swirling it around and sniffing it as if I knew what to look for. Taking a sip, I searched for some tasting notes.

"And what do you taste?" Kennedy said in a mocking sophisticated voice.

"Grapes."

She rolled her eyes. "Man, maybe I am out of your league."

"What am I supposed to taste, Kennedy the sommelier?"

She took another drink and smacked her lips as she looked skyward. "Hmm, let's see. Cherry, a little bit of cinnamon." She tasted again. "Or licorice."

I had another sip. "Okay, I'm getting another note. Tastes like… dry red wine."

She lowered her glass and gave me a teasing side-eye. "You're not worthy of this wine right now." And then she tossed me a wink.

The waitress brought out the charcuterie plate, and we drank more wine, devoured our appetizer, and surprisingly, still had room for our main courses. The food was amazing, worth every penny. The wine was delicious enough for me to take an interest in bumping up from a cheap Barefoot to something a little more sophisticated. But as satisfied as the food and wine made me, it wasn't the best part of the dinner. That was all Kennedy.

The way she stared at me with the candlelight flittering across her features made me believe that I was the most important person in the restaurant, more important than the fact that we were literally rotating. I'd never met anyone in my life who made conversation seem so easy, despite the multiple sporadic pauses in our timeline. We made up for all that lost time, sharing stories of our lives, all in an attempt to get to know the newest versions of each other. We were practically different people from the last time we were a thing. We had to rediscover each other all over again, and honestly, that was okay with me. I was excited to get to know the twenty-three-year-old Kennedy. I wanted to know about her European adventures, what her favorite countries were, her least favorite countries, the most beautiful thing she'd seen, any hilarious stories. Every word she spoke filled me up even more, and seeing her smile glow through the dim lighting when she told me about the Catacombs, Rome, the Anne Frank House, canal rides, bike rides, and French cafés, and how much she wanted to visit Thailand, made me feel as elated as she seemed to be telling them.

It felt like a first date, but at the same time, it felt like catching up with an old best friend. Our conversation never found a lull, and maybe that was why it took us a while to finish our plates because we were too busy talking and laughing. It was exactly like our dinner two years before. Easy conversation. Hard belly laughs. Subtle and not-so-subtle moments of flirting and blushed cheeks. I guess some things would never change.

"Can I say something?" Kennedy asked after wiping her mouth. "This was worth the wait."

The banter that had filled up most of our time quickly deviated. Her gaze darkened, and the corners of her mouth tugged upward. Just when I thought there was no more room left in my stomach, it had enough space to shift.

I leaned into the table and reached out. "The best part about this is that the night's not over," I said and caressed her hand with my thumb.

"And it's already, hands down, the best first date I've been on."

"It's only a date I've been planning for five years."

"Yeah, well, I'm still in awe."

"Was the bar set that low?"

"No, babe, that's not what I meant."

I pressed my lips together because if I let them roam freely, my smile would have eaten my face. She'd called me babe. I didn't even need another pour of pinot noir to keep my happy buzz going. That word did the trick.

"What?" Kennedy said when she noticed my grin.

"You called me babe."

A blush hit her cheeks. "I did, didn't I? I guess it slipped out."

"I like it. Keep saying it."

"Okay, babe."

After I paid, we decided to walk off some of the food on the High Line. Lights illuminated the handrails and benches that guided us through the elevated park. We weren't alone. Other couples had the same idea, walking around holding hands and enjoying the crisp fall night, and I wanted to keep walking if it meant that Kennedy's arm hooked around mine. Eventually, we settled on a bench and took in the sight of the brick buildings and steel structures towering over us that added a glow to the sky. I put my arm around her, and she snuggled into my side. We sat there for a few moments in silence, watching the other couples as our food digested.

"I never knew that Quinn Hughes was a romantic," she said and looked up at me. The lights sparkled in her eyes. "You've really evolved from performing arts center make-outs to two-star Michelin restaurants and a nightly stroll."

I nudged her side, and that garnered a laugh. "If only you knew that date I was planning back then. You would have been impressed."

"I'm sure I would have. You impressed me tonight. You do this with all the girls?"

I huffed. "Yeah, right. There really haven't been a lot of girls."

It was her turn to huff. "I doubt that."

"Swimming doesn't give you a lot of time to date. I'm not taking a Tinder date to a Michelin restaurant unless it's our tenth date, and it's going somewhere."

"What about tattoo girl?"

"Alexis didn't romance. I was lucky if we even went to any restaurant. Most of the time, it was a club."

"What about the other girlfriend?"

"Bethany? The most romantic we got was sneaking into each other's rooms during away meets. The only plus to swimcest is that you are equally busy. Plus, romance in college doesn't exist. You take them to the cafeteria on prime rib night and splurge on your meal plan dollars. And why are we talking about me romancing girls? You studied abroad in France, for crying out loud. You found a girlfriend there. I'm pretty sure that's the plot to a bunch of teen movies."

"I mean, the romantic in me really enjoyed kissing in front of the Eiffel Tower when it did its blinking light show at the stroke of every hour."

I gagged. "Lame."

She nudged my arm. "You're hating because you want that to happen to you."

"Mmm, no, not really."

"How about I take you to Paris and kiss you in front of the Eiffel Tower when the lights are going, and then I'll check in after."

"All right, it's a date. I'll bring you to the Paris Games and you can reward me with a kiss."

"Maybe I shouldn't reward you if you're not going to appreciate it. A bunch of other women would."

"Maybe I want to romance you in more nuanced ways."

She grinned and grabbed my hand. The same thick and riveting air filled the pause, much like it did two years ago when I didn't act on it. The moment flew back between us as gently as the breeze coming off the Hudson. This was the moment I'd been waiting for, one just as apparent as two years ago, only this time, I would act on it to erase the memory of the other one.

"Like a two-star Michelin restaurant," she said softly.

"By your favorite chef. With some of your favorite wine. Something less showy. Less clichéd. Something more intimate."

"I like intimate."

I slid my hand against her cheek and tucked a strand of hair behind her ear. I held her face for a moment, noticing her stare fall to my lips. My heart quickened as I leaned in and pressed my lips to hers. She kissed me back, soft and unhurried. It wasn't rushed or forced like my party. It was shy yet welcoming, patient yet craving. Our mouths opened; our tongues met. My stomach celebrated with backflips. My chest stuttered with electricity that always seemed to follow us around. Kennedy's hand rested on my knee and slowly grazed my thigh, sending a buzzing feeling through my body that encouraged me to deepen the kiss, allowing the passion to control the movements of our mouths. It trickled down my arms and legs. As the passion began melting me in my seat, I realized that we should take this to a more private spot than the High Line before we got too comfortable.

I pulled away, and Kennedy's eyes remained closed as she grinned. "Finally," she said.

"You're not patient, are you?"

She shook her head. "I've done enough waiting."

Just then, a raindrop landed on my face. It barely grazed my skin as I leaned in to kiss her again. She tugged my blazer toward her so we could pick up where we left off, and another drop hit my cheek. A heavier one. I pulled away, and Kennedy wiped her face.

"Is it raining?" she asked.

A few more landed on us, getting larger and heavier the longer we waited for more evidence. Then the sky lit up, and a crack punctured the humid air and unleashed a downpour. We shrieked and leapt off the bench. We ran down the High Line, attempting to seek shelter like the rest of the crowd. I whipped out my phone, called an Uber, and accepted the surging charge already factored into the price. We waited underneath the awning of an Indian restaurant. Our clothes were drenched and sticking to our skin, so uncomfortable yet hilarious at the same time.

On the ride back, she snatched my hand, and the humidity and rain stuck our palms together for the rest of the ride as our wet clothes glued us to the back seat. When we got to the hotel, still holding hands, we ran through the sheets of rain cascading onto the city.

Bursting through our hotel room door, I wasted no time tossing my blazer to the side and peeling off my white shirt. At the same time, Kennedy fumbled with the zipper on the back of her dress.

"Let me help you," I said through my laugh and walked up behind her to lower the zipper. I assisted in pulling the dress off her shoulders until it fell to her side. It was so wet, it reminded me of yanking off my tech suit after a race. Kennedy kicked the dress against the wall when she was finally able to break free, then turned around. My breath caught when I saw her black bra and bikini underwear. The cold hotel air met her skin and caused tiny goose bumps to break out on her arms and legs. Her eyes seemed as observant as mine, taking me in in my soaking black slacks and my bra.

She slid her fingers along the top of my pants before unbuttoning them, undoing the zipper slowly, and pulling them down until she found the tattoo on my right hip. I sucked in my breath as she touched the rings. I kept forgetting they were there. Twenty-three years without it, and it took Kennedy's soft, gentle fingertips drawing circles around each ring to remind me…in a sensitive spot that sent chills up and down my arms and legs.

"I really like this," she said in a low voice. "It's even better in person."

I swallowed even though there was no saliva in my mouth. "I'm glad you like it. Haven't fully enjoyed it until now."

She glanced up with fervor in her eyes. She didn't look at me with delicate anticipation or a sparkle of vulnerability like at the High Line. This look was determined, prurient, and desperate. As she squatted, her touch grazed down with my pants and pulled them off my legs. Once she tossed them carelessly aside, she pressed her lips against my tattoo and parted her mouth to take in all five rings. My knees almost buckled. Her hands wandered underneath the fabric of my underwear, clasped my bare butt, and pulled my waist closer until her mouth seized my tattoo so her tongue could trace the circles of each ring.

"God, Ken," I said breathlessly, biting my lip so the moans that were begging to come out could stay inside. I was afraid of letting her know how easily I caved at her touch.

"You feel so wonderful." Her warm words hummed against my hips. Her thumb brushed the top of my underwear, the exact spot that triggered a release of pleasure down my legs. She lifted her head and watched me react while rubbing me over my underwear.

"I…I can't do this standing up," I said in a wavering voice.

She stood. "You can't do it standing up?" She let out a little laugh. "You're an Olympic athlete. You can do anything."

"Not when you touch me like that."

"Then get on the bed, and let me touch you."

She pushed me on the bed and crawled on top. Her mouth met mine, and I snatched the back of her hair to deepen the kiss like the deprived person I was. I needed to feel all of her, so I flicked off her bra and glided her underwear down her legs before she did the same to me. I absorbed the sight of her for only a few moments before my desire overcame me. I pulled her in, capturing her right nipple, massaging her with my tongue in delicate circles, and right as she hardened in my mouth, I ended with a light suck and moved to the other nipple. She let out several moans of approval.

"God," I said and ran my hands down her back so I could clasp her naked ass. "I've wanted you so much—"

But instead of letting me finish kissing all over her body, she pushed me back, and once I hit the pillow, she propped herself over me and kissed my tattoo again before her mouth crept ever so slowly to my center, her bottom lip tickling the top of me. She stole a gasp out of me, and I forced myself to catch the second one after her thumb pressed into me right where I desperately needed it. I twisted against the sheets as the cries tickled against my sealed lips. Then her mouth covered me, and feeling her tongue caressing me, the wait after all these years, wrestled a gasp from me.

"Oh God," I muttered.

She slipped two fingers inside me with ease, and I moaned again as her tongue and fingers gradually picked up speed. I rocked against her fingers and reached for her free hand while she made me twitch and arch. I let go of the sheets and slipped my fingers into her hair and positioned her where I needed her the most, begging for more. She obliged. She made me feel so lost and dizzy so effortlessly. My whole body succumbed to the feeling of bliss and surrender. A cry burst out of me so quickly that I didn't have time to mute it with my arm or pillow. As I rode out the final spasms of my orgasm, she tightened her grip around my hand. I finally collapsed as I attempted to catch my breath.

"Holy crap." I panted and rested my arm on my forehead.

"There. Five and a half years later," she said. "What was supposed to happen after that date."

"I think that was the best orgasm I've ever had."

"Seriously?" I heard the accomplishment in her voice.

"I'm too tired to joke about something like that."

I sat up and dragged her into my lap. I could feel her arousal against my thigh. It was so sexy to feel how my sounds affected her as if I'd spent several minutes touching her. I pulled her in to resume kissing, and the softest murmur squeaked out of her when my tongue flicked across hers. I skimmed down the curves of her torso until I reached her thighs. I could tell she'd recently shaved her legs by how slick they felt. I grabbed her ass cheek, holding her close, and slipped my other hand in between us so I could play with her folds, teasing her and feeling her become wetter at my touch.

She hid her forehead in my shoulder, groaning at each graze against her center. As I sucked her nipples into hard peaks, her breathing picked up, and she undulated her hips against my teasing hand, asking for more. As her breath became faster and deeper, I knew the timing was right, so I entered her and basked in the sound and feel of her cry.

She tilted her head and raked her nails along my back. I pulled the most delicious sounds from her as she circled her hips around my fingers. Her body on top of my lap made me molten in my spot. I moved faster inside her, trying out different rhythms and techniques, learning more about what she liked. When I discovered her favorite, I used that motion to drive her to release. She nuzzled my neck, and I could feel the drops of sweat on her hairline. Her twitching muscles coupled with a jerk in her breathing. Right on the brink of her orgasm, I nudged her cheek away so I could have the perfect view. I wanted to watch her come as much as I wanted to hear and feel her. Her mouth parted. Her eyebrows rose in desperate need, begging me to finish her. I sucked in her bottom lip and pulled her tongue with my lips. With her bottom grinding against me and my insistent strokes inside her, she finally cried out sharply, and I reveled in the sight, touch, and sound of her climax.

I wasn't sure how I was going to leave her in thirty-six hours and not see her for two and a half months until we both flew to Aspen Grove for Christmas. The day was so perfect that it made it impossible for me to leave this moment behind. I wanted every single moment we had in the city to forever follow us.

She buried her head back in my neck as she collected her breath. I brushed a strand of hair out of her face and tucked it behind her ear.

"You're really fucking sexy," I said.

She kissed the scar on my chin before caressing it with her thumb. I remembered that she did that when we dated, and I loved it so much. It was the only time that I liked having a scar on my face.

We didn't leave the hotel for the rest of my visit.

CHAPTER NINE

I didn't know why I was so pissed off after the Indianapolis meet. I forfeited a week to be with Kennedy, only went to the pool three times, ate pizza, drank plenty of wine. Did I really expect magic to happen? Apparently, I did, and this time, I performed even worse than in Naples. Talia and Lillian assured me this was nothing serious, that given my vacation in New York and being exhausted from constant traveling, swimming poorly was a given.

I didn't accept that. No professional athlete accepted poor quality anything.

When I got back to San Francisco, I took my anger out on the pool. I made sure I kicked extra hard to smack my anger around, exerted more oomph into the walls when I did my flip turns, and glided my hands harder through the water. I could only imagine how horrible my form looked. David told me one day to take an afternoon off to do yoga with his wife, our nutritionist and instructor, Kendra. A one-on-one session with her to breathe out the ire. Yoga did have a strange way of working, but it only helped for a day.

I used to love the pool I trained in, especially during the summer. It was outdoors, which meant I got to tan in the process. I loved the sudden shock of swimming through a warm patch of water into a cool patch. It kept me alert. I loved slowly waking up during warm-ups, swimming eight hundred meters while thinking about my day, the workout, other random things. Mindlessly swimming was probably the equivalent to normal people commuting to work and letting their minds get lost in their music and the twists and turns of familiar roads.

But with my mind spinning with anxiety, the last thing I wanted was be alone with my thoughts. The water was the battery to kick-start a new day of nonstop tumbling. I didn't want to hear the thoughts that told me that I was, indeed, a one-hit wonder. That Tokyo had been my only time to shine. All those years giving up my social and love lives to a sport only gave me one week of happiness during my eight-year career. That I would spend the rest of my career trying to emulate that experience only for it to be snatched away by new and younger talent. I'd been primed as a swimming machine whose only purpose was to win medals. My only goals and accomplishments lived inside a chlorinated pool.

"Hughes!" David yelled, and right after I computed that he was talking to me, a burst of freezing water hit me square in the back. I leapt with a shriek, turning to see him aiming the hose at me, something he did when his swimmers took too long to jump in.

"Jesus, David, stop! I'm getting in."

"You've been staring at the pool long enough. Catch up to Papani and Verkler."

The nozzle pointed at me again, holding me hostage. I put on my goggles and felt the dread clench around my chest. "I'm getting in. Put the hose down."

"You have three seconds."

I rolled my eyes and jumped into my lane. The cold attacked my body in a way that didn't bring me the thrill it used to. The sun wasn't as warm as I remembered. The 800-meter warm-up gave me too much time with my thoughts. I stretched, kicked, and let myself go through the motions of the warm-up with my heart hollow instead of beating with motivation and excitement.

It was another morning of following the black line at the bottom of the pool only to end up in the same spot I'd started hours and miles in before.

David wheeled over the whiteboard with our workout. I closed my eyes and groaned at the long list of sets I had no interest in swimming. For the main set, right after the next five 100-frees, David squeezed in a lactate set, which was hell for swimmers. Far worse than burpees or ten-minute wall sits.

It added to my crankiness. Talia and Lillian laughed at me during the set as my face burned with what I could only imagine was deep red, given my heavy breathing and the pain in my muscles. David apologized, but it meant nothing because his mouth curled upward as if he enjoyed torturing us.

I did a lot of croggling during that practice, swim talk for crying into my goggles. The pool was the perfect shield, and I found that the only way to get through was to croggle it all out.

By the end, I was so fatigued that I stood in the steaming hot shower and cried while Talia and Lillian got changed on the other end of the locker room. I stayed in the shower until I'd cried everything out.

I had no idea how I could keep going through the next ISL meet, the ISL finals—if my team made it—and the world champs in Abu Dhabi. I had no idea how I could survive in the pool until Christmas.

I just wanted a fucking break.

I couldn't show up at the gym for dryland that afternoon. Practices right after the Olympics were less intense. We had a three-hour practice every morning, and on Tuesdays and Thursdays, we had an hour of dryland in the afternoon. But I'd reached my threshold. I locked myself in my room, slept until two, a half hour before we were scheduled to leave. There was so much dread inside me that without thinking a second longer about it, I decided to fake a migraine. I had no idea what else to do. I hated lying, and skipping practice was something I never did, not even when I got my usual January cold. But I needed an afternoon off. I was desperate.

David, I'm taking the afternoon off. I've had a migraine all day, and it's even worse now.

He responded. *Was it the lactate set? LOL.*

I don't know what it is. but I need to rest.

Can't you take some Excedrin? Work off the pain?

I've been working through the pain. It's probably because I haven't had enough rest. I'll see you tomorrow.

He could be mad at me all he wanted. I was allowed to skip a practice given the fact I never did. Last time I skipped was my freshman year of college when I got strep throat. Last time I did it voluntarily? Never. Guess there was a first time for everything. I deserved an afternoon of rest if the thought of getting back in the pool made me want to cry. David didn't respond, but I really didn't care. I threw the covers over my head and finished crying out the guilt I had for lying and skipping until it put me back to sleep.

In swimming, we weren't driven by financial factors unless we joined the very few swimmers with enough sponsorships to give us a livable paycheck. My performances at the world champs and Pan Pacs, in addition to Tokyo, made me one of those lucky swimmers with a handful of sponsorships under my belt. But even then, with eyes on us every four years, most of our biggest accomplishments went unnoticed by the world outside of our families and team. The thing that fueled us was internal motivation. We swam for ourselves. And if we lost our motivation, what did we have left?

I skipped the next morning. My excuse was that my migraine lasted all night, caused me to puke, and that I needed to go to the doctor. Obviously, that wasn't true. Instead, I slept until the excitement of FaceTiming with Kennedy woke me up. The best part of my day.

I didn't want to talk about swimming. I was up for any other conversation. Our FaceTimes were an escape from my life and a reminder of the one amazing thing I had to look forward to. I wasn't counting down to the world champs in December. I was counting the days till the world champs were over, and I got to go home for Christmas with her.

Apparently, my ability to suppress emotions was impaired because she knew the second we started talking that something was wrong.

"Babe, what's going on?" she asked with a fold in her eyebrows.

Usually, she greeted me with a weird thing she saw on the subway. But not this time. Even though I'd slept until two in the afternoon, I was still exhausted and down. Her voice was so nurturing and sympathetic, all I wanted to do was bury my face in her chest and cuddle her. Her embrace would be exactly what I needed to feel better, and right now, a break from the pressure in my head would be appreciated, no matter how short it was.

"Nothing's wrong," I said and feigned a smile. "Just tired. How are you?"

She tilted her head to the side and pursed her lips. "I don't believe you. What's wrong?"

I laughed nervously. I really hated talking about my feelings, especially when our time was limited. "Why do you think something is wrong?"

"Because I see it on your face. Your smile is not as big, and you look tired. You don't have that usual spunk."

"Swimming hours a day takes away all the spunk."

"You had spunk when we had dinner two years ago. You had spunk right before the Olympics."

"That's because I was about to go to the Olympics, and the girl of my dreams reentered my life."

She threw a hand on her chest. "Oh, what a line. Charmingly cheesy but it's not gonna fool me. What's wrong?"

Damn. I really thought that would distract her. "You're supposed to tell me what weird thing you saw on the subway. Stop breaking the rules."

"Stop diverting."

I groaned. "I'm just tired and stressed, Ken. That's all."

"Stressed about what?"

"I don't want to talk about it."

She straightened and leaned closer to the camera. "Well, too bad. You need to."

"I skipped practice yesterday and today. I faked a migraine."

"Oh wow. When was the last time you played hooky?"

"Never."

I could see the severity set in on her features. They became much softer, more sympathetic. "Why did you skip?"

"Because I need a break. I'm not excited to get into the pool. I dread it, like, really dread it."

Closing my eyes, I pinched my temples with my thumb and middle finger at a sudden pang. I could feel the reality sinking swiftly in my gut. Swimming didn't make me happy anymore. I was twenty-three years old. I was supposed to be full of life and dreams, and for whatever reason, I felt like I had no life. How could I be so ungrateful? I came back from the Olympics with five gold medals, the most decorated swimmer of the competition, and I found myself spiraling into a dark hole of depression, and I had no idea why.

It was like the Olympics sucked up all my serotonin, like a stimulant. When it was over, I was left with the comedown, the hangover, the depression from the depletion.

Maybe a much-needed break would provide me with clarity as to what the fuck was happening to me.

"Then take a break, Quinn. Everyone deserves a break. It's not an unreasonable ask."

I rubbed another round of tension out of my forehead. "I don't want to disappoint anyone."

"I don't think that's disappointing anyone. You need to think about yourself sometimes. Your mental health is the most important thing. Everything else is inferior."

I grunted and fell back on my bed, allowing my head to plop into my soft pillow. "I miss you. I wish you were here right now."

"I miss you too. A lot. Our week went by too fast."

"Hell yeah, it did. It was, like, the only week I've had since Tokyo that I didn't feel stressed out."

"I think you really need to consider taking a break. Weigh the pros and cons. Have you told anyone else about it?"

I scoffed. "Yeah, right. Everyone would flip out. Ugh, I really don't want to talk about this anymore. I just want to talk to you. It's the only thing I've been looking forward to all day."

"We only have two months to go," Kennedy said, as if it was a good thing. She wiggled her eyebrows, a playful smirk on her lips, trying to get me to laugh. But after thinking about those three meets I had to go to and all that practicing, two months my time was not the equivalent to two months her time. She seemed to forget that by the next time we saw each other, she would have to finish her documentary, present her thesis, and pass her classes. But school didn't seem to paint the stress on her face as much as my worries did.

"That's so far away," Ken," I whined.

"It will come here sooner than you think. And then we can go home, eat wonderful Swensons, drink hot chocolate in the glow of the Christmas tree—"

I laughed, remembering how Christmas was an ordeal for the Reed household. Her mom loved it so much. When we were kids, Mrs. Reed lit balsam fir and cinnamon candles all over the first floor, plugged in the Christmas tree, and baked us amazing sugar cookies that I would crave during the break. I wasn't surprised Kennedy was already daydreaming about us reliving that very scene we used to experience every year before she moved away.

"God, it sounds amazing," I said with a smile. "And the open-door policy doesn't exist anymore."

"But isn't your old bed a full? Mine is a queen. Just saying."

"Okay, I'm sold."

"And a new season of *Home Kitchen Masters* comes out, so we can have a binge party. And when I say binge party, I mean Swensons to-go, pj's, and all-day cuddles in my bed."

"God, that sounds perfect. It's so far away, it's almost depressing."

For the first time that day, the tightness in my chest unclenched. I wished so much that my mornings started with her, and my nights ended with her.

I couldn't sleep. I thought a lot about my looming decision because if I was going to take a break, it had to be now. We were a month out from the next ISL meet and the finals. Two months out from the world champs. I weighed the pros and cons of going, and every time I found a pro, my chest became tighter. I knew that meant something. I knew that meant my gut was screaming at me. Kennedy was right. My mental health was more important than the world champs. I could afford to skip it. I could still oblige my sponsorship contracts.

I knew what I needed to do.

CHAPTER TEN

I did it. I told David that I was taking a break from swimming, and that meant I wasn't going to finish the ISL season or go to Abu Dhabi. I explained everything the next day at practice and apologized profusely for letting him down. Sure, he was disappointed that I wouldn't be at those meets and disappointed that Amira would most likely take another world championship, but as I was about to cry, he rested his hand on my shoulder and told me, "Even world champions need a break. I want you to fall in love with the sport again."

I was so grateful for his understanding and support. An enormous weight had been lifted off me.

Before I flew back home, I needed to find a new apartment. As much as I loved living with Talia and Lillian, I really wanted to live on my own for a while since I never had. They would consolidate into a two-bedroom place, and I found a one-bedroom loft in the SoMa district that I knew I had to get the second I stepped inside. Right after I made the condo purchase official, I bought a plane ticket home for Thanksgiving so I could take a much-needed break, relaxing and humbling myself back home in Aspen Grove with my family for the holidays.

I hadn't spent time in Aspen Grove for more than a week since the start of college. Now I planned on staying for six weeks, hoping that would be some remedy for my mind. New stores and restaurants had popped up, like an industrial-looking craft brewery on the outskirts of town, a Chipotle that had me drooling at the sight, and a giant Whole Foods two blocks from Swensons in a building that had been vacant for quite some time. But despite those additions, it was still the same little town I used to hate when I was a teen but had learned to love during college. I loved the center of town, lined with colonial-style buildings already glistening with Christmas lights. As my dad drove me home from the Syracuse airport, I reunited with those familiar Aspen Grove roads weaving through the colonial charm, and I realized my hometown had so much personality tucked away. I hadn't learned to appreciate anything it had to offer until I was already homesick and missing its calm and quaint demeanor.

My house still smelled the same, greeting me the second I stepped through the garage door and into the kitchen. Mom had a big plate of homemade chocolate chip cookies waiting for me on the island, and when she saw me float to the plate as if under its gravitational pull, she leapt off the couch and scooped me up in her motherly embrace. I hugged her tightly, missing her more than ever. Same for my dad and brother. Liam's hard footsteps scampered down the steps, and I only had a minimal amount of time to process his six-foot self with his head of curly brown-blond hair running straight toward me. He plowed into me with a hug, picking me up and doing a full twirl before setting me back down. Despite having a decent accounting job, he still lived at home. He claimed he was saving money to buy a house, but I teased that he was mooching as long as he could. But I had to admit, making fun of him did help me feel a little better.

"Yay, my twin is here for six whole weeks," he shouted. "Six whole weeks of trouble."

"And I'm not training right now, so…" I flashed a mischievous grin at my parents. "I have all the time in the world."

Mom and Dad playfully shook their heads.

I went up to my room to drop off my suitcase. My parents had left it the same as it was when I moved out. The same full-sized bed in the corner pressed up against the soft aquamarine walls I'd insisted on because I was obsessed with swimming. My high school swimming plaques still hung on the walls, proving how dated the room was with the lack of my twenty-six other swimming medals. But hanging from a nail right next to those plaques were the first two medals I'd ever won—two bronze from the Kazan world champs when I was eighteen.

Tossing my suitcase on the bed, I circled the room as a flood of memories filled my mind. Most of them being those few short months with Kennedy. All the times we'd played with stuffed animals, watched Disney movies with a big bowl of popcorn, first slept together, and when she'd surprised me after states with a bag of Swensons. And then I remembered the little gem tucked under my bed. I crouched to find Honey Bear still lying next to the storage bins preserving school projects, artwork, and other miscellaneous items from my childhood. He was the teddy bear Kennedy had bought me when I needed stitches on my chin.

I hugged him and inhaled the top of his honey-colored head, which smelled like a mixture of my house and dust.

He would definitely be coming back to San Francisco with me.

As I waited for Kennedy to finish the last few weeks of the fall semester, I slept in like a normal twenty-three-year-old, on some days until eleven. While my family was at work, I went to the rec center to work out since I desperately needed to. I worked at my own pace, on my own time, because not working out drove me even crazier than all the strict diets and schedules. On some days, when I had an amazing workout on the treadmill, bike, or in the weight room, I treated myself to Swensons, indulging in their fried chicken sandwich or a blue raspberry slushie. Definitely not the combo meal, which included a sandwich, fries, *and* a drink. Even though I wasn't training, I couldn't overdo it on the unhealthy eating.

Kennedy finally came home in mid-December, three weeks into my stay in Aspen Grove. The second she texted me, I borrowed Liam's car and sped to her parents' house with a bouquet of white roses, lavender lilies, and baby's breath in a glass vase and two combo meals in a Swensons to-go bag to celebrate the fact that she got her master's degree. My girlfriend had a master's degree in journalism. She deserved all the flowers, and most importantly, all the junk food.

When she opened the door, her giant hug tripped me backward, and I almost lost my grip on the vase. She showered me with kisses that had me blushing to the maximum degree by the time I stepped inside, breathing in the wonderful scent of balsam fir and cinnamon, just like I remembered. I said hello to her parents, and I'm sure they spotted the evidence of the blush.

"These are for you," I said and presented her with the flowers and Swensons bag. "Ms. Master's Degree."

She smelled the flowers and then the Swensons bag before kissing my cheek, adding to the warmth on my face for her parents to see. "Oh my God. I'm not sure which smells better."

"It's probably the food." I raised the bag. "We can eat these together. Binge on *Home Kitchen Masters*?"

"Finally!"

She grabbed my hand, and we scampered off to her bedroom where her suitcase sat next to her bed. She put the flowers on her white desk next to another vase of roses that I assumed were from her parents. She plopped on the foot of her bed, wasting no time shoving the warm, salty fries into her mouth. I joined her, ripped back the foil, and bit into the fried chicken sandwich with its perfectly warm, crisped breading with the right amount of seasoning in each bite, the pickles, onions, lettuce, tomatoes, and their secret sauce drizzled on top. God, it was like sex.

"Thank you so much for the flowers," she said and rested her hand on my thigh. "They're beautiful. You make me feel spoiled."

"With flowers?"

"I never got flowers from other people I dated. Well, except now, Brielle thought it would be a good time to send me flowers," she said, gesturing to the bouquet of rainbow roses next to mine. "She never did it before. They came before I even got here. My mom put them on my desk. I told her to toss them, but she said she wouldn't throw out a nice gesture. I'm gonna toss them anyway."

"You do whatever you need to do."

"I need to make room for flowers from someone I actually care about." She hooked her arm around mine and kissed my shoulder.

"I'm really proud of you, Ken." She made a goofy face as she shoved a handful of fries in her mouth. "What? I'm serious. You got your master's degree. That's amazing."

"It was just a year and a half program—"

"Stop selling yourself short. Let me be proud of you."

"All right, you can be proud of me. But after I tell you more news."

"Good news?"

She nodded, swallowed another bite of fries, and washed it down with a large sip of chocolate malt. "It's amazing news."

"What is it?"

"I got a paid internship working on this documentary. Guess what city?"

My heart raced at the anticipation. "San Francisco?"

"Ding ding ding! Can you believe that? In San Francisco. With *you*." She poked my side. My mouth dropped.

"Seriously?" My voice cracked, but I swallowed the tears. I refused to cry in front of her, especially when this was amazing news for her, for us, some kind of clearing in my hazy future. I'd felt so down, and then Kennedy was in front of me, telling me this amazing news, and so much happiness filled me up all at once it was almost jarring.

"Seriously. I'm not unpacking that suitcase," she said with a point. I was speechless. All I could do was stare as she waited for a response. She bumped me with her shoulder. "This is when you celebrate."

"Kennedy, that's…that's amazing. I'm even more proud of you."

"You just bought a condo. I just got a paid internship in the very city in which you bought said condo. I think we're about to make big steps after Christmas."

She intertwined her fingers with mine. Tackling adulthood was a little less scary with the promise of Kennedy being near me.

"So are you going to live with Jacob, or were you going to—um—live with me?" I asked.

She bumped my side again, a grin pulling on her lips. "I was hoping with you. You have a better face than Jacob. Plus, I really don't want to hear about what weird technology he's making at work. When you get him going, he doesn't stop, and none of it makes sense. He also lives an hour away, and my internship will be in the city. But if that's too much of a leap—for us to live together—then I don't have to. I completely understand if you don't want to."

"No, I want you to," I said almost too quickly, but I didn't care. I knew what I wanted. I wanted to be happy. I wanted something to look forward to, and being with Kennedy was a fast track to feeling normal. "There's definitely enough space. Loft bedroom. Huge windows. Hardwood floors. Do I need to show pictures to convince you?"

She scratched her chin and looked up. "Yeah, I'm really going to need pictures. It's the only way that it will officially sell me."

We crawled back to her pillows, and when we lay down, she rested her head on my shoulder as I pulled up all the pictures I'd taken when I bought the condo. Handing her the phone, I pressed my forehead against her cheek, inhaling the smell of shampoo and her wonderful natural scent. I couldn't imagine falling asleep and waking up to her every single day. It felt too good to be true.

"Quinn, this place is beautiful. Look at these windows."

The windows crawled up the vaulted ceiling. Two rows of normal-sized ones on the left and on the right, two giant ones stacked on top of each other. Light hardwood floors spread throughout the open kitchen and living room. Stainless steel appliances. Granite kitchen countertops. A balcony, and from the seventh floor, I caught a glimpse of the Bay Bridge in the distance.

"Does this mean I sold you on being my roommate?"

She kissed my cheek. "I want to be your roommate." With a moment to think, she pulled away and shook her head. "I can't believe this."

"What do you mean?"

"Think about it, Quinn. Think about everything we've been through. You were my best friend when we were kids, we were each other's first kiss, then the pact we made in high school...everything is coming full circle now. I can't believe we're going to be living together."

"We're going from playing house to actually living it."

"We spent so many hours playing house," she said with a laugh.

Way back when, we would play in each other's basements. I was always the husband, and that was because we auctioned that role off with three rounds of rock, paper, scissors. Obviously, I lost. I had to make my role official by proposing to Kennedy with a watermelon Ring Pop, her favorite flavor, and, in return, she placed a blue raspberry ring, my favorite, on my left hand. Anytime we got our hands on the candies, we'd put them on our fingers and get into character. She was an English teacher. I was a professional swimmer. We had a golden retriever named Buddy. For being a stuffed animal, Buddy had quite the life. He had a whole backstory, courtesy of Kennedy's wild imagination. It had to have been the writer living inside her.

Buddy was the runt of the litter and ran away from his siblings and mom because they were mean to him. An older couple who couldn't care for a little pup like Buddy rescued him from the side of the road took him to the shelter, aka Kennedy's room. More specifically, her bed, where she lined up a handful of stuffed animals to represent different crates. She'd always wanted a dog, and even though I really wanted the pet dolphin right next to Buddy, she'd told me I had to give the wife what she wanted.

"Happy wife is a happy life, Quinn," she'd said. She had just come back from her cousin's wedding when she'd learned that phrase. So I had to acquiesce to her wishes, and we'd brought Buddy back.

"You were a bossy wife," I said.

She feigned shock. "You never cleaned the dishes."

"Because I spent all day swimming, and then you made me walk Buddy."

Her shocked expression quickly morphed into an impish grin. "What are your thoughts on a real Buddy?" She wiggled her eyebrows up and down.

"No way, not right now."

"But in the future?"

"When I'm a retired swimmer, and we have a yard big enough for Buddy to roam."

"Are the suburbs in our future? The California suburbs?"

"Do you want them to be in our future?"

She bit her lip and nodded. "I always pictured raising a family somewhere in New York. Like, outside the city, so we had a house and a yard, but then my partner and I could have a date night in the city, away from the kids."

"Kids?"

She nodded. "You want them, don't you?"

"I think so but, like, kids in the far future. I can't even think about having kids until I'm retired and have a house in the burbs after I've spent my twenties living in the city."

"Oh, man, I totally agree. I want my whole twenties to live life, travel, nail down a good job."

I breathed a sigh of relief. "Oh thank God."

"You were really that worried?"

"Yes! We've never talked about kids before, and if you had an inkling of baby fever soon, I don't know—"

"God, no. We're twenty-three. Way too young to be having kids."

"Well, I feel like a fourth of our class already has kids."

"I'm glad we're on the same page in the baby department. Like, we're still another era away from that happening." After my sigh of relief, she jumped onto my lap and pinned me to her bed. My heart rushed at the surprise. As she leaned forward, her hair pooled over my face, enveloping us in a secluded world within the secluded bedroom.

"You're bringing me home with you," she said softly. "You can't run away from the idea now."

I shook my head. "I'm never running from you."

The rest of our time in Aspen Grove was everything I wanted it to be. Kennedy and I spent almost the whole time together, mingling with our families, secluding ourselves in one of our bedrooms to binge Netflix while cuddling. We even went out with Liam and our good friend Gabriel to the new brewery to spend the night catching up and reminiscing about childhood. I spent Christmas Eve with her family, including her brother Jacob and his wife Ava. I hadn't seen Jacob since I was thirteen. Christmas Day, Kennedy spent the day with my family. We went out to the brewery again with Liam, Gabriel, and Gabriel's girlfriend of two years to celebrate New Year's. The holidays back home were wonderful and humbling.

As much as I wanted to start my life with Kennedy in a brand-new condo, in a brand-new city for her, I was getting used to the quiet life in Aspen Grove. I couldn't believe I never fully took advantage of everything my town offered back when I lived in it. I was born and raised there, lived in the same house since I was born, and I couldn't wait to move across the country when I had the chance. Home was so comforting, reliable, and my family had a huge part in that feeling. But it was also quiet and laid back. Life moved much slower than in a bustling city. It really helped ground me, helped me focus on the most important things in life. It wasn't a stupid time on a scoreboard or a medal. It was having loved ones by my side, caring for other people and myself, and belonging somewhere. I was so excited that I didn't have to fly home by myself, that Kennedy was coming with me with her life stuffed in multiple bags. We were going to find a place to belong... together.

But as much as I was looking forward to that, I was terrified about picking up my life where I'd left it back in San Francisco: lost in the dark.

❖

I stood on my new balcony, bundled in the blanket my parents gave me for Christmas. Kennedy and I had just moved into the condo. It was the first week of January, and darkness had fallen over San Francisco, but the city was one of the few things that looked even more beautiful through the darkness. Life still carried on. Music still played from various restaurants and bars down the street. People still walked around the neighborhood with their dogs, on the phone, breathing in the water coming off the bay. Lights still twinkled and illuminated the city.

Two hands slipped in front of my stomach and pulled me into a tight embrace. I smiled when the smell of Kennedy's shampoo kissed me before her lips landed on my cheek. We had spent the whole day unpacking, got our bed set up and most of our bedroom, but still had to tackle the coffee table and entertainment system, but we were so exhausted.

"What are you doing, my little cocoon," she said and then kissed the back of my neck, forcing the hairs to stand up and beg for more.

"Hiding," I said. "From you and our mess of a living room."

She laughed. "You know a lot of that was your fault with all those Christmas presents you gave me."

"Those weren't Christmas presents. Those were move-in presents. Big difference."

She'd unwrapped the gifts when we moved in the day before. Thank God for Talia and Lillian. I bribed them with fifty dollars each to wrap all the presents I had delivered to our condo and place them inside with the spare key, so when Kennedy and I walked in, she saw all her move-in presents in their designated room for her to unwrap. People who got a six-month paid internship on a documentary about LGBTQ+ history in San Francisco deserved a bunch of gifts.

"But all I gave you was that medal display frame," she said. "You weren't supposed to buy me anything."

We'd agreed before Christmas that we weren't going to go crazy on presents because I'd just bought a condo and Kennedy was moving cross country. But…I lied and got her stuff anyway. A lot of things. The tone in her voice indicated guilt, but I loved what she got me. It was a glass display case with six separate frames for each of my Olympic medals. The icing on the cake was a wooden sign that said

"World's Okayest Swimmer" to hang right above the frame. It hung in our bedroom, the first thing I'd nailed to the wall because I loved it so much.

I'd bought her something new for every room. For the kitchen, I got her a French press since the one she'd used in Brooklyn had been her roommate's. Turned out, she needed a lot of coffee in the morning to function. In the living room, I'd bought her a rustic pallet bookshelf filled with all her favorite classics: *The Great Gatsby, Animal Farm, 1984, A Brave New World, Slaughterhouse Five, Lord of the Flies, The Outsiders.* And no bookshelf was complete without all seven Harry Potter books. I left plenty of room for her to decorate and add books as she pleased. For the balcony, I'd bought her all the things she needed to have her garden: lettuce, peppers, tomatoes, peas, green beans, and of course, spinach to feed me. In our bathroom, I'd gotten her a whole basket of Lush bath bombs and salts so she could have her Sunday bubble baths. Maybe I could join her a few times in the tub that was definitely big enough to share. And then in the bedroom, of course, I was the present. Wink. Wink. Because I could be adorably cheesy sometimes.

"Let me do things for you, okay?" I said when I faced her. "I wanted to do all of that, and I'm able to do it. I just expect you to give me a few extra kisses in return."

She gave me an attack of really short pecks, ending it with a longer one, a kiss more passionate and loving than the twenty others.

"Now I have one more present."

She grunted and rolled her eyes. "Oh my God, you have a problem. Seriously, stop buying me things."

I reached into my sweatpants pocket and pulled two Ring Pops. She threw her head back in laughter as I gave her the watermelon ring.

"Since we're making our house-playing days official," I said. "We need to have our Ring Pops, just like old times."

She unwrapped her candy and gave the ring back to me. "You have to propose."

"Even though I already did when we were nine?"

She sucked in her lips, and her growing grin indicated she was enjoying this as much as we had when we were kids. I rolled my eyes and acquiesced. "Kennedy Renee Reed, will you make me the luckiest girl in the world and be my live-in girlfriend? Can we finally make all of our years playing house official?"

She tossed her hands over her heart and feigned shock. "Oh my God, a thousand times yes," she said facetiously and stuck her left hand out so I could put the ring on her finger.

She made the proposal official by tasting it, and I followed her by putting my ring on and doing the same. I closed my eyes for a moment as I enjoyed the taste of my youth. I studied the ring on her finger, and sure it was just a Ring Pop, but I liked that something representing our relationship was on her finger. It was a fake proposal, but why had my pulse twitched faster than it should have? Why did a smile linger a little longer than the quick taste of nostalgia? My mind sent me back to the jewelry store the day before I left Tokyo and that blue topaz ring. The feelings were similar.

Warmth traveled through me. Here we were together. In our own place. Our own balcony. Our own city. All those years of playing house, all those summer nights throughout our childhood being so excited when our parents allowed us to have a sleepover, that was all real now. She was part of my life, and after the past few weeks of spending every day with her, I never wanted to be without her again.

"It's kinda funny that we used to play house, and we were always married," Kennedy said softly, a warm smile pulling her lips upward. "It wasn't until after those days that I realized I had a crush on you. If I'd known then that I was going to like you, I would've tried to get you to kiss me."

"Oh, would you?"

"Yes, I would have."

"Maybe it was because you finally saw how hard I worked as a professional swimmer to put invisible cheeseburgers and fries on my wife's plate that you realized how much you loved and appreciated me."

"Hey, I worked too. I was an English teacher, remember? And look at you now. You really are a professional swimmer."

My smile loosened. Even when I was a kid dreaming about being an Olympic swimmer, I couldn't come up with a real job for house like a teacher or a cop or an accountant. I latched on to swimming so hard from a young age that I didn't know my life without it. I'd always thought that immortal happiness took the form of a gold medal decorating my neck. There was no Plan B. And now I was at an age when I wished that there was a Plan B, but instead, I'd put all my eggs in one basket.

"Yeah, I'm a professional swimmer and nothing else," I said, and then realized as my words hung there how self-pitying I sounded.

"Quinn, that's not even true."

"But what am I, Ken? I've only focused on swimming my whole life, and for what? A few medals? A swimming career that will get me to one more Olympics, two if I'm super lucky? Swimmers don't last for that long. I have no idea what I'm supposed to do with the rest of my life."

She rubbed my arm. "There's plenty of time to figure it out. I mean, does any twenty-three-year-old know what they're doing?"

"I don't know. Do they?"

"I don't think so. We just got our training wheels off, Quinn. We're all riding into the adult world for the first time on our own. I feel like it's normal to struggle a little bit."

"But you're not struggling."

"Define struggle. I decided to go to grad school partially because I still didn't know what I wanted to do with my journalism degree. Broadcast? Print? Neither of those sounds exciting to me. I still don't know what I want to do with it, and I'm lucky that I have this internship for the next six months, but I have no idea what the hell I'm going to do after it. I'm kind of banking on making connections through the filmmaker, but that might not happen. So I'll feel as lost as you do in the summer."

I had no idea she wrestled with those thoughts, and I felt like a horrible girlfriend for just finding out and not giving her more time to talk about her issues.

"I didn't know you felt that way," I said softly.

She shrugged. "I worry, but I'm hoping for the best. But you want to know what I think?"

"What?" I asked, enjoying her still rubbing my arms in the most nurturing way.

"I think you've been so used to having everything written out for you, like every minuscule detail of your day-to-day schedule was decided by coaches and practices and diets. Right now, you're staring at a blank page for one of the first times in your life. It's scary for everyone, but it's especially scary for you because you've always had something to work for."

"That's exactly it. What I worked for, I've already achieved, and it didn't transform me like I thought it would. It sounds so selfish and ungrateful, but I can't help it."

"I don't think you're selfish or ungrateful. I thought grad school would answer all my questions, but it didn't. If it wasn't for this internship, I would be terrified and scared too. I think you should give yourself more credit. You're in a lot better shape than you think."

She kissed me on the cheek, and I let out a sigh of relief. It was nice to hear that she thought I was in good shape because all my thoughts told me that I wasn't. I wanted to be more than a machine. Kennedy had wanted to major in journalism because she wanted to bring attention to certain issues that needed attention. Back then, it was LGBTQ+ rights, the environment, immigration, and women's rights. Talia studied community health and prevention research in hopes of one day researching the cancer that took her mom's life when she was only fifteen. Lillian was pre-med and wanted to do physical therapy after swimming. The people in my life all had these amazing goals to better the world, to have their career impact so many people for the better. And here I was just thinking about myself, going after a medal, and now after ten years of being on the national team, I wanted to make a difference too?

I was so angry at myself for chasing after something so superficial. Half of the reason why I majored in psychology was to better understand how the brain worked and to use my knowledge to beat myself at stresses, doubts, and anxieties about swimming. I was so used to looking through a narrow swimming lens that I didn't even think about what I could use my degree for other than my sport. Why couldn't I have thought long-term when I was in college? Before it was too late?

I kept questioning myself until the early morning. I couldn't even fully enjoy Kennedy curled up into me with her arm slung around my body. Even the soft, rhythmic patterns of her breathing tickling my neck as her head rested on my right boob didn't rock me to sleep. I'd been running my fingers through her hair for an hour, hoping to put her to sleep so she didn't know it was another restless night for me. I started to worry if I would ever get out of my funk. How much longer was it going to take for me to equilibrate from the Olympic fantasy I'd been living in for the past two years? How the hell did I find a purpose that defined me as more than just being a swimmer? What if I never found out? What if I was going to feel this miserable despite having all the amazing things that I had?

I had no reason to feel this way. I had family and friends who loved and supported me. I had a home. I had a wonderful girlfriend. I'd accomplished the things that others spent a lifetime dreaming about. Whenever I found the strength to applaud myself for my swimming accomplishments, looking at my medals hanging on the adjacent wall, an evil voice in my head told me that scraps of gold and silver didn't count as real accomplishments.

My thoughts spiraled for hours until it wore my brain out, and I finally went to sleep.

CHAPTER ELEVEN

Here was how I spent my free days without any sort of training: I woke up to Kennedy stepping out of the shower around seven thirty. The first thing I saw was my beautiful girlfriend standing in front of the closet—*our* closet—with a towel wrapped around her and another one twisted on top of her head. On good mornings, she would see me stirring and stretching, and she would jump on me. She smelled like fresh shower and body wash and would kiss all over my face as her wet hair towel draped over me. As she put makeup on and dried her hair, I started the coffee and made her scrambled eggs. Little Kennedy had always loved scrambled eggs with bacon bits, but adult Kennedy loved it when I added spinach, onions, and peppers. So really, it was a "messy omelet," we joked. Then I made us protein smoothies with almond milk, bananas, whatever kind of berry we'd decided to buy that week, protein powder, and spinach so she could drink it on the ride to her internship. I added her scrambled eggs to her lunchbox so she could eat when she got to the studio, put her coffee in her thermal mug, and drove her to work.

After giving her a kiss good-bye, I went to the gym—treadmill for forty-five minutes, a spin class or a hot yoga class, followed by another forty-five minutes in the weight room. It was a good afternoon when the buff gym rats didn't walk up to me, usually the guys in ripped tank tops or the ones who always had to grunt while they did a rep. Half of them checked me out in the mirror, and I had no idea if they were checking out me or my workout. On the bad days, a few of them had the arrogance to give me unsolicited advice, and a number were just flat out wrong and had no idea how their bodies worked.

One January day, I waited patiently for the squat bench press machine that some beefcake had been hogging for a good fifteen minutes. He would do a set with two-hundred pounds, grunt, pace around the machine about two times while he collected his breath too loudly, and repeated. I found other ways to fill in the time, like pull-ups and dumbbell presses. When I finished those, he was still using the machine. That was when I decided to take a water break and stared him down until he noticed me.

"You waiting for this?" he asked.

"Yes," I said flatly.

"Okay, let me take these off," he said and headed over to the plates.

I raised my hand. "No, that's okay. You can leave them."

His dark eyes scanned me from head to toe as he sucked in his grin. I weight trained twice a week for forty-five minutes and had been doing that since I was fifteen. I could squat two-twenty, bench press with seventy-pound dumbbells in each hand, and do pull-ups in a forty-five-pound weight belt. But despite that, Beefcake laughed as if I was full of shit.

"Nah, come on," he said, about to take the plates off.

"I'm not joking. Leave them on," I said as he slid off a fifty-pound plate.

"You know I have two hundred pounds on here, right?"

I laughed. Beefcake had tons of muscles but no brains. "I know how to count," I replied. "If you are that set on helping me, can you add ten pounds to each side?"

"Ten pounds?"

"Yes. That would be great."

"That's two-twenty."

"I'm well aware."

"You're saying you can squat more than me?"

I buzzed my lips, deciding to let my snarkiness shine during this really awkward moment for Beefcake. "If you squat two hundred, then yes, I guess I can do more than you."

Beefcake's dark brown eyebrows drew together as he acquiesced to adding twenty pounds and then gestured for me to go ahead, almost as if to prove my worth. I offered him a tight smile, wrapped my fingers around the bar, did five perfect squats at two-twenty, and marveled at his agape mouth when I finished my set.

"Jesus fu—"

I never *ever* bragged about my Olympian status at the gym...or to strangers in general. That would be classless. But something about Beefcake really pissed me off. His tight scowl. His patronizing tone. The fact that he hogged the machine for fifteen minutes for me to outdo him, and then he gave me this look as if I'd said something derogatory. If I was going to pull out my Olympian card on any stranger, it was going to be for Beefcake.

"Girls can lift," I said with a sneer. "Don't look so shocked about it."

"But—"

I leaned into him, but not too close because his skin glowed too much, which meant he reeked of sweaty man musk. "Not to brag, but I did just come back from the Olympics. Five golds. Now, are you done with this machine? Because I would like to finish my set."

With his mouth still open, he waved for me to continue, and I did as he slung his sweat rag over his shoulder, gawked at me for another five reps, and finally walked away.

That was how I turned what could have been a bad gym day into a really satisfying one.

Then I usually came home, ate some kind of salad, but since I wasn't training, I treated myself to cheese or croutons, mediated for twenty minutes, and showered. Then came an afternoon of boredom when the extra pep from the mornings and workout fizzled out of my system, and all the free time allowed the anxiety I had about my life and career to take over. I tried to nap it off, usually waking up at five when I started cooking dinner. Something about having a delicious meal for my girlfriend right when she came home was exciting to me. I really enjoyed cooking her food, much more than just for myself.

But on the bad nights, after a full stomach and after watching *Jeopardy* with Kennedy on the couch, taking turns with who got to rest their feet on the other's lap, the worry became so loud in my head that sitting on the couch became stifling. For solace and time alone, I decided to shower. As the bathroom collected steam, and the streams of hot water pounded on my back, I would sit on the ground and sob. I didn't want Kennedy to see or hear me because part of my irrational anxiety was that I wouldn't get better, and she would regret moving out here to be with someone who was depressed. I was terrified of losing her for a third time, and at the same time, I was terrified my life had no direction. It made me feel even worse when I would come back downstairs and lie to her about it. The first few times, I played it off as how I was switching to night showers. But obviously, that wasn't true. My actual showers were right after my workouts in the morning. My nighttime showers were nothing more than a crying session masked by running water.

One evening in early February, as the existential crisis formed in my head, I drew myself a bath, stealing one of the lavender bath bombs I'd bought Kennedy as a move-in present. After situating her bath pillow on the opposite side of the faucet, I dimmed the lights, lit a few candles, and submerged into the warm, foamy water. I'd never taken a bath before. At least not with a pillow, bath bomb, and warm water. My kind involved buckets of ice and almost made me cry from the pain. I realized then that I had been missing out on the luxury and calmness of a bubble bath. No wonder Kennedy always had one on Sunday evenings to combat the Sunday Scaries.

I closed my eyes, but I couldn't turn my brain off. Every part of me under the water was relaxed. I dipped under the purple foam, hoping the silence would flick my brain off. Being underwater used to be so therapeutic. I didn't hear anything. It was just me and my thoughts. And when my thoughts were the only thing I could hear, being underwater was like throwing myself into a small room so I could hear the worst things I thought about myself being screamed in my ear.

I pushed back up and wiped the foam off my face. And lost it. My whole body cracked. I sobbed, letting all those months of holding back worries, doubts, problems, fears, and anxieties into the tub.

I'd grown to hate the sport I fell in love with as a kid, the sport that first sparked my dreams, the sport that taught me resilience, failure, self-control, and motivation. The sport that had given me so much but at the same time had taken everything away. I sat in the tub, finally allowing myself to feel the emptiness I'd been running from since I settled back into reality after the Olympics. I allowed myself to choke on my cries until I had nothing left.

Twenty minutes in, my body still quivered when I heard the front door close downstairs. Kennedy was home, and I didn't even have dinner ready. I sat up and splashed handfuls of water on my face to erase the puffiness ballooning my eyes.

"Quinn? Quinn?" Each call grew louder as she ascended the spiral staircase and into our bedroom. She knocked on the door and poked her head through the crack. "Quinn?"

"Hey!" I said way too chipper, overcompensating. I wiped my face one last time. "How was work?"

She opened the door and stood in front of the tub. "Work was fine. Very busy but good. What are you doing?"

"Trying out one of these bath bombs."

She studied my face and cocked an eyebrow. "Are you okay?"

"Yeah, I'm fine."

"Were you crying?"

"No. I just got some of this bath bomb in my eye." I cupped some foamy water into my hands to show as proof. "It's not tear-free."

"No duh. It's all perfume-y and glittery."

"I'm sorry dinner isn't ready. I guess I—" Got too carried away crying? "Just enjoyed this too much. Maybe we can order something?"

She waved a hand. "I'm not really worried. Devon and I went out for sushi today and stuffed ourselves, so I'm not starving." Her stare dipped to where the soap met my breasts right above the nipples. "Plus, food can wait when my girlfriend is naked in a tub."

I grinned. "Want to join? The water isn't really warm anymore. Maybe we can draw another? Grab some wine, get another bath bomb?"

"Man, you really know how to take a bath. Let's do it."

I was already in new water when Kennedy came back with two glasses of wine. She pulled her shirt above her head, and I sank farther into the water as I watched her strip. She unhooked her bra, and despite the countless times I'd marveled at her breasts, I reached for my wine to replenish the lack of moisture in my mouth. She unbuttoned her jeans, but I still couldn't peel my eyes away from her breasts. I didn't think I could ever get tired of looking at her naked, and I still couldn't get over that I could see her naked anytime I wanted.

Once her clothes were off, she gently glided into the bath, and I hated the foamy water that concealed her nipples.

"Oh, hey," she said, and her right toes tickled my upper thigh.

"We've been living with each other for a month and haven't taken a bath yet," I said before taking another sip of wine. "Yet at our first high school sleepover, we were quick to hop in the shower together."

"Ah, teenage hormones."

She relaxed her legs against the sides of mine. Water droplets latched on to her neck and the tendrils of hair that didn't make it into her messy bun. She reached for her wine over the edge of the tub, took a sip, and smiled.

"So, you're a night shower-er and the occasional bath girl now?" she asked with teasing in her voice.

I ran my fingers through the top layer of foam, drawing a dent of lines and feeling the lightness in the air evaporate. "I wanted to see what the hype was about," I said, hating that I fed her a lie, but I wasn't in the mood to talk. I didn't want to taint our first bath in our first home with a sob fest. I didn't want to talk about my problems that really didn't feel like problems. I loved my evenings with her, and I wanted to enjoy a bath with wine and a beautiful naked woman. So I pressed on, "I have to say, I like it a lot better than ice baths."

"Those sound like hell."

"The longest six minutes. Plus, pretty naked girls are never involved, so…" Then it was my turn to tickle her thigh.

"I feel like a true adult right now. Taking a bath with my girlfriend after work with a glass of wine."

"Tomorrow, we'll be applying for Social Security."

"Wow, life really does fly in the blink of an eye."

I splashed her and hit her perfect breasts. "Tell me about your day."

She sent a wave back at me. "It was really good. I'm excited. Devon and I brainstormed location shots. I reached out to our interview subjects to schedule dates. Oh, and while we got sushi, Devon was asking how I was adjusting here and recommended I join a social sports league. Apparently, those are a thing?"

I shrugged. "I wouldn't know, but sounds cool. Making new friends as an adult is so hard."

"I know, and I really need a group of friends. You know, so we can talk about you and go to brunch. Oh, and Napa. I forgot there's Napa." She playfully facepalmed her forehead. "Anyways, I looked into it, and there are drinking leagues, competitive leagues, gay leagues, all-girl leagues."

"What a time to be alive. Sign me up for the competitive lesbian league, please."

"I think I'm going to do it. The girls league. No analyzing, just doing it because I want some friends."

"I think it's great, babe. I can come to your games and flip out at the ref for making bad calls or giving you a yellow card."

"It's very rare for the goalie to get a card. I've only gotten one, sophomore year of high school."

"That's hot. How about you do that again, and I'll reward you."

She laughed. "No, Quinn, you don't want a card."

"I know you don't, but I want you to get one."

"I don't think I can get away with that in a competitive league. There's a trophy at the end. That means I need to be on my best behavior."

I played along and grunted. "Ugh, okay, you win that trophy, and we can set it up on your bookshelf downstairs. Deal?"

She reached out her hand for a shake, and I accepted. "Deal." She kissed the back of my hand. "Now, how was your day? Are you sure everything's okay?"

No, it wasn't. I'd just cried for a good twenty minutes, but I didn't want her to worry. Her plate was already taken up with her internship and trying to settle in a brand-new city and finding a life outside of work and me. She didn't need my issues on her shoulders because she was the type of empathetic person to absorb my feelings and make them her own.

I plastered on a convincing smile. "What makes you think I'm not okay? You're naked in a tub with me. I'm doing amazing."

"I'm serious, Quinn," she said and caressed my ankle with her thumb. "You seem…I don't know. Off?"

"I'm tired. That's all."

"You'd tell me if something was bothering you, right?"

No.

"Yes," I lied, but gave her calf a reassuring squeeze. If I really needed her, of course I would lean on her. But nothing was worth mentioning that I hadn't already voiced. She didn't need to know the tiny worries pricking at my mind.

"Because I don't want you to bottle up your feelings. You're used to doing it, and it's not healthy. It doesn't really accomplish anything."

"It does temporarily. Enough for me to swim or do something I need to do."

"Yeah, but hasn't bottling stuff up gotten you to this point? Feeling overwhelmed and blue every single day?"

"It happens sometimes, Ken," I said. "People feel blue. It's actually really common in the sports industry. At least they told us that in my psychology classes and mental training. This isn't anything out of the ordinary after the Olympics."

"Depression?"

I nodded. "You work so hard, and then bam, it's over. All the buildup, the hype, the rush, it comes to a crashing halt. Think Cinderella the whole evening, and then picture her a minute past midnight, and she's left with nothing but all those memories."

Her eyebrows furrowed, and that concerned look took over her face again. "So you feel like Cinderella after midnight?" she asked in a low, cautious tone.

I hesitated for a moment, knowing this bath was heading in the direction I didn't want it to go. But that was something I thought she needed to know to put my depression into perspective. "I do."

She ran her hands through the water as silence squeezed into the tub. I drank to occupy some time while she ruminated. Seeing her long expression and how helpless she seemed was the exact reason I didn't want her to see inside my brain. She would try everything in her power to make me happy when I had no idea what that even looked like. My idea of happiness was distorted into external motivations rather than internal. I felt like I needed to relearn what it was really like to be happy, something that didn't involve medals, world records, or winning.

"I don't want you to feel like that," she said. "Tell me what I need to do to help you feel better."

What would make me feel better was to not focus on my sadness. I'd already cried it out and didn't want the evenings to mesh together with my usual depressing afternoons.

I leaned over to scoop her into my lap. When I pulled her, her eyes widened, and the flat expression on her mouth curled upward. There was that smile that I loved, kicking her concern to the curb. "I think we should christen the bathtub," I said and started kissing the soft column of her neck.

"Quinn," she said through her giggles. Her legs wrapped around my lower back, the water splashing against the side of the tub. "I was trying to have a serious conver—"

I sucked on her favorite spot, the nape of the left side of her neck. Every time I pulled it into my lips, her head relaxed to the side. Caressing slowly and methodically up her thighs to her waist, I pressed my lips against hers, and her kiss lit me up with a surge of endorphins. I quickly deepened it, begging her mouth for entrance with my tongue. Her legs clasped tighter as I used one hand to keep her stable while sliding the other in between us and across her center.

Right as she released a breathy moan, I pulled away and met her eyes as they darkened with desire. "You still want to have a serious conversation?" I whispered against her ear.

She let out a low needy groan as my hand pressed into her where she begged for it. She buried her head into my shoulder. I rubbed deep circles on her and then pulled one of her nipples into my mouth, sucking it into a hard peak before moving on to the other one.

"Quinn," she murmured, but I kept giving her nipples attention with my tongue because I'd been drawn to them ever since she took off her shirt. "We're getting water everywhere."

"I don't care," I said, spreading her folds and slipping a finger inside her.

She gasped, and the sudden insertion jolted her head back while her hips bucked into my hand. As she started grinding, she directed my face back into hers. She sucked in my bottom lip, running her tongue along it, which had my lips buzzing with sharp electricity. She was able to send warmth from my center, up my spine, past my neck, and made the back of my head tingly with her kiss. She filled me with so much hunger that the feeling was almost brand new because no other woman was able to elicit that kind of desire from me.

"Quinn, I want your mouth on me," she said against my earlobe. And then I was completely unwound and undone.

We stumbled out of the tub, and she grabbed a towel to pat down her body. I'm not sure why. Where we were going, we didn't have time for pat-downs. Her mind probably went out of the moment and thought about soaking wet sheets, but I wanted her to stay in the moment. I yanked the towel out of her hands, flung it to the ground like the nuisance it was, and hoisted her in my arms. She gripped her legs around my waist as I carried her into the bedroom. But before we fell onto the mattress, I needed to kiss her. With her still wrapped around me, I pushed her against the wall, and we crashed into the kiss that was a mixture of frustration and surrender. Her mouth fell open with ease, and in return, filled me up with the passionate urgency I craved. I slipped my hand from behind and placed my fingers back inside her, pulling a sigh from her. I felt the evidence of her arousal, and from the shudder down my spine and the jolts to my center, I probably felt the same.

"Fuck," she muttered and pulled her head back until it rested against the wall.

I moved my fingers faster and attached my lips to her warm, damp skin, kissing her collarbone and down to her breasts. As I gently bit her nipples, my strokes still insistent, her nails dug into my skin and raked hard against my back. It painted the picture more vividly for me about everything I was able to make her feel.

Once my arms started to shake, I pulled away from the wall and fell on the bed with her. The water dripping off her body soaked her and suctioned us together when I crawled on top and positioned myself between her thighs. As I started moving against her, and her nails dug into my back, it didn't take long for either of us to finish. Her cries were enough to put me right up against the edge. We'd only been grinding on each other a few moments before I came and released every single emotion I'd bottled up. My legs and arms tingled so intensely that I had to bury myself under the sheets from the shuddering. She joined me and scooted her naked body against mine, cuddling into me as we collected our breath.

I realized I'd been stroking her arm and hand in silence for at least ten minutes. Her breaths were heavy and content. Resting my cheek against the top of her head, I noticed her left hand in between my breasts. I studied her fingers, how skinny and still they were, how small her hands were. I kissed her forehead and continued to skim her skin until I stopped at her ring finger. I remembered how my lungs caught when she wore the blue topaz months back. Through the darkness in my head, she was the light in front of me. In the evenings during training, that was my time to wind down and get into the monotony of my schedule: cook dinner, watch an hour of TV, meditate, bed by nine o'clock. Repeat. But with her, the evenings made me feel alive. I slogged through the whole day just to get to the moment she came home, and we enjoyed dinner, cuddled on the couch, and she fell asleep with her head on my shoulder, left arm draped over me every night. I had no idea what the future held, but the only thing I really knew was that I wanted her in it. I didn't want these evenings to ever end because I didn't know how anything could replace the comfort and excitement I felt when she was next to me.

"Kennedy?" I said, hearing the vulnerability rattling my voice.

She looked up at me, but even within the tired smile, I saw so much happiness in the curve of her lips. It made my stomach somersault. "Yeah?"

There were things I didn't want to tell her, things I didn't want to delve into during a sexy, relaxing bath, but I promised myself that anything she really needed to know, I would tell her. I wouldn't tell her that my afternoons were my time to dwell. I wouldn't tell her how much it terrified me thinking of the smallest possibility that she would leave me. But I would tell her the important things, the feelings that weighed so heavily in me that not talking about them would only send me spiraling faster.

I rubbed her hair and took a good look at her eyes struggling to stay open. My heart raced at the words dancing at the tip of my tongue, but they needed to be said.

"I love you."

She propped herself up on her elbow. Through the darkness, she zeroed in on me. A creased brow only lasted for a moment before a smile formed on her lips again, as if the words had finally settled in. She gently rubbed my cheek and ran her thumb down my lips. "I love you too, Quinn. Very much."

She kissed my nose, then my left temple, my forehead, my right temple, before moving softly to my lips; she was so reverent, I couldn't help but feel the amount of love she had for me. It was overwhelming in the best possible way.

God, was I in love with her.

She buried her head in its usual spot, in between my shoulder and collarbone, and squeezed me tighter, making me squeak. I hugged her back with as much love as she gave.

That was the moment when I knew she was the woman I wanted to spend the rest of my life with.

CHAPTER TWELVE

At the first lightness in the air after a few unusually cold weeks, we finally were able to plug in our patio lights, set up the furniture, and invite Talia and Lillian over for a few drinks. Both of us suffered from cabin fever, especially Kennedy. Her soccer games kept getting canceled because of the freak weather. They'd had their first game, and I had to admit, Kennedy in her bright pink goalie uniform, rejecting shots left and right, was incredibly sexy. I couldn't believe it'd taken me this long to watch her play. After their win, we'd all gone out, and I was happy that she clicked with her team. She'd been so excited for practice and her following games, but the weather really amplified. Her second game had been canceled because of a dusting of snow. Actual snow. That never happened in the city. Her third game was canceled due to a heavy rainstorm that flooded the field. I blamed her for the weather, though. Everything was fine until she moved here.

Extroverted Kennedy was dying being trapped inside, especially knowing she had ten other girls trying to orchestrate another post-game bar adventure.

With the mid-March air finally at normal sweater weather temperature, Talia and Lillian saved us with a night of drinking, eating, and socializing. Since I hadn't gone to practice in months and I was no longer living with them, I had only seen them a few times for lunch or yoga. I was actually curious about updates with Lillian's fireman and the smallest bit curious about if Talia was still texting my brother.

Now that I was practically wifed up, I needed to live vicariously through them.

"Wow, the condo is gorgeous," Lillian said as she and Talia took in the space and complimented the Scandinavian décor that gave the place a pop of personality.

"Oh, that's all Kennedy," I said when I brought over my attempt at a charcuterie board. That was what defined true adulthood, right? You invited your friends over, gawked about interior design, and showcased your best attempt at charcuterie over margaritas. I considered it a huge step into the adult world, and with zero design skills, unlike Kennedy, I was impressed by how aesthetically pleasing my board was.

At the sight of food, the party assembled around the coffee table with Kennedy's homemade guac, margaritas, and flatbread. I situated myself on the floor next to her as Talia and Lillian sat on the couch.

"I figured it was Kennedy," Lillian said as she sliced some brie and spread it on a cracker. "You couldn't decorate to save your life."

"She was forbidden to have any authority in decorating," Kennedy said. I gave her a frown, and she blew me a kiss.

"Any time I went into your room, I felt my personality die a little," Talia said.

I rolled my eyes. "Okay, that's a little dramatic."

"You had nothing on your walls. Just a pride flag above your bed."

"It brought color into my room."

"Yeah, see, this is why she wasn't allowed to decorate," Kennedy added. "She was only allowed to approve or disapprove."

"It shows," Lillian said. "The place is beautiful, Kennedy. Nice job. And this food looks amazing. This flatbread—" She took another bite and closed her eyes to fully savor the taste.

"I'm really dead weight in this relationship," I said. "She knows how to decorate *and* cook amazing food."

"You're really here just to look pretty," Kennedy said with a wink.

"Pretty much. But my charcuterie is pretty impressive, right?"

All three of them studied it for a moment and then gave a satisfied nod.

Kennedy looped an arm through mine and kissed my cheek. "It's the most beautiful board I've ever seen."

"You're lying."

"So, Kennedy, how are you liking San Francisco?" Talia asked.

"A very cold San Francisco," Lillian added. "We promise it isn't usually this cold."

"I love it so far. I've been busy working on this film."

"Which is so cool, by the way."

Kennedy turned a light shade of pink. "Yeah, it's been really fun. It's been busy. Good busy. Especially now that we're interviewing people."

"And she just joined a soccer league," I bragged. "She's the badass goalie."

"Can we come to your games?" Talia said. "We'll be the best cheerleaders."

"Yes. Please do. That is, if we ever have a game again. We only had one, and the other two were canceled. It's been years since I've been on the pitch, though. I'm a little rusty and will need all the encouragement."

"She's lying," I said. "She did awesome at the first game. How many shots did the other team have, and you blocked them all?"

"Beginner's luck," she said.

I shook my head. "Nope. All talent and badassery."

"Hey, Quinn, follow your girlfriend's lead, and get back in the pool," Lillian said with a teasing grin as she tossed a chip at me.

I knew that was coming. "I'm enjoying sleeping in and eating chips and guac, thank you," I said and found the chip on my lap.

"You given any thought about that?" Talia asked before another bite.

"Not really," I answered. "David wants me to come be a part of his swim camp in a few weeks. So I agreed to that."

"I think it's great, babe," Kennedy said. I'd told her about the idea when David first brought it up a month ago. I'd never coached before, unless I counted swim lessons in high school.

"Maybe you'll fall in love with coaching," Kennedy said.

"Maybe. I did really like teaching swim lessons," I said.

"And these kids are already qualifying for the Olympic trials," Talia said. "I think you'll be great at it, and they're going to basically die when they see you. You're the queen of the Tokyo Olympics."

"Well, we miss you in the pool," Lillian added. "Fukuoka world champs is four and a half months out. You thinking about staying out of those?"

"Don't allow Amira Kőszegi to win gold again," Talia said. "Ugh. If she wins two more golds at worlds, then she's a ten-time world champion."

"Then good for her," I said and took a large drink. Sure, I was annoyed when Amira won two more golds in the 200 and 400-free in Abu Dhabi. Her races were really close, almost losing to the second-place swimmer. Her times were a couple of seconds slower than her Tokyo times, and that comforted me a little bit that I wasn't the only one not swimming my best. But I cared more about my mental health and taking a break than whatever Amira Kőszegi was up to in the pool. I thought her accomplishments bothered my teammates more than they bothered me.

"Maybe come to practice again and see how you do?" Lillian asked.

"I already know I'm going to sink," I said.

"You don't know that. I highly doubt you're as out of shape as you claim to be. Don't you still work out every day?"

"Yeah, but that's not what I'm worried about."

"Then what are you worried about?" Talia asked.

I hadn't really told them the reason for dropping out of Abu Dhabi. I kind of just did it and told Talia and Lillian I really needed a break for a few months. But I never addressed why.

In sports, we were taught that pushing through any kind of adversity would make us stronger. Have a stomach cramp? Keep swimming. Can't breathe the last few meters, and it hurts? Kick faster, it will end sooner. Too tired from working out six hours a day? Jump in the cold pool. It will wake you up. Hell, even when I faked my migraine, David had told me to pop an Excedrin. There was always something for us to do to subdue the pain. Resting or asking for help was never an option, and maybe I feared that opening up to my two best friends, two athletes, would result in them telling me to suck it up and just push through it.

But some things I couldn't push through.

My sigh came from the pit of my stomach. "I don't know. I guess I'm another victim of post-Olympic depression. I mean, Lil, you had it after Rio, right?"

"I did, and right when I got my bearings again, I tore my ACL and fell into an even worse depression."

"Then how did you get out of it?"

She tossed back a drink as if fueling herself for diving into her feelings. It hit me right then and there: the effects of sweeping all of our problems under the rug. We were programmed to push through it. Not to deal with it. And now that we were unboxing the feelings, I felt uneasiness stiffen the air. I'd known and lived with Lillian for six years, yet I didn't know the majority of her turmoil post-Rio or post-injury. I knew she'd been depressed, but we hadn't talked about it as much as we probably should have. The guilt didn't hit me until I finally asked her about it two and a half years later. Why the hell hadn't we talked about it?

"It was hard," she said, her usual teasing, happy voice softened and lowered. "I mean, you guys remember, I couldn't get out of bed. I won gold in the 100-breaststroke in Rio, but I got second in the 200, third in the 400-IM. I was so pissed off about that after Rio but had Tokyo to look forward to. And then it was all over for me just like that." She snapped her fingers. "A year and a half out and everything changed. There were times I wondered if I would ever swim competitively again. Abu Dhabi was a great assessment but still proof that I'll have to work my ass off for the next four years for Paris, and honestly, if I make it to Paris, it'll probably be my last chance. An ACL injury really knocks off the last few years of your swimming career."

She'd never told us this before. I felt so ashamed. I wished so much that I could lift her spirits about her career, but she was right. Once we hit thirty, we were practically grandmas. We reached our peak in our early twenties, and then it was a slow decline. The three of us would be twenty-seven for Paris. I'd be shocked if Lillian won gold in Paris after a severe injury, swimming against uninjured athletes in their early twenties. I could see the extreme disappointment in her eyes as if she'd confronted the cold hard truth for the first time.

"You know what you're going to do after?" I asked, throwing out a lifeline for her to grab and show me the way.

"Yeah, I'll get my master's degree in physical therapy. Maybe even a doctorate. I'm not sure, but I'm definitely going to do physical therapy."

"What about you, Talia?"

She shrugged and popped another bite of flatbread in her mouth. "Probably the same thing. I want to do cancer research, so I'll need a master's degree."

She was in better shape than Lillian and probably could have pursued the 2028 LA Games if she wanted to. She could easily be a thirty-one-year-old Olympian if she didn't injure herself in the next eight years.

"See, that's the thing, I have no idea what I'm doing," I said. "I was so focused on winning gold that I had no other plans. I've been bred to swim. I feel like my worth is defined by medals. And I feel so greedy and wrong for being depressed after Tokyo. It's just that I sacrificed everything to get here—my social life, my love life, being a normal twenty-three-year-old—and I didn't realize it until I got home."

Kennedy rested her chin on my shoulder. "Quinn, I didn't know you felt this way."

I ran my hands down my face. "Because I don't like talking about it." Her grip loosened as I grunted. "We're taught to push through our pain. We're not taught how to be vulnerable. Vulnerability doesn't win medals. Life is so much more than the fairy tale we've been living in. I've spent twelve years with a fairy-tale mentality, and I'm now realizing it's all wrong."

"I get it, Quinn," Lillian said. "After Rio, after my ACL. You're not alone."

"But I feel so alone. I feel like, for the first time in my life, I have no direction. I'm just…floating. Barely floating."

"People feel alone when they're depressed," Lillian said. "I felt even more alone when I got injured. I know you and Talia were trying to encourage me, but sometimes, I wanted to yell at you guys because you weren't injured and didn't understand the fear of never swimming again. There's something out there for you, Quinn. Don't feel like your only purpose is swimming."

"That's how I feel. An overworked machine."

Kennedy's arm slipped off mine when she got up to go to the bathroom, leaving me in a heavy silence with Lillian and Talia looking at me with the same worried eyes Kennedy had since after the games. I hated when people looked at me like I was broken, and sure, I was broken down to the core, but I didn't want sympathy. I wanted solutions. I wanted to find a way out like Lillian had. A little bit of hope flared in me knowing that she'd worked it out. I wished I had what the answer was. I didn't want to have an unknown number of years of feeling miserable and waiting for the solution to pop up.

I didn't want to spend the rest of the night rolling around in my sob story. I wanted to enjoy the time with my friends and girlfriend, eating, drinking, and laughing, and after Talia and Lillian assured me again that I wasn't alone, and I could talk to them at any time, Kennedy came back with a new drink in hand. We spent the remaining time playing drinking card games, fully taking advantage of the last few weeks of the lull in training.

But the weight of our conversation didn't leave when Talia and Lillian did. As Kennedy and I cleaned up and got ready for bed, we shuffled around in an awkward silence that I didn't pick up on until we finally got into bed. She was too quiet, and studying her face, I wondered if her dazed look indicated that something was wrong.

As she settled into her spot on the bed, she plopped her head on the pillow, a sigh seeping out of her, and then looked up with the same worried expression she'd been giving me for months.

"Hey, Quinn?"

I positioned my arm out for her to cozy into me. It was our usual position when we got in bed, and the fact that she didn't jump into my arms worried me. Instead of resting her head on me, she shifted her body and fixated on me.

"Yes, babe?" I said and rubbed her arm. I wished that was enough to comfort her and push away any fears.

"You know you can talk to me about anything, right?"

"I know."

"It's just that…well…you seemed so open with Lillian and Talia, and I really don't feel like you're that open with me. It's like when you're with me you have this…well…this wall up or something. You never want to talk about things."

Shit. She was worrying. It was all over her face and rattled her words. My heart pounded as the fear coiled around my gut. Kennedy stared, begging for answers. And really, could I blame her? It'd been two and a half months of living together, and I'd managed to get out of any conversation that strayed down the path of opening up to her. But with everything I told Lillian and Talia out in the open, I'd revealed my hand. I had to backtrack and make her feel better so she wouldn't think she was the reason I was unhappy or realized I was too depressed a person to be with. Moving to a new city was a big deal, and I didn't want her to regret it. She made me so happy. I looked forward to our evenings together, having her tell me all the boring parts of her day that were interesting to me, cuddling on the couch while we watched TV. I woke up every day for those moments. I wanted to make her as happy as she made me.

God, I had no idea what I would do if she left me.

But admitting that my mind was anything but solid would be admitting that I wasn't "the greatest female swimmer in the world." That label meant I was living the greatest life, strong, and bathing in ultimate athletic success. In truth, that training had broken me in unnoticeable, nuanced ways I was never taught to look out for. I still wanted to cling to the idea that everything was solid even though I knew it wasn't true. I wanted to trick myself back to good mental health because that was the easiest way to mend it all.

But as I attempted to trick my brain, I'd created a wall between me and my girlfriend. It wasn't because I wanted to keep her out. I just wanted to protect her from the other side.

"I'm sorry. I'm not good at talking about my feelings." I spoke truthfully and held our clasped hands in front of my chest, trying my best to ease her worry.

"I know, but I'm your girlfriend. You should be able to talk to me."

"I know, it's…it's just hard. I don't want you worrying about me or regretting moving out here."

Her eyebrows pulled together. God, see what happened when I told her how I felt? Her frown popped out, and it terrified me.

"Why would I regret moving out here?"

When she said it out loud, it sounded so irrational, but it was a fear I couldn't shake.

"I don't know. Because it's a huge change for you, and you're already stressed about finding friends and establishing your life out here, and I feel guilty that I'm the only one you can fully rely on. I'm in this funk that I can't seem to get out of, and you might leave to go back to New York to be with friends and family and people who aren't depressed—"

"I want to be with you, Quinn," she said with her eyebrows still scrunched together, but this time, the firmness in her tone and the seriousness in her frown made an impact on me about how delusional my anxiety was. "I've wanted to be with you since our first kiss. We all go through bad times. I mean, you stood by me in high school when I was still figuring out who the hell I was, and I hurt you in the process."

"You didn't hurt me—"

"I did, Quinn, don't even deny it now. I couldn't stand up to my friends because I was so insecure. Senior year was so hard for me in more ways than I ever let on. But you still stuck by me."

"I didn't, though. I broke up with you, and then when you came out and asked for a second chance, I still said no."

"None of that is the point I'm trying to make. The point is, you saw me at one of the lowest moments of my life, and I'm going to be here for you at your low moment. I want you to be honest with me. I want to help you get back to the old you. I really miss her."

She kissed our intertwined fingers, and I tried comforting her by caressing her hand. "I miss her too."

"I want to know what you're thinking, even if it's dark. You're supposed to be able to share that stuff with me. Don't you trust me?"

"I do trust you. I trust you more than anyone."

"Then can you try? It's like you have this wall up. It's been up for months now, and I keep wondering when it's finally going to go away."

"I don't want to have a wall with you."

"Then talk to me. I want you to get back on track. I want you back to your normal self."

When she worded it like that, with a tired tone, it sounded like she wasn't happy. She made it sound like I was a second full-time job. I knew that she didn't say those words exactly, and deep down, I knew that was not what she felt, but my broken brain reworded her sentence and translated that my paralyzing depression made her unhappy. Or maybe that was what I wanted to hear to reaffirm I was right. I had no fucking idea, but I was getting sick of feeling this way and allowing my brain to reword what people told me into a bunch of nonsense.

"I want that too," I said. "I just…I don't know how to get better."

"Try talking about it? With me? A therapist? What? Why did you roll your eyes?" I didn't even know I'd rolled my eyes until she checked me and flashed a scowl. "What's wrong with seeing a therapist?"

"Nothing's wrong—"

"Then maybe you can start looking for one? I really think you should. I'll look for one with you. We can both get one."

"I don't need a therapist. I need to figure out what the hell I'm going to do when my swimming career is over."

"A therapist can help with that. You said you want to get better, Quinn. How can you be depressed for almost five months and be okay with that?"

"I'm not okay with that," I said a little too defensively.

"Then do something about it!" She lifted herself to square her body with mine. "I don't know why you're acting like therapy is the dumbest idea. I said I would get one with you. We can do this together."

"I don't want to see a therapist."

She opened and closed her mouth, and when no rebuttal came out, a frown took over her face. "So…you want a solution, but going to someone to help you discover that solution is off the table?"

"You don't need to be patronizing—"

"I'm not being patronizing. I'm trying to help you. Someone has to because you're not doing it yourself. I feel like instead of fighting against the current, you're letting it thrash you around."

I shifted too and crossed my legs to get comfortable. Apparently, this wasn't going to end anytime soon by the harshness in both of our voices, and if Kennedy thought I was a useless piece of debris floating around, then I definitely wasn't happy.

"That's what you think?" I asked.

"Why are you acting so surprised? What have you done that's a step toward feeling better?"

"I dropped out of the world champs. You know how big a step that was? You know how hard it was to tell my coach that at the peak of my career, I need to pull away from the sport and take a break? Or let my teammates down? You know how scared I was? I almost didn't do it. Talk about letting something thrash me around."

"I get that's a big thing to do, but that happened in November. It's now the second week of March. What have you done to find solutions? You worry about your life after swimming, which is a valid concern, but what have you done to solve that? You already shot down my suggestion of therapy. So what's the alternative?"

"I…I don't know—"

"You don't want to go to therapy because what? You were trained not to ask for help? Are you one of those athletes who thinks they're better than asking for help?"

My eyebrows furrowed. "No—"

"Then I don't know how you're going to get those answers if you won't talk to me, won't talk to a therapist—"

I rolled my eyes, shook my head, and got off the bed. It wasn't comfortable anymore.

"Quinn? Where are you going?"

"I don't know. Wherever the current takes me, apparently."

She grunted and chased me, grabbing my hand as I snatched my sweatshirt from the floor, but I yanked it out of her grip. "Come back to bed."

I pulled the shirt over my head. Kennedy followed me into the walk-in closet as I shoved into my tennis shoes. "And have you continue to tell me I'm not doing shit? That I'm just letting life beat me up? How is that helping me?"

"So you can realize that sweeping things under the rug—like you're used to doing—is very detrimental to your break."

"I really don't want to continue this conversation," I said and walked around her to head downstairs.

"Quinn, come on—"

"I just need to walk."

"No, you're running away from your problems," she shouted over the loft railing. "Come back, and let's talk about it."

"I'm not running away," I yelled. "I'm taking a walk. Jesus."

I snatched my keys from the hook mounted to the wall, continued out the front door, down the elevator, and into the damp early spring night. Mist saturated the air, and a thin fog hung low around the tree lines. The streetlights flickered off the shallow puddles on the sidewalk as I buried my hands into my sweatshirt pocket and continued walking without a destination. The misty rain clung to my face, and the cool air sent a shiver down my spine. The weather was horrible for a ten o'clock at night walk around the neighborhood, but I really needed some air to calm down.

I did a few laps around the block, passing the craft brewery about fifty paces right out my condo's front door, the market at the corner about to close, the yoga studio next to the market that attracted so many hot women that it made the weekend mornings that much more enjoyable, and the hole-in-the-wall Chinese takeout place that had amazing Kung Pao chicken that Kennedy and I ordered at least once a week.

I loved my neighborhood and all the sights, sounds, and food smells that came with it. I also really loved living with Kennedy and establishing our favorite places. The market was our go-to if we were craving Halo Top ice cream. We took the neighborhood and turned it into ours, and it made me feel like a new San Francisco resident, living vicariously through Kennedy. Watching her falling in love with the city felt like falling in love with it all over again. At the same time, I was falling in love with her.

Then my thoughts latched on to Kennedy and training.

She was my girlfriend, my best friend, my partner, and she thought I wasn't doing enough. Half of me agreed with her, so why was I so angry? Why did I have a tone with her when I understood what she was saying? Why did I run away when she was trying to help me and understand me?

You want her to tell you that you're doing amazing. You're still searching for validation that confirms you're still a winner, Rational Me said.

I couldn't believe how childish I'd acted. What the hell was I doing? I hated that I was so good at sweeping things under the rug. Later was always more convenient. I guess it was part of my swimmer programming. But I couldn't expect to get better or fall in love with swimming again if I wasn't willing to deactivate that suppressing gene in my DNA.

The last thing I wanted was to be mad at Kennedy. I had no idea what I wanted to do or what my future looked like, but I knew one hundred percent that Kennedy was my person. Two and a half months into living together, fully enveloped in the pact we made, I knew I could be with her for the rest of my life and not feel left out of the dating scene. If anything, I needed to get my ass off the couch and look for that answer to my problems, even if that meant I spent the whole day wandering the city or the internet looking for it. I had to do it for her and ease the anxiety that told me if I didn't get out of my funk, she would leave me for a happier life back on the East Coast.

Didn't I have enough rest since I dropped out of Abu Dhabi? Plenty of time to sleep in, catch up on *Killing Eve*, *Stranger Things*, and the last season of *Orange Is the New Black*, enough time to store away pop culture references and topics to make me feel like a normal twenty-three-year-old?

The answer was yes because now, whenever I woke up, I wanted the day to fast-forward to my evenings with her. And as much as I loved our evenings, I wanted so much more to live for.

Realizing how stupid my walk was, I did a one-eighty and went back home. I needed to suck it up and have this conversation, apologize for my petulant behavior, tell her I appreciated her helping me. But when I got back inside, all the lights were off. I used my phone's flashlight to lead me up the spiral staircase.

"Kennedy?" I whispered as I crawled into bed. "Ken?"

She was either sleeping or pretending to be, leaving me to curl up on the farthest end of my side without leaning against her, feeling ashamed that it was my fault we were both going to bed angry, our fight unresolved. The nights were the worst part of the day. That was when all my anxieties woke up and frolicked. With the fight still lingering, it was like a stimulant to my worries. I knew I wouldn't be getting much sleep.

"I'm sorry," I said, in case she wasn't already asleep.

CHAPTER THIRTEEN

I didn't realize how much of an impact my break from the pool made on me until I walked into the locker room. The chlorinated air filled my nose and settled the nerves bubbling inside me. It was like stepping into my house after months of being away, and the smell of home brought instant nostalgia and a sense of calm. I wasn't expecting that at all.

Kennedy was right. I needed to try. The best way for me to get out my anger was always swimming, especially during a brutal practice. I relied heavily on my workouts when I had a bad day. There was something about exerting tons of energy in the pool or weight room that really helped drain my toxic emotions. As I squeezed into my suit, I wondered if my depressive emotions were still accumulating because I hadn't turned to my regular outlet. For the first time since the Olympics, I craved a brutal workout. I might not have been ready for that lactate test months ago, but I was hoping that one was waiting for me on the whiteboard. A workout to slap me in the face and tell me to wake the hell up.

David looked up from writing the sets on the whiteboard, jumped up from his squat position, and pulled me in for a welcoming hug. "You're back," he said and patted me on the back.

"I'm back."

He pulled away and allowed his smile to grow. "What does this mean? Are you in for Japan?"

"I'm not really sure, but I woke up today wanting to swim. So here I am. Give me a lactate set. I'm ready."

"I don't have one scheduled for today, but maybe I can tweak something around for later in the week?"

"Don't listen to her requests," Lillian shouted from behind as she pulled her Berkeley swim cap over her head, shoving her messy bun underneath it. "She's literally the only one who wants a lactate set."

"But if you ask, you shall receive," David said.

"I won't show up for the rest of the week if that's the case," Talia added.

"That's fine. I'll just make sure to have a backup hell workout for next time. I'll go through my old practices, pull out the ones I flagged that made any swimmer of mine barf, and there you go."

"You actually do that?" Talia asked with rounded eyes. "You flag your barfing workouts?"

David flashed a malicious smile. "I do. I'm very proud of it. Now, you guys wasted a minute. You have one more, or I turn on the hose."

Lillian and Talia gave me a playful scowl.

"We hate you," Lillian said and leapt into the five-foot pool in true cannonball fashion, which I'm pretty sure she did on purpose to get me wet.

After I sandwiched my goggles in my eyes, I leapt into the pool, and the cold water empowered me to trudge through my thoughts. During that 800 warm-up, some clarity settled in me. How I'd been so incredibly unfair to Kennedy the night before. She was right. I'd been allowing the water to thrash me anywhere it wanted, but when the hell was I going to stop?

Afterward, my limbs felt like Jell-O, which informed me that they would be sore tomorrow. I left the pool feeling weightless, for once having the energy to continue upward in my day. It made me optimistic, added an extra pep in my step. I decided to use that energy for the better. Since I had a lot of apologizing to do, I ran to the store to grab all the ingredients for Kennedy's favorite meal: Serena DeLuca's gnocchi with pomodoro sauce. And then I traveled to several wine stores to find her a Petit Verdot. I cleaned the apartment, did our laundry, and when dinner time neared, I read the recipe to make sure I didn't mess it up because last time we cooked together, I mistook two teaspoons of salt for two tablespoons, and holy sodium, we went through our red wine and Brita water very quickly. This dinner had to be perfect, just the tiniest thing to show her how sorry I was about the night before.

As six o'clock approached, I had the table set, wineglasses out, gnocchi and sauce broiling in the oven. Then my phone went off on the kitchen island right after I finished pouring the Petit Verdot.

It was a text from Kennedy. *Hey, a reminder that I have soccer practice tonight. Should be home around 830.*

I let my phone topple on the kitchen island and faced the oven; the timer had two minutes left until I was going to scoop a nice heaping spoonful on her plate next to the spinach salad with her favorite red wine vinaigrette.

But now this whole dinner that I'd put so much time, thought, and effort into had to be delayed. The gnocchi would get cold, the taste would be ruined by the microwave, and the salad dressing would make the spinach soggy. All because I couldn't remember the soccer practice she told me she had on Mondays from six to eight. It was my fault for not remembering, and the failure triggered the depression. My anxiety told me that because I didn't remember, the food wouldn't be as good, and Kennedy wouldn't fully appreciate the meal and would continue to be mad at me and leave me. I knew this was irrational, but I could feel the progress I'd made starting to unravel. I kept telling myself not to let my disappointment overshadow the progress. I'd gone to practice. I'd felt amazing afterward. I was looking forward to going to practice the next morning. That was progress. That was something to be proud of.

She came back around eight thirty, busting through the door in jogger pants and an old Aspen Grove soccer sweatshirt. Her hair was pulled back into a ponytail, baby hairs sticking out in every direction as proof of a good workout. Even disheveled from practice, she looked so beautiful.

"Hey," she said through her huff and tossed her duffel bag on the floor. There was still uncertainty in her tone. "It smells good in here."

"Yeah, I made dinner. That Serena DeLuca gnocchi recipe you like."

She found the plates I put on the kitchen counter with the feta strawberry spinach salad on top and the red wine vinaigrette drizzling from the salad pile.

"Is that the red wine dressing I love?"

I nodded. "And some Petit Verdot on the table."

"Wow, Quinn. You went all out tonight."

"I wanted to have a nice meal with you. But I forgot about your practice so I have to heat it in the microwave."

I got off the couch, unwrapped the foil over the gnocchi dish, and put it in the microwave. She observed me, and the longer she lingered, the more worry filled her stare. She had been speaking with uncertainty ever since she walked through the door, and we'd been awkwardly shuffling around everything left unsaid from the night before.

When the microwave went off, I grabbed the dish, spooned a large helping on both plates, and set them on the table. Kennedy slipped into her seat, her eyes still on mine as I scooped up my first spoonful to assess if the microwave ruined the flavor or not. I closed my eyes and basked in the delicious taste and perfect amount of heat.

"I'm sorry if you made this a thing and—"

I raised my hand. "It's not a big deal. Really. It's my fault for not remembering."

She seemed to feel the uneasy ground too. This was all my fault. "This is really sweet of you," she said. "And you cleaned the condo?"

"And did laundry. It was a pretty productive day. I also went to practice."

She almost choked on her first sip of wine. "Oh my God, you did?" I nodded. "How was that?"

"Pretty great actually. Put me in a good mood. Gave me the energy to do all this stuff."

She reached for my hand underneath the table, and I took in her fingers. She kissed the back of my hand. "Babe, I'm so proud of you. How are you feeling? You going to go back?"

"I think so. I want to."

She smiled, a genuine smile that didn't quiver in worry. "That's great!" She kissed my hand again before letting go to take a bite. A soft moan seeped out of her as I watched her face marvel. "Geez, this tastes amazing."

"I didn't ruin it with salt this time." She laughed and took another bite. "How was your practice?"

"It was really good. Feeling less rusty."

"Because you're a badass goalie. I'm sad that I'm not going to see your game next weekend."

"Well, that's if the weather doesn't jinx it again. But it's okay.

You're going to the camp, and I think that's going to be really good for you, especially since you got back in the pool today."

"I think it's going to be good for me too."

"The girls are already planning our next bar adventure. They want to do a brunch. They said your presence is required. Also," she said and took a bite of salad, "you need to stock this dressing in the fridge. Do that and keep making these gnocchi. Those are your only two jobs."

"You really like the dinner?"

She groaned again, and I could feel it in my stomach. "It's amazing."

"Gotta keep my babe happy."

Despite the light banter, something uneasy still hung in the pauses of the conversation. I felt as if I couldn't fully dive into a conversation about the delicious meal I'd aced or ask her questions about her new team without addressing the elephant in the room. The argument sandwiched a huge space between us. It felt as vast and deep as an ocean, and I struggled to find a way to swim across.

"Ken, I'm really sorry about last night," I said softly.

She lowered her spoon and looked at me sympathetically. "It's okay."

"It's not. You were right, and it wasn't fair for me to snap at you."

She rested her hand on my knee. "Quinn, it's okay. We all have our moments."

"But I've been having moments for months, and you shouldn't suffer from it. Your first few months living with me in a new city shouldn't be like this, and I feel awful for giving you that."

She retrieved her hand, glancing at her plate and pulling another sip from her glass. "You're going through a hard time. I want to be there for you. But sometimes it really worries me that I can't do anything about it. That's all."

"But you are doing something about it. You're always there for me. I know I have an amazing support system, and that's helped a lot."

"Is it bad that I feel like it's not doing enough?"

Her comment hit me hard, like a belly flop off the diving board. The uncertainty in her tone reached her eyes, and I could feel myself spiral into all these thoughts that told me she wasn't happy being with me. How did I tell her that my depression had nothing to do with her?

How did I tell her that being with her had actually prevented me from reaching rock bottom?

I squeezed her hand. "You know how much I look forward to our evenings? I go to sleep and just want it to be the moment you come home, so I can spend the rest of the night with you. Being with you is the best part of my day."

"I want you to look forward to the whole day. Even without me."

"I know. I'm going to practice for the rest of the week, and if it doesn't make me cranky, I might tell David I want to go to Japan."

She offered a loose smile, but it didn't reach her eyes. A low burn ran through my stomach knowing that what I said hadn't put her at ease. "Okay but that's not a solution to the actual problem. What happens after Japan? You're going to say 'oh well, this depression is normal. It will pass like last time.'"

"No," I said a little harsher than intended. I just wanted to celebrate one baby step at a time. I wasn't expecting more criticism.

"Are you going to be able to lower your guard and talk to me?"

"I'm talking to you right now."

"No, right now, you're being defensive."

"Because I feel like nothing I'm doing is good enough for you. I went to practice today. I'm going for the rest of the week. I thought you would be happy for me."

"I am happy for you. I'm glad you went to practice, but that's a temporary fix. You're worried about what you're going to do after swimming. It's been four months since you started your break, and where are you with answering that question?"

I opened my mouth to fight back but realized I didn't have an answer. Instead of saying anything, I chugged the rest of my wine.

"My point exactly," she said. "I love you, Quinn. You know that. I've wanted this for a long time. I moved my life out here for you. But you know that this affects me too, right? Seeing the person I love not being herself, spending months being hopeless, and then not opening up to me for whatever reason, that affects me too. I don't understand why we can't go to therapy together—"

"Because that's not going to solve anything."

"How would you even know when you've never bothered to try? How can someone who studied psychology think that?"

"The therapist isn't going to understand anything. If you're not an athlete, it's hard to understand how you can be depressed after coming back with five fucking gold medals—"

"You find a sports psychologist, then they'll understand—"

"They'll tell me to acknowledge that I have anxiety and say to myself that all my irrational fears are 'anxiety talk,' like that diminishes everything that's a valid concern. Or they'll tell me to write down all my thoughts in a fucking bullet journal or something—"

"A bullet journal?"

"I'm not going to start a fucking bullet journal. I did it once for a class, and my eyes haven't stopped hurting from rolling them for a whole semester. Or they'll tell me to practice mindfulness. I've tried that plenty of times, and my mind doesn't stop tumbling, and the worries don't go away. I go to yoga twice a week, I meditate every day, and look at me. Does it look like those have worked?"

"No—"

"My point exactly. And then in one last ditch effort, they'll tell me to go read, *Eat, Pray, Love* and use my frequent flyers miles on some spiritual journey through India because that will finally cure me."

"You really think that's how therapy is going to go?"

"I can talk and complain all I want to someone, but it's not going to change everything I've given up for this sport. Until recently, I had no love life. I barely have a social life. I'm not getting those years back. Therapy isn't a DeLorean that will take me back in time so I can use college to do something outside of floating in a pool."

"Are you kidding me? Quinn, listen to yourself. You think sitting around and waiting for inspiration is going to solve your problems more than therapy? You know therapy is the shortcut to rewiring everything you've been told to do as an athlete. If you don't want to live in a fantasy land anymore, you need to lose this 'no pain no gain' mentality because it's complete bullshit. This is not some injury that will fix itself."

"If it's not a serious injury, no one cares. They expect you to suck it up and work through the pain."

"Mental health isn't a serious injury? It's a pretty big one, especially for the sport that you say is ninety percent mental."

"Can't we just enjoy this meal without talking about this?"

"Because you're too good for therapy? You think constantly

pushing things under the rug is really that healthy? You can get away with that in swimming, but you can't get away with that in the real world. Look at where it's gotten you. You're a shell of yourself."

I set my spoon on my plate. The clatter hung in between us, adding to the tension. Her eyebrows were firmly set, and her beautiful eyes drilled me for an answer.

"Swimming has wired your brain to process things in an unhealthy way," she said. I clenched my jaw while focusing on my gnocchi. "Therapy will undo all of that. It will help you think healthy, and that will change your inner monologue that tells you you're just a swimmer and there's no future for you, because none of that is true." She squared her shoulders and dipped her head as if trying to get my attention. "I want this to work more than anything, Quinn. I started from scratch to be with *you*. That alone should tell you how much I love you and how much I want to make this work. But if you're not going to try to work on yourself, how am I supposed to believe that you'll do the same thing for us? If you don't fix yourself, you're putting us at risk, and it will go downhill with you. Given everything I've given up for this, that *really* hurts me."

The stinging hit my eyes at the same time a toxic warmth rushed through me. Was it hurt? Guilt? Anger? They were too similar to differentiate. I was taken aback. It was like her words stapled me to my seat. I never remembered her being so forward with her feelings. She hadn't been like that for the majority of our friendship because then I would have known about her feelings for me long before senior year. I had no idea what to do with her words. My worry about not making her happy just blew up at our kitchen table, and the fear of her leaving stung my eyes. I tried so hard to keep her from hurting, and it didn't even work.

"I never meant to hurt you," I said and swiped at my leaking eyes.

"I want you to get help. I told you last night that I'll do it with you. We'll both do it."

"But...that's not going to—"

She pointed at me. "Don't you dare say it's not going to help. Jesus, Quinn, stop denying that it'll help without even giving it a chance!"

She pushed her seat back, and the chair screeched along the hardwood floor. She put her hands on top of her head and paced around the island. My tears fell into my hands as I dug my fingernails into my palms over and over again.

"I don't…" She paused, opening and closing her mouth as if she wanted to say something at the same time she wanted to stop it. "I don't know how we can keep going on like this if you won't talk to me."

"I do talk to you, Ken!" The words grated against my throat. My voice was hoarse, my throat was raw and scratchy from holding back tears, but they all came out at once.

"You don't. You bottle things up. Every time we talk, it's like I have to claw my way through whatever wall you have. Why is there a wall in between us? What did I do?"

"N…nothing!" I coughed a sob and buried my face in my hands.

"That's a lie, and you know it. You really need to prioritize things. I've tried everything in the book to help you, and you keep shutting me down. I'm running out of ideas. I didn't move out here to watch you waste away in this condo."

I wiped the moisture on my face. Her words were pressing on an open wound. "Waste away?"

"You're not you!" She threw her hands in the air. "This isn't you. God. You know what? I can't do this anymore. I need to breathe and take some time." She stormed past me to the spiral staircase. Each step had a pound to it that I wasn't sure if she was making on purpose or not.

"You're running away? Are you ever gonna grow out of that?" I yelled up to her.

She leaned over the railing, and despite a floor separating us, her glare packed a punch. "Excuse me? Grow out of what?"

I swallowed. The anger was in control, and Rational Me was on a smoking break. "Running away," I said. "That's what you do when things get tough. You did it when you kissed me the first time, you did it in high school when you came back, when we dated, you always fucking run away."

"Are you seriously bringing up high school right now? Are you ever going to let go of the fucking past? Or do I need to worry that anytime we fight, the things I regret most in my life will be used against me as if I've forgotten about them? Is that why there's a wall up? Are you still pissed about high school?"

"I'm pissed because you're running away like you've always fucking done. We fight, and what do you do? You bolt."

"Oh, okay, we're going there?" She stomped down the staircase, and that finger marched its way over to me until it poked me in my chest. "If you think you're dating the same person you did when we were seventeen, you're in for a rude awakening because I've learned not to tolerate shit from people. Learned that in my last relationship when all I did was get shat on and blamed for everything, and I refuse to be blamed for things that aren't my fault. If you want to be like my ex-girlfriend, I'll gladly leave like I did with her."

She pounded back upstairs and left me with guilt so heavy, I was unable to move. All I wanted to do was to protect her, and instead, I'd pushed her away.

I snapped out of my shock when she came back down with a bag slung over her shoulder. My heart dropped to my stomach, and the tears flooded my eyes like at a broken dam.

"What are you doing?" I said in a panic, and my scratchy throat throbbed again.

"Not staying here with you."

"Kennedy, I'm sorry—"

"You know what, maybe this was a mistake."

It was like her words slapped me in the face. "What?"

"Maybe we dove too fast into this."

"Into what?"

"This," she said and gestured between us. "Us. I think going from zero to one hundred and living together was too much." She looked up, crying freely. It hurt me even more to see her feeling the same pain as me. "I can't sit around and watch you do this to yourself anymore and drag me into the middle of it when I didn't do anything wrong. This has been going on for five months, and you keep refusing to get help to change it."

She swept past me into the entryway and snatched her keys off the rack.

"Please, Kennedy, don't leave." I cried as I followed her to the front door. My throat was already raw. "Please, don't leave. I'm sorry."

"I'm staying with Jacob," she said and wiped her eyes before exhaling, as if she needed that for encouragement. "We need space to calm down."

"What? For how long?"

She looked skyward as her eyes watered. "I don't know. Think about things. Until you can admit that you need help. I need to go—"

"But, Ken—"

Once she closed the door, I toppled to the floor, curled up in a ball, and cried.

In the empty and silent condo with the home-cooked meal still scenting the kitchen.

CHAPTER FOURTEEN

I went from my girlfriend shooting daggers at me and leaving me alone with the weight of guilt in our condo, to a bunch of kids from thirteen to seventeen eyeing me with a starstruck sparkle in their eyes. David's camp went from Friday afternoon to Monday morning, and kids from as close as San Francisco and as far as the East Coast flew into Berkeley for it. He had it once a year, usually in a different California city. All these kids were on the elite level, destined to crush high school and state records—if they hadn't already—and could easily qualify for the Olympic trials, and they wanted to gain knowledge and experience from someone who had coached thirteen Olympians throughout his career.

I didn't join the camp until Friday evening, four days after Kennedy left. I sent her one text the morning after our fight, begging her to come back, and she said she still needed space. I was thankful for this camp now. It would give me a much-needed distraction from my lonely condo and empty bed. A king-size bed was far too big for one.

Now I walked down the steps to where David stood in the lecture hall at Berkeley, waiting for the campers to take their seats; the chatter hushed, and one hundred pairs of eyes widened and studied me. This rush of embarrassment washed through me. I wasn't used to being gawked at, and I felt all sorts of insecure. Did I have toilet paper on my shoe? A stain on my shirt? Was my tag showing? No, these kids were gaping because they were completely enamored, and after feeling lonely and ignored by the love of my life, it was a nice juxtaposition.

When David started his forty-five-minute pep talk, he introduced me, I waved, and they gave me ecstatic waves back. I didn't talk much, just said the occasional sentence or two, backing up his points about hard work, failure, and learning from failure. I didn't want to give too much away because I was going to tell them my own story on Sunday night. After the talk, a bunch of kids ran up to me and asked if they could take a picture with me. The chaperones said they would have plenty of time for pictures later, and they all needed to head back to the hotel for lights out.

But I liked rebelling because it was fun.

"We can squeeze in a few more," I told those waiting for their turn, giving them a wink before the selfie.

Their eyes lit up at my rebellion.

The next morning, when I walked down the pool deck in my suit, cap, and goggles, the same reaction from the night before happened. Instead of putting on their caps or jumping into the pool like they were supposed to, they stopped, pointed at me, and chattered with wide smiles.

"Are you going to be swimming with us, Ms. Hughes?" one of the girls asked with infatuated eyes.

That pulled a smile from me because not only was I Ms. Hughes to someone, but I made them excited for jumping in a freezing pool at eight in the morning during spring break. I think the only way I'd be excited to jump into a cold pool this early would be if I was swimming with Michael Phelps or a really hot girl like Olivia Wilde.

"Is that okay?" I asked.

Her eyes grew as she nodded joyfully.

"You guys better get in soon," I said. "This guy likes to turn on the hose and spray you with freezing cold water if you take too long."

I hooked a thumb at David, and their enamored eyes became terrified.

"Go! Go! Go!" I said, clapping, and they all jumped in the water.

David put me in charge of watching over the three thirteen to fourteen age group lanes. My job was to coach them through the sets and correct anything they could improve on. Mostly, I told them to close their fingers during freestyle to have a better grip on the water or not to take a breath after they did their flip turn because it made the turns faster.

For the last forty-five minutes, I hopped into the fastest lane and led them in swimming the main sets.

"Go easy on us," said the original leader of lane one, a boy who had to have been eighteen.

"It would be my honor to get lapped by Quinn Hughes," one of the girls said, and the lane rewarded her with laughs.

I didn't go easy. Their parents spent all the money for them to attend this camp, so I was going to make sure they got their money's worth.

These kids were so fast, they weren't too far behind. Actually, they were giving me a pretty good workout.

During lunch, I grabbed my tray and sat with the other coaches. As I scooped a spoonful of cherry Greek yogurt into my mouth, I checked to see if I had any messages from Kennedy. It was killing me that our last text was Tuesday afternoon, and it was now Saturday. Every silent day, I worried more if this would be the end of us, that she would spend the rest of her internship with Jacob before moving back to New York. I had no idea if I needed to give her more space or if I was supposed to fight. But since she didn't see me as a fighter anymore, I thought I would power through and send her a text.

I really miss you, Ken.

I slipped the phone back in my pocket and finished lunch with my heart pounding like a weight in my chest.

The afternoon was dedicated to dryland. Since it was a gorgeous day, we met outside on a soccer field littered with medicine balls. After two laps around the field for a warm-up, David had us doing multiple sets of push-ups, planks, sit-ups, lunges, and burpees. I was sweating with the campers while the coaches put us through quite a workout.

"Do burpees ever get any easier?" a high school girl asked as we took a water break.

"Not in the slightest," I said and squirted water in my mouth.

"So this means I should quit now?" she said with a teasing grin.

I patted her shoulder. "They're not meant to be easy, so that won't change, but your tolerance will."

"Good to know. Thanks, coach."

Then we were on to the medicine balls. David instructed everyone to partner up. I spotted a girl in the thirteen-fourteen group looking over both shoulders. All the couples grabbed medicine balls as she hung her head and kicked the grass. I'd always hated partnering up, especially in camps like this where I didn't know anyone. Since I never went with a friend, I was always by myself, and anytime I was told to find a partner, anxiety snaked my stomach and chest. My heart broke for her as she kicked the grass shamefully as if mad at herself.

"Hey," I said softly, and she perked up, her eyes rounding as if she couldn't believe I was right in front of her. "You want to be my partner?"

With arched eyebrows, she nodded. I smiled and found a medicine ball. I squatted, holding the ball out in front of me, sprung up, and gently passed the six-pound ball.

"What's your name?" I asked as she caught it.

"Taylor."

She followed my lead and tossed the ball back. I could feel the loneliness emanating from her. Come to think of it, if she was the girl I recognized from the morning session, she'd had a magenta cap and walked onto the deck with her head down amidst the cliques lingering on the bulkhead. While I coached the first half of the practice, many of the kids were smiling, chatting, and she was the quiet girl in lane two toward the back of the line. I had to stop her once to tighten her streamline. She'd given me a thin smile and a nod and continued without saying anything.

"Nice to meet you, Taylor. I'm Quinn."

She gave me a half-smile, catching the ball. "I know. I watched you during the Olympics."

"Oh yeah? What event do you swim?"

"The 50-free and the 100." She paused. "And fly now, I guess," she said with a quick eye roll.

I laughed. "You guess?"

"Yeah, my coach is pushing me to do it."

"And you don't like it?"

She shrugged. "It's hard. I only ever swam it in practice or the IM. I don't really like it. I like the 50 and 100-free better."

"I don't really like fly either. But I have lots of respect for those who can do it. You must be a badass if your coach wants you to swim fly."

She shook her head. "No way."

"Way. Only the most badass swimmers swim fly. It's a fact."

We took a break when David called. The next set of twenty throws was overhead. After our water break, Taylor started the first toss. I figured I would keep talking to try to keep that smile on her face.

"So, Taylor, where are you from?"

"Kansas City, but I just moved to Palo Alto last fall."

"How do you like California?"

The sadness crept back on her face. "It's fine, I guess. It's hard to make friends in middle school when they've all known each other since elementary."

Kennedy popped in my head and all the moving she'd done in her life. She'd moved when she was seven from the suburbs of Buffalo, moved to New York City right before eighth grade, moved back to Aspen Grove sophomore year, moved to Syracuse for college, moved to Brooklyn after college, and then moved to San Francisco. In the past, she'd mentioned how hard moving was for her when she was a kid, how it had been hard to fit in with her Manhattan school, and how'd she cried when moving to Aspen Grove. Remembering her tales, I felt for Taylor.

"What about your swim team?" I asked, tossing the ball.

She shook her head and threw it back without answering. Now I understood why she was so quiet. The poor girl struggled to make friends in her new city, and a sympathetic pang gnawed at my chest. As someone who felt like an outsider for much of middle school and high school, I felt a sudden connection.

"There are four girls from my new team here, but they seem really close, and…I don't know."

"You should talk to them."

She shook her head. "They're always together, and they partnered up so quickly."

"I'm sure they'll take you in."

She shrugged. "I don't know. There are four of them, so why would one of them partner with me?"

"If you sit with them at lunch or dinner, introduce yourself, and get to know them, you'll give them a reason to partner with you."

She didn't say anything. I got a sense that she was painfully shy, so walking up to a group of longtime friends was even more daunting.

After dryland, we all set out on a hike on Grizzly Peak Trail, and despite the campers swarming around me, trying to get my attention and asking questions, I made it my mission to push through to Taylor, who hiked near David and the rest of the coaches in the front.

"Hey, friend," I said when I finally caught up to her after allowing the other campers to take selfies with me.

Her gloomy expression turned bright. "Hi!"

"You're hiking this trail like a pro. It must be all the badass butterfly skills."

She laughed. "I'm really not that good at the butterfly. It's something my new swim coach threw at me."

"My coach in middle school threw the 200-free at me, and now it's my event."

"Yeah, and you're really good at it."

"Can I tell you a secret?" Her eyes widened at the sudden softness in my tone. "I really hate the 200."

She pulled away and let out another laugh. "But you won the gold in it."

"I still hate it. It's a horrible event. Is it a sprint? Is it long distance? Who the hell knows? It's having an identity crisis. But hey, maybe the fly is going to be your new stroke. I bet you're going to be a future gold medalist."

"Don't say that. That means I'll have to swim the 200-fly, and that's the worst event in all of swimming."

"That's true, but those who swim it are true badasses. My good friend Talia swims the fly, and she's much cooler than me. Badassery."

"Talia Papani? I really like her. She's pretty too."

"She's gorgeous and an absolute beast at the fly. And guess what?"

"What?"

"She also hates it. But shh! Don't tell anyone. That's our secret."

"But you guys are so fast and make it look easy."

"Lots of practicing, Taylor."

Ever since I let her in on some secrets, talking was easier as we traveled up the hill. She told me how she hoped to go to the Olympics, either Paris or LA, but doubted if she could qualify for Paris as a seventeen-year-old. I informed her that plenty of seventeen-year-olds were in the Olympics, that age didn't mean anything. She said that at really important meets, she would be so nervous and scared that her times would be bad, and she worried that would always prevent her from going to the Olympics. I told her how I'd missed London by three seconds, how I'd missed a medal in Rio. How every successful person had an arsenal of failure stories.

"You're going to have bad races, bad meets. Those are inevitable but good," I said. She seemed confused. "You're your own worst critic. If you tell yourself you can't do something in swimming, you won't be able to do it. Sometimes I forget that too, but it's really important to ingrain it in your head."

Her eyebrows furrowed as we marched up a steep incline. "Can I ask you why you didn't go to the world champs in December?"

I let out a nervous chuckle and scratched the back of my head. How did I explain this to a girl who was filled with so much doubt without scaring her? "I was so tired. I'd been giving a hundred and ten percent for years and realized I hadn't really lived much outside of the sport. I felt really down, in a rut. I just wanted a break and reevaluate my life."

She glanced at the dirt trail and kicked a small pebble. "Swimming's helped me," she said softly. "It's the one thing that makes me feel confident."

"I know how that feels. That's how I felt in high school."

She looked back at me. "Really?"

I nodded. "People were mean in high school. Made fun of me for not making the London Olympics. But the best way to shut them up is to keep going and prove them wrong."

She grinned. "I think you proved them wrong."

"I think I did too."

"Are you going to the world champs this summer?"

"Um…that's a good question. I…uh…I'm not sure yet."

"Why?" she asked like going should have been a given.

I trudged through the burn in my calves and leaned on the large stick I'd found to assist my out-of-shape body up the damn hill. Taylor made the hike seem easier than it was. "I have doubts of my own."

"Because you became your own worst critic too?"

"Exactly. It's a demanding sport, and it made me wonder if I gave too much to it. I overworked myself, forgot to enjoy the little things in life, and being so focused on winning and being the best, I lost touch of reality. Kind of made me not love the sport anymore. And that's when I started feeling like a failure."

She looked at me as if I was crazy. "How are you a failure? You won five gold medals in Tokyo. You're so good."

"No one thinks they're the best. I can tell you, if you're here at this camp keeping up with all the swimmers your age and older, you're exactly where you need to be if you want to qualify for the Olympics."

"Then I can tell you that you're anything but a failure."

Her words marinated in me, and the things I'd told her moments before were shouted back at me. *I'm my own worst critic.* And nothing would change unless I learned to rewire my brain.

The terrain finally leveled at the top of the hill. An opening cleared in front of us, and San Francisco poked out in the distance, sitting in a thin layer of fog. The camp scattered all over the clearing, soaking up the sights of the city and our surroundings below. Wiping a layer of sweat off my forehead, I grabbed a water bottle out of my bag, squirted some into my mouth, and offered Taylor some.

"You should go to Japan," Taylor said, taking a seat crossed legged on the ground. I joined her. "Prove yourself wrong. Fall in love with the sport again."

"And you should go talk to the girls on your team. Go right up there, say hi, offer them some water, and ask to sit with them."

She turned to observe the four girls laughing. "What if they say no?"

"Then I'll spray them with the hose at practice tonight."

That garnered a grin. She thought about it for a long moment, playing with some pebbles as if assessing the pros and cons of what she'd proposed, and at the same time, my pro list for seeking help grew longer. Then, after drawing in a breath, she held out her pinkie. "If I go up to those girls, you have to go to Japan."

I thought about it for a moment and followed the feeling in my gut. "Deal," I said and hooked my pinkie around hers to seal the promise.

She glanced over her shoulder at the girls again and then looked back at me with terrified eyes.

I gave her a thumbs-up. "I believe in you. We've chatted each other's ears off today. Go do the same to those girls."

She thinned her lips, and I offered my water as a conversation starter. She nodded, grabbed the bottle, and walked over to them very demurely. I was worried she would back out at the last minute. She waved, and the girls perked up. I sucked in a breath like a terrified mom, afraid my kid was going to be rejected. I didn't breathe during the first few seconds of the exchange, and when Taylor extended the water, the girls smiled and shuffled around in their circle to create space for her. Once she sandwiched herself between them, I buzzed my lips, finally exhaling, and my insides swarmed with assurance. She did it, and I was so fucking proud.

Now you need to uphold your end of the promise.

I pulled my phone from my pocket and checked it for the first time since lunch. My heart was ready to leap out of my chest when I saw I had an hour-old text from Kennedy.

I miss you too. A lot, it read.

If Taylor could leap out of her comfort zone, then so could I. Glancing back at Kennedy's text, I was reminded of everything that I still had and everything I could lose if I didn't dive into my uncomfortable zone. Because at least I wouldn't be alone if I tried. It was much better than being alone completely.

Instead of texting back, I texted my agent, Lucy. *I think I want to start therapy. I think it's time. I want to love swimming again.*

❖

The next evening, I drove to camp to tell the rest of the campers the whole conversation I'd had with Taylor. They huddled into the lecture hall where I was scheduled to tell them about my journey to the Olympics. Now that I had speaking time, they stared at me, hawk-eyed, probably seeking inspiration. Most possessed athletic prowess beyond what was normal for their ages. This camp was designed for Olympic hopefuls, and my journey had been very similar to theirs. Starting young, clinging to my memories of the Beijing Olympics, dedicating much of my high school life to the pool; that eventually paid off because I won my first two medals at the world championships in Kazan when I was eighteen. I stressed the power of pushing through doubts and failures, mentioning all my failures, from London to my disappointment in Rio. There were more failures than successes, but the ones who made it to the Olympics not only mastered their sport, they mastered their failures. I wished someone would have told me that when I was younger. It would have lessened the blow.

As the kids headed out to enjoy their last hour before the lights went out, Taylor hopped down the steps with a bright smile on her face.

"Hey, Quinn?" she said as I slung my bag over my shoulders.

"Hey, Taylor. What's up?"

"Thank you. For everything."

I gave her a half-smile. "What do you mean?"

"I mean, for talking to me. Telling me to keep going. Pushing me out of my shell. The girls invited me to their room last night, and we played card games and..." She glanced over her shoulder and found David talking to a group of high schoolers. She turned back to me and gave a mischievous smirk. "We stayed up until midnight talking and playing games. I ate lunch and dinner with them today, and one of them invited me to a sleepover at her house next week."

I held out my fist for her to pound it. "There you go. I'm so happy for you. That's amazing."

"Maybe this is the start of me making some friends out here."

"I think it is. You need confidence, Taylor. Once you start believing in yourself, amazing things will happen."

She glanced at the ground for a moment before looking back up. "Are you going to keep your promise?"

"I pinkie promised, didn't I?"

"Yeah…but…you're supposed to believe in yourself too. You remember how you told us that the Beijing Olympics and Dara Torres inspired you?"

"Yeah?"

She kicked the toe of her tennis shoe into the ground as she struggled to make eye contact. "Well…um…just so you know, um, the Tokyo Olympics were my Beijing Olympics. And…um…you inspired me. Long before our hike yesterday."

My heart swelled at the same time the stinging hit my eyes. I could have started crying, but I tamed my flaring nostrils and the pulling in my throat.

"Taylor, that's…that's really sweet of you."

"It's true," she mumbled.

"I believe you. I really appreciate that," I said with a pat on her shoulder. "I really needed to hear that."

I don't think she knew how much her words resonated with me, how much I needed the last push in the right direction. I'd been desperately searching for inspiration. I'd accomplished Olympic gold and had realized how much of my life I'd given for those slabs of metal. I needed a new purpose. I had no idea that this camp would open my eyes to how much my story could influence others. I'd never expected to meet a teenager whose insecurities reminded me so much of mine: what I was going through currently, what I went through at her age and throughout high school. If I expected her to push through it, crawl out of her comfort zone to make friends, and own the butterfly when she didn't think she was good enough, I needed to do the same. Because kids were watching me more closely than I thought they were.

I wanted to be the person I'd desperately needed when I was younger.

I had to go to Japan. For Taylor, for others, for me, and for my thirteen-year-old self.

"I'll be back in the pool on Monday," I assured her. "I promise. Hey, maybe I can come cheer you on in your next meet? Show off your badass fly skills to me?"

Her eyes lit up. "Seriously? You would do that?"

"Why wouldn't I? You're only an hour away. That's nothing. And maybe I can bring my friend Talia. She can give you the secrets to mastering the fly."

"Really? Oh my God. That would be so cool!"

"Consider it a date."

She rammed into me, showing off all the strength inside her. She wrapped her arms around me and thanked me again as I hugged her back. Her tight, comforting embrace told me how much my words resonated with her, and I squeezed her back, hoping that she could feel how much her words resonated with me.

We'd found one another at the right moment in our slumps.

As I sprinted to my car, I whipped out my phone. *Are you free right now? I want to talk. In person.*

Once I got in and started the car, my phone dinged with Kennedy's response: *Yes, I'm free.*

Can I please come over? I want to see you and talk. I promise no fighting.

CHAPTER FIFTEEN

I pulled up in Jacob's driveway with my hands suctioned to the steering wheel from my clammy palms. Lights illuminated the townhouse windows, Kennedy's safe space for the past week. Her hour-long commute from Santa Clara to Berkeley had been a major commitment to avoid me when it would have taken just a half hour to Uber if she'd stayed in the city.

On the fourth ring, I took in one last heavy breath and held it.

"Hey," she said softly, sounding so unsure.

"Hey," I said, my voice rattling. "Can you come outside?"

Silence. For a split second, I thought the call dropped. I watched the outline of her head peering through the window.

"Okay, one second," she said.

My breath finally escaped.

I got out of the car and rested against the door to brace for this conversation. She came out in sweatpants and my navy Berkeley sweatshirt. I laughed at how bold it was to take one of my favorite sweatshirts when we got in a fight. But since I always allowed her to wear it, I didn't think she did it out of spite. It could have been an accident. I told myself that she took it to have a bit of me.

She stopped a couple feet short of my car, crossed her arms, and through the darkness, I saw her struggling to make eye contact, flitting from me to the driveway.

"I wanna talk. For real this time. No yelling."

She hugged herself tighter, and I wasn't sure if it was because she was cold or because she felt so uncomfortable. It broke my heart thinking of the latter. "Sure, go for it," she said, her voice still soft, and her eyes falling to her shoes.

I assessed the distance between us, a distance two strangers would have stood at to have a conversation. A distance that was a gaping hole for people who had ten years of romantic history and who were supposed to be in love. This was my girlfriend…I thought. I thought we were still technically together. Whatever the technicalities were, this space between us, those tightly crossed arms, those civil sentences, weren't supposed to bind us. We were so much more than civility. I was madly in love with her. Had been since I was seventeen, when the spark of love I felt when we slow danced at our senior prom had fully bloomed. It had become such a part of me that I couldn't imagine my life without it or her. The only way for me to kill this awkward space was to swallow the lump in my throat and spill my guts. This was my last shot, and I was ready to tear down this wall and have her in my arms again.

"I told Lucy that I want to see a therapist. She emailed me a list of some in the area that specialize in helping athletes, and I scheduled my first session. It's on Wednesday."

Her arms loosened, and she painted on the smallest smile. "What? Really?"

I nodded. "I'm tired of feeling this way. I want to get my life back."

"Quinn, that's…that's amazing. How did you…what changed?"

"Well, for one, I missed you," I said, biting my lip to steady the shaking in my voice. God, I hadn't even said two sentences of my confession, and I was already starting to lose it. "Like, so unbelievably much. I've been absolutely miserable without you, and not having you to come home to or fall asleep with…it was a big wake-up call. I was just so scared of telling you everything and scaring you back to New York. And I realize now that I scared you away by not telling you everything, and I'm sorry. I never meant to hurt you. I was just really afraid of losing you."

A part of me thought the silence would prompt her to say how she missed me back, but she didn't say anything. And I was determined to barge through the thick walls to get the truth out of her because I knew how she felt. I knew she loved me. She didn't have to say it. How she'd acted the past few weeks showed me how much she cared because if she didn't love me at all, she would have done more than stay with her brother. She would have broken up with me. She would have told me that the hell I was putting her through wasn't worth it. She would have been back home the second it got hard, but instead, she'd pleaded that I get help, and even when I'd continued to refuse and stared at that boulder, she still left the door open for me to waltz back in. Kennedy stayed. That was love.

"I also met this camper. This girl, Taylor," I continued. "She reminded me so much of myself when I was thirteen."

"How so?"

"She doubts herself so much when she has no reason to. She's a really great swimmer with so much ambition. She just needs to believe in herself. I feel like she needs someone to guide her and believe in her to help her realize that she has so much potential if her inner voice doesn't get in her way."

"And that's your own problem," Kennedy said quietly.

"I know. After I told the camp my journey, Taylor told me that Tokyo was her Beijing Games. Tokyo inspired her to go after her own dream, and I was the one to do that."

Kennedy's eyes softened. "Really?"

"Really. That…it really meant so much to me. Having someone look up to you and believe in you like that really does something. I think this is something I want to keep doing. Coaching kids."

"Then do it, Quinn. You'd be amazing at it."

"I want to learn how to love swimming again, and trying to help kids fall in love with it this weekend kind of helped me in the process. I want to get better so I can do that. I want to get better so you can come back. I'm in love with you, Kennedy. I told you that back in high school, at prom, and guess what? I've never stopped loving you. Not for a second."

She let out the cry and covered her mouth with her hands. The gloss in her eyes grew thicker in the glow. I hoped more than anything that those tears were happy ones and not ones that were going to stab me in the gut.

"You're the best thing that's ever happened to me." I continued to fill the silence by spilling everything I felt about her. I would keep telling her how much I felt until she responded. Telling her would be the easiest speech. "All I want to do is make you happy. I'm one hundred percent committed to being with you and being the best girlfriend, and I promise to always fight for us. I've never wanted anything more in my life."

She squeezed my hand. "I've never wanted anything more than this, either," she said through her sniffling. She wrapped her arms around my neck and pinned me against my car as she relaxed into me. I hugged her back and buried my face in her shoulder, taking in a deep inhale. My Berkeley sweatshirt smelled like her. I grabbed her tighter, making sure that smell would never leave me.

"I'm so sorry," I said into her ear. "I never meant to drag you into this."

"I missed you so much, Quinn."

"I missed you too. More than you know." She pulled away and wiped her eyes with her sleeve bunched over her knuckles. "I love you, Ken. So fucking much."

She caressed my cheek. "I love you too."

Hearing those words felt like a hug around my heart. Saying "I love you" to her filled me up so much that I couldn't hide my smile. The first time I told her I loved her at our senior prom, we couldn't even kiss or hug or celebrate the fact because we weren't together. Now, almost six years later, she looked back at me as if granting me permission to cup her face and show her how much I missed her and how much I loved her. And I did exactly that. I kissed her as if that was all I'd ever wanted to do. I kissed her as if promising that the rest of our months wouldn't resemble the last few. I kissed her as if she was the love of my life because she was. No other girl would have that title. It belonged to Kennedy Reed, and it would always belong to Kennedy Reed. And she welcomed all of it. I could feel it in the way she kissed me back so tenderly and passionately that she loved me as much as I loved her. She pushed her waist against mine, securing me against the car. Our worlds came crashing back together and fit right into place.

"Spend the night," she said, softly yet authoritatively, when she pulled away.

"At your brother's house?"

Her eyes darkened. "I can't wait anymore. I did enough waiting."

I opened my mouth to say something, something like there was no way we could waltz into her brother's house and have make-up sex. But then she played with my hoodie strings, and my weakness for her face, her eyes, that mischievous smirk, all wrapped up in my Berkeley hoodie made it easy for me to grab her hand in approval because I needed her also.

She led me through the front door where Jacob and Ava sat on the couch, shifting in their seats and focusing their attention back to the TV and a rerun of *The Office*.

"Yeah, so…um…this is a funny part," Ava said to her husband and gestured to the muted TV.

He glanced over his shoulder. Our eyes locked, and he followed every inch I took farther into his house.

"Oh hey, Quinn," Jacob said mildly but in a protective tone that informed me we had a pending conversation.

"We're finishing our chat in the guest room," Kennedy said without stopping, still tugging me through the hall.

But we did anything but chat. The door locked, and she threw me onto the bed. We peeled each other's clothes off and kissed every inch of each other's skin until we couldn't take anymore. We'd had amazing sex in the past, but I don't think any were as intimate and intensely passionate as this one. Our sessions usually had phases. Phase one: I want to devour your naked body. Phase two: You feel so wonderful, and I'm so in love with you. Phase three: You're so sexy; now make me come. But this time it was different. It started out with phase one and then remained at phase two the rest of the time. Our kisses were deep, our movements were alternatingly fast, slow, gentle, and fervently rough. My center undulated against hers, and sweat covered our bodies, but I didn't care. It made our moments that much sexier. More intimate. We were so closely connected, so lost in each other's worlds, that it was the first time I'd experienced a simultaneous orgasm with my partner, and it took us both by surprise. It made me cuddle into her afterward, holding her tightly so she could never leave again.

As always, she fell asleep before me, and I found so much peace and comfort feeling her chest rise and fall with each breath. I noticed about twenty minutes after she had fallen asleep, twitching against me, that a grin still lingered on my face from feeling her breathing and her body heat warming me like a second blanket.

For the first time in a long time, I fell asleep with a smile I couldn't get rid of.

❖

That next morning, I woke at seven, attempted to go back to sleep, but couldn't. My beautiful girlfriend slept peacefully next to me, curled into my body, breathing heavily. And then I remembered that I was in her brother's house. Hadn't spoken to him since Christmas and then fucked in his guestroom. I mean, fucked seemed really casual and fun. Sleeping with Kennedy the night before was one of the most intense and romantic sex sessions I'd ever had in my life. But either way, by the stare he gave me when I stepped into his house, I knew he viewed me as his sister's girlfriend whose antics had pushed her away for a whole week.

So yeah, I kind of needed to do something to make up for it.

I went out and grabbed four coffees, a variety of bagels, some apples and bananas, and two fistfuls of creamer and sugar packets. Okay, and I made an extra stop at CVS to pick up a watermelon and a blue raspberry Ring Pop to charm Kennedy. The plan was to leave everything on the kitchen table and sneak back into bed with her so that Jacob and Ava could discover the loot of breakfast goodies and maybe reconsider harping on either me or Kennedy for the previous night.

But things never worked out the way I wanted them to.

Just as I crept back into the silent house, there was Jacob starting the coffee. He was still in his pajamas—basketball shorts and a gray T-shirt that said "Silicon Valley Nerd"—with his hair disheveled. But as dorky as he looked, his expression was anything but. Back were the furrowed eyebrows and staring green eyes, giving me a look as if I was the bad guy who'd broken his sister's heart. Which was pretty accurate. I had a lot of explaining to do.

"Coffee and breakfast?" I said way too nervously, raising the tray and paper bag.

He pursed his lips and nodded. "Nice save." He stopped tending to his coffee and put his empty cup away. "I'll take one of those with you outside."

I gulped. "Okay."

We stepped through the sliding glass doors onto the balcony with its potted plants and flowers hanging from ceiling hooks, nice touches that I'm sure were all Ava.

Taking the first sip of steaming coffee, Jacob rested his back against the wooden railing and raised an eyebrow. "So," he said. "You and my sister."

I drank to replenish the moisture in my throat. Here came the older brother lecture. "Yeah?"

He squared his body on mine...probably for intimidation purposes. He'd housed his heartbroken sister for six days because of me. I didn't blame him. I would have done the same to Liam's girlfriend if the roles were reversed.

"I'm ready for the grilling, Jacob. Lay it on me."

His smile grew, but it was one of those smiles that came right before someone was about to lecture you and point out how wrong you were. "She's been really upset, you know."

"I can only imagine."

"A lot of crying."

I closed my eyes at the sudden pang in my chest. "I'm sorry, Jake. I never wanted to do that."

"You know how much she loves you, right? She'd do anything for you."

"I know. I can feel it."

He took another sip, looked skyward as if debating telling me whatever he was thinking, and then let out a deep sigh. "You're different, you know that?"

"What do you mean?"

"Ken isn't an open book."

"Oh, I'm well aware of that."

"I gave up years ago trying to find out how her dating life was going because I couldn't get as far as the name of the person. And with Brielle, all I got from her was, 'Oh she's good. We're fine. I saw her last weekend.' I couldn't tell you one thing about the girl besides the fact that she was in law school. But with you, I don't even have to ask. She's been bringing you up all the time. Like, I know you still cry when you watch *The Lion King*, and you can recite a whole scene from *Angels in the Outfield*, and it takes you, like, two hours to find a restaurant to go to when you want to eat out because you want to make sure it's perfect."

"No one wants a crappy restaurant. I've watched *Kitchen Nightmares.*"

"I can go on," he continued without missing a beat, "but I think I made my point. She's an open book when it comes to you, and it doesn't take a genius to figure out why she's like that about you and not anyone else she's dated."

"I'm sorry you have to constantly hear about me," I said, half-joking. He smiled and took another drink. "Just know that I love her. I've known that since high school, as crazy as it sounds."

"It doesn't sound too crazy. Makes sense…because she told us the whole story. Beginning to end. No detail left behind."

I raised an eyebrow. "Seriously?"

"I mean, granted, the only way for Ava and me to crack her was by giving her a couple glasses of wine and boom, open book. Guts and feelings spilled all over the table. She completely adores you, Quinn. Lesson I learned from all that wine. She's absolutely head over heels for you."

My face turned hot. I looked at my coffee because I couldn't look him in the eye, too embarrassed to admit the truth to my girlfriend's brother. "Well, the feelings are pretty mutual."

When I glanced at him, a content grin thinned his lips. "Even though she was annoying, part of me was relieved that she's found someone who makes her so comfortable opening up to us when she's never been like that. That's how I know you have this immense power to hurt her, so I can't help but be protective."

"Jake, I'm really sorry. I already promised her—and I'll promise you right now—that's not going to happen again because she's, like, the greatest thing that's happened to me."

"Greater than all your gold medals?"

"The medals are a consolation prize." My answer forced a smile out of him, and he shed his protective, older brother persona. "I really love her, Jake."

"I can see that. She loves you too."

I glanced at the patio, feeling the truth that hummed through my chest ready to burst into the open. "Can I tell you something?"

"Sure. Go ahead."

I'd never said the words before, not even to Liam or Lillian or

Talia. I didn't share with anyone the secret that I'd kept locked up for the past month, but if anything, everything we'd gone through reassured me that it was the right thing to do. Kennedy Renee Reed was the only girl for me and the only girl I wanted to be with. I knew it the moment I saw her before Tokyo. Once she reentered my life, I never wanted her to leave again. I had zero doubts that anyone would ever come close to her.

"I bought a ring."

His mouth fell open. "What?"

I nodded as my heart sprinted in my chest. Nervousness mixed with fresh excitement and adrenaline. "I want to marry her."

"Holy shit," he said and covered his mouth. "You have the..." He struggled to say "ring," but I nodded to fill its absence. "Oh my G... when? When did you get it?"

"A month ago." It was a few days after our first bath together, the night we said we loved each other. I knew it then. "I haven't been more confident about anything in my life."

"When are you going to do it?"

"I don't know. We're still so new. I mean, she just moved out here three months ago, so it kinda seems crazy, but then it doesn't at the same time. We've known each other since we were seven. We've had feelings for each other for ten freakin' years. I mean, am I really crazy?"

"I don't...I have no idea. If you feel it in your gut, who am I to say it's wrong? I knew Ava was the one two months into us dating. You and Ken have more history. It makes complete sense to me."

"I have no doubts about Kennedy, and I know she feels the same way."

"Do it, Quinn. Go ask my sister to marry you."

My stomach swelled with so much joy, I couldn't contain my smile. I had this overwhelming urge to cry when I got his approval. The reality of what was happening quickly set in. I'd bought Kennedy a ring, and I was going to ask her to marry me.

I wanted to fast-forward to the perfect moment and ask her. I was ready for the rest of our lives together.

"When I have an inkling of the perfect time to ask, trust me, you'll be the first to know. I might even ask for help."

He clasped his hands on his scruffy cheeks. "Holy shit. I can't believe this. You're going to be my sister-in-law."

"Don't tell anyone. Not your parents. Maybe Ava, as long as you two sit on the secret until I figure out the right time. I haven't told anyone yet, not even my brother."

He zipped his lips. "I promise, I won't say anything, sis."

Chapter Sixteen

Taylor made me reiterate my promise when Talia and I watched her kick ass in her 100-fly a month later. And then to show her I was upholding my end of the promise, I invited her and her four friends to join one of our practices at Berkeley. She got to swim in our pool and learn all about mastering the fly from Talia. We loaded them up with Team USA and Cali Condors merchandise before treating them to lunch. I was happy to hear that she and the girls were now best friends, and she even admitted she was starting to like California. I was so happy for her, and she said she was happy I was going to Japan.

"I'll be watching," she told me at lunch. "Just in case you back out last minute. I will know." She winked.

Even though the practice with Taylor was fun, training for the Fukuoka world championships was the most brutal thing I'd ever put my body through. I had four months of catching up to do, and that meant beating myself to a pulp to get where I needed to be.

David's workouts abused me, which was good. If I'd earned a dollar for the number of times I puked on the side of the pool, I could have covered the utility bills for the month. This made David happy, and I knew he flagged each workout for his barf collection to use against us at later practices. I bathed in ice regularly, not the warm baths with Kennedy that I really wanted. There was no room for error when it came to my strict diet plan, so Ring Pops and Chinese takeout weren't allowed. My alarm was set for four thirty Monday through Friday. My yoga mat saw sunlight for the first time in months after hiding in the closet. Sundays became food shopping and meal prep day. And the fridge was loaded with spinach, kale, fruits, lean meats, and veggies. My therapist was happy to hear that my swimming schedule was back in place, how it showed signs of me falling in love with the sport again. I saw her once a week, and Kennedy saw hers once a week as well. We talked through my anxieties, how to rethink them and steer my brain away from basking in them, and discussed my future, what I wanted to get out of it, what would make me happy and unhappy. I told her I wanted to coach, told her about Taylor and how she'd really opened my eyes, how I was thinking about applying for the position of assistant coach on her elite club team, and how coaching gave me a sense of purpose.

My mind had been pieced back together just in time for Japan.

When I arrived in Fukuoka, I felt so overwhelmed, it was almost stifling. All my doubts came rushing back. I only signed on to do one event because of my break, and I didn't want to overwork myself. That was the 400-free. Against Amira, who'd won in Abu Dhabi and had been training ever since Tokyo. She probably thought she had an edge…and she did, honestly. I felt like David about to swim in a pool of Goliaths.

The morning of my race, after a quick call with Kennedy, who gave me words of wisdom and positive vibes from her hotel room down the street, I joined the rest of Team USA at the pool. My stomach churned like it did when I'd had way too much dairy. The pressure mounted in my shoulders and tightened my muscles, and I really wished Kennedy was around to knead the tension out of them. She gave amazing massages. But since she was in the stands, Lillian was an amazing Plan B and gave me a three-minute shoulder massage as Talia spouted inspirational quotes as if we were in the climax of a sports movie.

Like the Olympics, the announcer introduced each swimmer, and out they came onto the deck. The congealing anxiety and nerves made it feel as if a rock was buried in my stomach. My heart wouldn't stop shuddering. Amira was right in front of me with headphones on, jiggling her arms and legs one last time before the announcer called her. Here she was moving freely, as if this was a typical Tuesday, and I felt as if I was weighted in my spot, ready to barf for the cameras the second I stepped on deck.

How about that for an entrance?

I didn't barf when I walked to lane six, though the feeling lodged in my throat never left. I turned up the volume to my iPod hidden in the pocket of my Team USA warm-up jacket and focused on the music. I dried off my block so I wouldn't slip and find another way to humiliate myself. Once my clothes were off and my headphones dumped in the basket behind my lane, I took in the sight of the natatorium. It wasn't nearly as daunting as Tokyo, which seated fifteen thousand people on a worldwide stage. This was smaller at five thousand seats and was broadcast on two channels only the most dedicated sports lovers paid for.

As the announcer introduced lanes seven and eight, I felt as if I was in the process of vomiting. To my right, Amira jumped up and down in a last attempt to loosen up. In my head, I thought about the goal time that David had given me. Four minutes and five seconds. It was thirteen seconds slower than Tokyo and the current world record, three fifty-two, but this wasn't about me winning, beating Amira, or bringing home a medal. For the first time, I wasn't competing for external motivations. My therapist and I had really honed in on that in the months leading up to these world champs. Now that I'd accomplished the things I wanted in my career—like world championships, Olympic gold, and world records—I needed to rewire my brain to focus on other things.

I needed to compete for myself, solely for how it made me feel. It made me feel powerful, fast, and free, and that was what I was looking for when I hit the wall.

I celebrated the fact that despite my four-month break, I was in the final. Hadn't seen that coming, honestly. I was pretty proud of myself. I celebrated the fact that I loved the grueling training I'd put myself through to be on this deck. I was excited to go to practice again. Like for the first week of school, I was excited to get back into the swing of things and learn. I celebrated the fact that the most important person in my life had traveled across the world with me. This was the very moment Kennedy and I had been talking about ever since we were kids, how she wanted to be in the front row, cheering while I donned red, white, and blue with the American flag on my latex cap. As I took in the five thousand people, I found my girlfriend with the rest of the Team USA families. I smiled that she'd squeezed into the front row, arms dangling over the railing with her phone in position to record.

And then I glanced down. The sight of her shirt tore me open and made me breathless just a few short moments before my breathing would be limited.

The shirt. She was wearing the shirt. Scrawled across her chest were the words, "my girlfriend," with a black-and-white photo of me she'd stolen off Instagram.

Thirteen years of talking about the shirt and never having the opportunity to wear it, there it was. It finally happened. The sight of it warmed my chest and hit my eyes, but I couldn't break out in tears right before my race. I needed to turn the urge into adrenaline and power through this race, trying to beat four-oh-five. The faster I swam, the sooner I could admire that shirt.

I was ready. The shirt was the final straw.

The official blew four short blasts. My brain flicked into race mode. No more smirking. There was no smirking in swimming. There was no smirking seconds before I had one race—one chance only—to prove to the world and myself that I could go through the four shittiest months of my life and still come back from it.

The eight of us stepped onto the blocks and dangled our arms, waiting to take our marks. I took one last breath, deep enough to shove any remaining nerves and doubts out of my body. The crowd hushed.

"Take your mark," the official announced. All eight of us clutched the blocks.

Buzz.

We dove into the water. As always, diving gracefully without my goggles falling was one hurdle I knew I could achieve in any race. I used every fiber of my leg muscles to butterfly kick ahead of Amira to my right and the Australian on my left.

My swimming career might only last another four to eight years—or hell, not even that long—but I was sure as hell going to make the most of it because only a handful of people in the world could say they were professional swimmers and Olympic medalists. Until the day came that I announced my retirement, I was going to give my career as much energy and stamina as I had given each of my races. So when I popped my head up for the last time, I could look back at the scoreboard in my mind, at everything I'd accomplished, and tell myself, you gave everything you had until there was nothing left to give.

And I was going to apply that same mentality to this race. Any race could be my last, and I didn't want to have regrets.

Swimming against Amira and the Australian was one of the most challenging races I'd ever swam. For the first half, I lagged by half a body length as the two of them were neck and neck for first. I even counted myself in fourth place at one point. I kicked until it burned. By the second half, I made it back into medal territory, and the last fifty meters, I decided to nearly suffocate since each turn to get air slowed me down by a fraction of a second. I wanted to beat four-oh-five so badly, I couldn't afford that fraction.

So I sent my body into full beast mode.

From the corner of my eye, Amira, the Australian, and I were neck and neck. As the water splashed, I could hear the crowd, that was how close the race was. Coaches whistled. The crowd screamed. Teammates roared. I could have sworn that through it all, I heard Kennedy. I thought of her, my family, my teammates, and Taylor, knowing all of them were watching. I picked up the pace. I held my breath tighter. My face was on fire. My throat muscles yanked and cried out for oxygen. My hamstrings felt as if they were coiling down to a thread. My chest was ready to implode. I mustered the pain and the negative thoughts in that last fifty meters to get to that cross waiting on the wall.

Once I smacked it, I lifted my head and sucked in all the hot, humid air. Warm water trickled out of my ears, and I heard the screaming of all five thousand people packed into the stands. They jumped up and down. Amira and the Australian panted as they stared at the scoreboard. The Australian victoriously tossed her hands in the air. Finally, I made out the times on the scoreboard on the other end of the pool. My chest squeezed.

Lane six: second place. Three fifty-eight.

I'd lost to the Australian by half a second, but I didn't even care. My mouth fell open at the sight of three fifty-eight. Somehow, after all the shit for the past few months, I was able to get a time five seconds slower than my Olympic time. I was able to swim a race that had my blood pumping with the thrill that I loved so much. My body and mind felt amazing to the point I was a little disappointed I didn't have another race.

I congratulated the Australian, gave Amira a friendly hug, and then hoisted myself out of the pool, still gasping for air as I looked for Kennedy. She'd managed to find an American flag and hopped up and down, smiling the widest I'd ever seen as the stars and stripes rippled above her.

A half hour later, the three medal winners were escorted back out for the ceremony. Even as the Australian national anthem played, something I would have moped about a year ago, I couldn't stop smiling. I was sharing this moment with my girlfriend, something I'd wanted to do since I was eleven. I'd beaten my goal time. I could see Taylor freaking out back in California, and I knew that girl was a huge part of my success.

When the last note of the anthem rang throughout the deck, the crowd roared in applause. I shook the hands of the Australian and Amira and then hopped off the podium to go to the girl who really mattered. As people leaned over the railing to offer congratulating hands, I ran up the bleachers where the coaches and press sat, and extended my arms up to Kennedy. She clasped my hands after dabbing her damp face. Seeing her there in that shirt, holding my hands, the stinging met my eyes again.

"You look so ridiculous in that shirt," I said and kissed the backs of her hands.

She laughed. "You don't know how many people took a picture of this shirt. I hope this makes me Tumblr famous."

"Are you ready to star in some fan fiction?"

"Star in some what?"

"I'll show you on the plane ride home. In the meantime, come here."

I stepped onto my tippy toes. She leaned so far forward that it almost worried me. The railing pinned her at her waist, and the top half of her hung over so I could cup her face and bring her in for a kiss. I almost forgot that the press was beside me until the clamor of lenses shuttered, but I didn't care. That wasn't going to stop me from kissing the love of my life.

"I love you, Ken," I said through the noise of the crowd and the fluttering of lenses. "I couldn't have done this without you."

It was her turn to hold my face. She brushed a lingering tear sliding down my cheek. "You could have because guess what?"

"What?"

"You're so fucking incredible. You turned the darkest moment of your life around and proved to yourself that you're not a one-hit wonder. I think you're finally able to see what I've seen in you all along, what all those kids like Taylor see in you. You're so much more than a swimming machine, my love. You're an inspiration. You inspire me too, and I'm so lucky that I get to be with you and witness it every day."

Her words made me crack. I started crying, then laughed at my crying. This was all I'd ever wanted since I was eleven, to share this moment with the best friend who'd promised to be by my side. It was worth the long wait. Not only was my best friend in the stands, but she was also my girlfriend, the love of my life, the woman I wanted to spend the rest of my life with. I could feel the love and support pouring from her. And I wanted to show her exactly how much I loved and appreciated her, especially for never giving up on us.

I told myself that once we got back home, I would start planning the proposal. I had to ask this woman to marry me.

CHAPTER SEVENTEEN

One year later

"Oh my God, I'm going to vomit," I said.

My parents, Liam, Mr. and Mrs. Reed, Ava, and I watched on Mrs. Reed's iPad. Jacob had specifically built his own hidden camera for today's purpose. It had been his own hobby for the last few months. Talk about commitment and dedication. I thought he would assist in tricking Kennedy or offer up some ideas, but no, this guy built his own hidden camera because that was what Silicon Valley nerds did to help get their little sisters engaged. Ava had sewn the camera on his button-down so both of our families could watch it happen in real time.

My palms wouldn't stop sweating while Jacob escorted Kennedy around Aspen Grove. She'd thought it was just a brother-sister errand run for a cookout with both of our families in my backyard that evening, but she would soon realize we were in town for something much bigger.

As I watched and started to feel physically sick, Jacob parked right outside my parents' house. I told Kennedy to meet me there so I could tag along to the grocery store. He trailed behind her. He knew part of his job was to always walk behind, so all of us could see her reactions. My driveway was the first stop, and Kennedy halted when she made out the pink chalk marks.

Jacob played his part. "What is it?"

She faced him. Her eyebrows folded as she pointed to the writing. "It says 'This is where we first met.'"

"This is where who met?"

Kennedy turned and noticed the box of chalk on the left, where the driveway met the grass. I had an arrow drawn to where a note stuck out between the sticks. She bent and read it.

"What does it say?"

She showed him a picture wrapped up in a note: It was when we were seven, a few months after she moved in. We were in our bathing suits on that very driveway, cheeks slightly burned from the summer sun, and we were holding a watermelon slice. My arm was around her, and both of us had crooked smiles from adult teeth growing in.

"Look at how cute Quinn is," she said, and that comment made my neck perspire even more.

"You were a really cute kid," Dad said.

"Glad to know I grew out of it."

"Someone had to tell you the news," Liam added and then cackled.

Back on the iPad, Kennedy looked at the note. "It says, 'This is the spot where we first met. You asked to color with Liam and me. I drew a dolphin, and you gave my dolphin water. You said dolphins needed water to swim. That's the moment I knew you were special. I couldn't explain why, but I instantly felt drawn to you. I knew it had to mean we would be best friends, but I had no idea you would be so much more. A present is waiting for you where I cracked my chin open.'" She looked at Jacob quizzically. "What the hell is all this?"

The camera moved from what I assumed to be a shrug. "I don't know. I guess she's not home?"

She faced right, looking down the street where we had sped down the hill and I'd flown off my bike, hit the curb, and cracked my chin. "I guess not, but I see something over there." She pointed, and her eyebrows creased again. "Let me go check it out."

As they walked a few homes down, I threw my hands over my face, feeling another wave of intense butterflies.

Liam's warm sturdy hand patted my back. "You can't barf, sis," he said, and I could hear his wide smile. "This plan is amazing. I might even steal it for my future wife."

"Steal it, and I'll kill you."

"Oh, I see it," Ava cried, drawing my attention back to the iPad. "I see the bear."

I'd propped Honey Bear against the mailbox with another note taped to his stomach. I'd explained why to the house's new owners. The wife had thrown her hands over her chest and said she felt honored to be a part of the wonderful moment.

Kennedy laughed. "Oh my God, is that Honey Bear?" She picked him up, patted the top of his head, and unstuck the note. "I have no idea what's going on. Why is he here?"

"Why are you asking me? She's your girlfriend."

"Yeah, but clearly, I can't explain why she's leaving notes all over the neighborhood and Honey Bear out in the open for someone to steal."

"Maybe the note will explain."

"'You bought Honey Bear when I needed seven stitches. I thought you bought him because you were my best friend. You later told me it was because you liked me. I had no idea until that night you kissed me on your patio when we were thirteen. Go to that patio and ring the doorbell. Don't worry. The Rosens are a really nice family. They even have an Australian shepherd!'" She turned to Jacob again, eyebrows still together, but a grin landed on her face. "Our old house? Oh my God, this is the most complicated errand ever."

"I guess we should go back to the house?"

"I guess so. I need to see their dog."

Their old house was only about two homes away. Carrying Honey Bear, the two walked up the driveway. My stomach swirled in another rush of nerves. She stepped onto the patio where she gave me my first kiss the night before the Reeds moved to New York City. For a moment, I got lost in the memory, and I could feel the buzz on my lips, the thrill she gave me. Twelve years later, she was still able to give me that buzz.

She rang the doorbell and smiled when she heard the dog barking.

I'd explained to the Rosens what I was doing and why I was asking them to hold a note for me. Mr. Rosen had been more than grateful to partake in the moment, and he'd congratulated me on the Olympics. He'd let me pet his adorable, merle-colored shepherd with bright blue eyes. I was so grateful that everyone in the neighborhood was so accepting and on board with my plan.

He was the one who opened the door and let a tooth-revealing grin etch his face. It was no surprise Kennedy's eyes fell to the dog, and her smile mirrored his as he opened the door. The dog licked her hand.

"You must be Kennedy," Mr. Rosen said and handed her a note. "I've been holding this for you."

"Do you know what's going on?"

He shook his head, but of course, he knew what it was. "I have no idea."

The two chatted about how she used to live in the house, and our families groaned about Kennedy's charisma at a time we didn't want her to talk with strangers. We wanted her to open the damn note. I was the only one who didn't mind because the more she talked to Mr. Rosen and petted his dog, the more time I had to breathe through my rapidly coiling stomach.

Finally, she opened the letter and found another picture. She didn't show it to Jacob, but we all knew it was a photo of the two of us in the basement of the Rosens' house, in the little closet underneath the stairs that we deemed our secret spot. Kennedy and I locked ourselves in there when we were kids, told ghost stories, and doodled on the wall. Mrs. Reed had taken a picture of us during one of our sleepovers when we were ten. We'd lined the floor of the closet with pillows and blankets, and Mr. Reed had put up fairy lights. We'd sat in the glow with our doodles and random names of boy crushes—most of them Kennedy's—and spent hours there.

"Read it," Jacob demanded.

"Oh yes, right, sorry." By the way her eyes skimmed each line and her smile grew, I could tell she got lost in the memories. Sometimes, I still had dreams about that closet. I wondered if she did too. "'We still talk about our secret spot, the Harry Potter closet in your old basement. We spent hours in there telling ghost stories, writing crushes on the wall, and hiding from Jacob. It was like our own little world. Now go to the restaurant where we had our first real kiss. Ask for the Kennedy Special.'"

"Where's the place you had your first real kiss?"

I noticed Kennedy's nostrils flare as her smile widened, softly and thinly, almost as if something settled in her. My stomach flipped when she bit her bottom lip and looked down at the note and picture.

"Ken?" Jacob repeated.

She glanced at him, eyebrows arched, and eyes brimming with tears.

Did she know what was happening?

"Oh, yeah. Sorry. It was Swensons. Senior year." She paused and gave her brother, and unknowingly the camera, a furrowed brow. "You sure you have no idea what's going on?"

"No," he said with an annoyed grunt. "I just want to run to the store and get back to the Hugheses. Can we please go to Swensons and get this thing over with?"

Kennedy rolled her eyes and headed back to the car. "Yeah, okay, when I stop getting these notes."

"I'm hungry," he whined.

"Jacob deserves an Oscar for his performance," Mom said.

Everyone laughed but me. I laughed on the inside, but this was the final destination. Once they left Swensons, I had to get off the couch and head to my backyard to ask her the most important question of both of our lives.

On their way there, everyone in our living room checked in with me. Smiles wide. Tears still filling their eyes. I kept wiping my sweaty hands against my shorts and noticed I was shaking.

Mom sat beside me and grabbed one of my hands. "Aw, hon, you're really that nervous?"

The lump in my throat tripled in size. This was all suddenly real.

"Yes, I'm fucking terrified." I paused when the parents blinked through my expletive. "I'm sorry. I'm terrified."

"I must say, Quinn, I wasn't as nervous as you are when I proposed to your mom," Dad said and kissed the top of Mom's head.

I frowned. "Well, geez, thanks, Dad," I said. Mom nudged him with her elbow as he laughed. Glad my dad found my nerves as entertaining as what was unfolding on the iPad.

Then Ava squeaked when she announced Jacob and Kennedy had pulled into Swensons.

"They're there! They're there," she shouted. The parents swarmed around her holding the iPad. "The last destination." She turned to me, focusing on anything but the iPad. "Quinn, are you ready?"

"T-minus twenty minutes," Dad said and squeezed my shoulders.

I jumped up on my feet. "I need to go barf. Be right back."

I couldn't finish watching. I had to excuse myself to breathe. My heart had never felt so heavy in my life. Quick and weighted. As my fingers curled over the bathroom counter, I closed my eyes and slowly breathed, held it in, then exhaled.

This reminded me of the moments as an assistant coach to Taylor's club team when the swimmers' emotions and doubts peaked. With the help of my own therapy and working through my internal thoughts, I was able to help them push through their insecurities. I was coaching thirty swimmers from thirteen to eighteen this summer. They had raging hormones and short attention spans. If I could coach them, I could coach myself through this proposal.

I'd already visualized this moment countless times, just as I did with all my swims. I'd been practicing my breathing techniques to calm my nerves ever since we got to the San Francisco airport to begin our trip back home. I did it one last time now, practicing the speech in my head like I'd been doing over and over for months. I knew it most likely wouldn't be the same speech I gave her in the moment, but I wanted to do everything to make sure it was as close as it could be.

While I practiced my deep breathing, I imagined what was playing out on the iPad. She and Jacob would go up to the Swensons drive-thru window, and with her eyebrows hinting at her confusion while her smile told of her intrigue, she would ask a worker wearing a white soda jerk hat and a fire engine red button-down for the Kennedy Special. Inside, she would find her last clue. A large fry seasoned with their delicious mysterious seasoning and a note that said, "This was the place where you told me you liked me since we were eleven. We kissed right here, and when I think about our first real kiss, I get butterflies. It's been eight years, and those have never gone away. Enjoy the best fries in the world on the way back to the house where we made our pact."

"Quinn," Liam shouted down the hall. "Get out of the bathroom. They're heading back."

Oh my God, this is happening. In twenty minutes, I'm going to have a fiancée.

Both our moms and Ava dabbed their eyes as I ran to the backyard. The stringed patio lights were on, despite the fact it was six thirty p.m. in July, and the sun still had two more hours in the sky. Dad had mowed the grass that afternoon, and the smell of freshly cut lawn permeated the air. I could feel our families watching through the sliding glass door as my heart slowly reached a crescendo. I had the idea for the proposal nailed down right after we'd come back from Japan, inspired by how I'd had wanted to ask her to our senior prom. I'd run my plans by Taylor and her teammates. They all said my plan was "dope" and "iconic." And somehow, Kennedy's parents had kept the secret since Christmas, when I'd asked them for their blessing.

I swallowed nonexistent saliva, feeling my pulse twitch in my neck. Sweat stuck to my fingers, which really needed to have the ability to grip the ring so it didn't fall. God, that would be so embarrassing.

My breath caught when Kennedy turned the corner. The tears formed the moment I saw her. No matter how hard I tried, I couldn't hold them back. The first one fell, and then I ignored the rest because her face was stained too. Her eyes shimmered in the glow of the patio lights, and she stopped a few feet in front of me.

Everything in my brain drained. I forgot about my sweat, the food I really wanted to eat, the water I desperately needed to drink. The only things remaining were the words I wanted to say.

"I don't bite, you know," I quivered through my laugh.

She lowered her hands and erased the space between us cautiously, almost fearfully, but the corner of her mouth showed me that she knew what was happening.

"Quinn…what are you doing?" she asked low and soft, and her wavering voice sounded like my own.

"Hanging out in my backyard."

"You put me through a scavenger hunt?"

"I did. I couldn't put you through one to ask you to prom, so I figured I would use it to ask you something else."

Right as she smiled, a cry escaped. She attempted to hide it with her hands, but it was already out in the summer air. A new round of tears formed. She quickly swiped them from her eyes, seemingly embarrassed that she was crying. The long streams continued down my face, but wiping them away was pointless when I was so fucking happy, nervous, excited, and hopeful for the next moment.

I thought I had this speech nailed down. Every word. Every pause. Every smile I'd flash. I'd known this girl since I was seven, and somehow, I lost the ability to talk and tell her everything. I let out a slow breath, finally accepting the fact that no matter how many times I'd practiced this, how it had played out in all the scenes I'd fallen asleep to the last few months, the words were lost in my brain. I had to surrender and let the unfiltered words dancing on the tip of my tongue out because those were the truest words I could give her at that moment, one of the biggest moments of our lives.

Maybe the unfiltered words would be much better than the rehearsed ones.

I reached for her hands, and when she grabbed hold of mine, I brushed both with my thumbs. "Ken?"

She sniffed and tried to fix her damp face with her shoulder but failed.

"Don't even try to wipe your face because it's not gonna work. I've accepted the fact I'm going to be a mess, and you're not going to make fun of me until later, okay?"

She choked on a laugh, sucked in her lips, and nodded.

Here went nothing.

"We made a pact seven years ago at my house. We said if our paths crossed after college, we'd try again. Ken, I've thought about that pact so many times since we made it. So many times, that during those five years apart, you still felt like mine, as much as you did when we were together. The second you told me you were in town, that was the moment I knew that this was it. This was our paths finally crossing. This had to mean something. We had so many things in our way at the time. Ex-girlfriends. Long distance. Depression. But we made it through all those roadblocks. We can admit that it was really hard, especially the first few months of you being in San Francisco. But being with you, loving you…it's been the easiest thing I've ever done. You came back into my life three different times, and each time, I've been so incredibly happy. Anytime you're not with me, my days just float by, blurred together with no direction. Seven years ago, when we made that pact, we were saying good-bye to each other again, and Ken, I don't ever want to tell you good-bye. I knew that right before I left for Tokyo. I couldn't say good-bye to you again."

Her nostrils flared, and the muscles in her jaw flickered. "I don't ever want to say good-bye either."

"I knew I loved you when we slow danced at prom. I knew that I never stopped loving you when all I did was wonder when our paths would cross. I knew that I was in love with you when you told me you got the internship, and my response was being a crying mess. I was so incredibly happy."

"Me too, babe. Me too."

"You were there for me during the lowest point of my life, when I was terrified of the future because I had no idea what it would look like.

I had no idea what my purpose was. But now I'm not terrified of the future if it means you're in it. I want to be with you for the rest of my life, Ken. You've been on my mind constantly and consistently since high school."

Another cry slipped out of her. She retrieved her hands to cover her mouth again, probably attempting to mute the rest of the sobs blubbering in her throat. It allowed me to reach into my pocket and snatch that velvet box that had been poking me in the butt cheek this whole time. I let out one last heavy breath before holding it in front of my stomach.

I gulped at the dryness in my mouth. God, I needed water.

When I opened the box, Kennedy's stare grew at the sight of the blue topaz surrounded by little diamonds on the platinum band. "Oh my God," she said through an airy exhale and rested both of her hands on her stomach.

"You remember this ring?" I asked. But she couldn't even speak. Seeing the glaze in her eyes caused mine to water too.

"Quinn…" she said in her quivering voice.

"Kennedy," I began but my stupid throat started closing up because I couldn't hold it in anymore. It was like our whole relationship flashed through my mind, and I saw the Kennedy Reed who was my childhood best friend in a fishtail braid and a crooked kid smile, asking to color with Liam and me on our driveway, to the Kennedy Reed in high school who was so beautiful I had to train myself not to look at her in the hallways, to the Kennedy Reed she was now, standing in front of me seconds before I asked her to be my wife. Right as those words were on the tip of my tongue, my blink cut the tears running down my face. "Damn it." I wiped my face, and she let out a nervous laugh.

After a staggered exhale, I decided to go for it. "Kennedy, I'm so in love with you. I'll be in love with you for the rest of my life. Will you marry me?"

"Oh my God," she said and let out the cry I could tell was hanging in her throat. "Quinn…"

"That's not an answer."

"Yes, God, yes!"

A wet blubber escaped me when I heard the words that made it official. "Do you promise?" I asked, crying harder because she'd said yes, and I wanted to make sure I heard it correctly because if I did, I was going to be the luckiest woman in the world.

Kennedy let out a giggle and cupped my damp face. I looked into her beautiful watery eyes that still glistened from the patio lights. "Do I promise to marry you? Yes, I promise."

She pulled me in for a kiss, and I wrapped my arms around her neck so I could kiss her back before I needed to give her the ring.

Once I made our engagement official, I took my first look at that gem on her ring finger, smiled, and noticed her smile had grown even wider, if that was possible.

"It's...I...I loved that ring, this ring," she said.

"I know. You said you always wanted another blue topaz. Now you have one forever."

"I can't believe you remembered."

"Of course I remembered. I remember everything about that day. I didn't want it to end."

"But it was so exp—"

I pressed my finger against her lips to shut her up. "You deserve this ring. Just please don't lose it," I said with a laugh and freed her lips.

"I love it, Quinn. So much. And you. I love you more."

She clasped my face and reeled me back in. We wasted no time celebrating our engagement with another kiss.

Kennedy Reed was my fiancée, and the rush of warmth in my chest never felt so fucking good.

"Ah!" Liam screamed behind us, ruining the moment as he always did and promising to ruin many more moments in our future.

I'd gotten so wrapped up in the moment, I'd completely forgotten our families in the living room, witnessing it all unfold, including the intimate celebratory make-out. I shuddered despite the fluttering in my stomach.

They poured out the back door. Both of our moms cried as hard as we did, their eyes almost unrecognizable underneath their tears. Liam bulldozed into me and picked me up to twirl me around and then did the same to Kennedy. There was a lot of hugging, crying, and smiling. My dad held Kennedy's yellow Polaroid camera and snapped a candid picture and then wiggled it around impatiently to see how his first shot turned out. Everyone applauded Jacob for his superb acting. The dads grilled steaks and burgers. Everyone drank lots of champagne. Liam took another Polaroid of Kennedy sitting on my lap while flaunting the ring.

"Ah, so basic," Liam said when he handed us the picture. "Perfect for the Gram."

The new pictures added to the collection I'd used for the proposal. Our families passed them around and beamed at the memories. We ate a delicious barbecue on the back patio. Laughed, cried, and drank more champagne. I guess the parents had really stocked the fridge. Good thing Kennedy said yes, or that would have been really awkward.

As the day flickered into night, Dad fixed up the fire pit, and I cozied into the chair with a beer in hand. Kennedy came over with a fresh glass of something red, probably a Petit Verdot. She slung one arm around my neck and took a sip.

"So I'm thinking a fall wedding," Kennedy said. "Here in Aspen Grove. The leaves changing colors in our pictures. Burgundy and navy blue for our colors. Oh, and we can use all of our pictures as centerpieces." She pointed to the pictures on the table next to me.

"You already have a Pinterest wedding board up, don't you?"

She grinned. "I've had one since I moved in with you."

"That's disgusting."

She tickled my side. "Don't ruin our engagement night by being a jerk."

"You're going to have to deal with that for the rest of your life. You've already come this far."

"Yeah, and I think I might have said yes too soon."

"Don't even joke. My nerves are still going."

"Aw, babe, really?"

"I wanted to vomit all day. I still feel like you're going to say 'just joking.'"

She kissed my cheek. "I'm not taking my yes back. It was the most perfect day and the most perfect proposal."

"Was it really?" I asked. She responded with a nod and nudged my forehead with hers. "When did you know you weren't going to the grocery store?"

"When I found Honey Bear chilling out under that mailbox, I was like 'what the fuck is going on?' But it probably wasn't until I got to my old house when I started really wondering if this was some kind of scheme. I had no idea, Quinn. We've only really talked about it a handful of times."

"I know, that was the point. You know I bought the ring like a month after you moved?"

"A month?"

I nodded. "Told Jacob I had the ring the morning after we…well… officially made up in his spare room. Oops. And your parents have been dying with this secret since Christmas when I asked their permission."

She pulled her head back, seeming to doubt the truth. "Really? This whole time? You even asked permission? What a gentlewoman!"

I kissed her nose. "Remind me to text Taylor. I had to get this plan approved by the kids. You know, make sure it had the stamp of cool approval."

"Taylor even knew about this?"

"Of course. And she's been waiting for an update. Apparently, she's the messenger for the whole team."

I snapped a picture of the Polaroid Liam took of us and the ring and sent it to Taylor, who would send it to the team, who would all be ecstatic based on how loud they'd shrieked when I first told them. Throughout the summer, I'd rounded up the swimmers with team dinners, nights at the movies, trying to establish a sense of community during a time they'd really searched for it. I could picture the next dinner or outing and having them swarm around me for the juicy details.

I was excited for it. They were a fun group.

"You're really cute, you know that?" Kennedy said.

"What? Why?"

"Because your smile is so big right now."

"Because I just got myself the most beautiful fiancée," I said and kissed her cheek.

"No, you're smiling because you found something that makes you happy. You know that you smile anytime you talk about Taylor or the team? Those kids really love you, Quinn. I'm so proud that you found something that makes you really happy."

"Me too. And I've got you so I'm really the luckiest person in the world."

She kissed me before resting her head on my shoulder.

It was hard to believe there was ever a moment when we'd lived in different worlds, a time we'd lived on opposite ends of the country, and a time where we'd hardly existed to each other at all. All the twists and turns, ups and downs, light and dark days were all paths that had led me straight to her. From the first time I'd met her that summer evening when she'd ridden her teetering bike to our driveway. She'd given my childhood color. After she'd given me my first kiss; she'd given my adolescence its first bout of intense lust. When we'd reconnected right before Tokyo, she'd given my heart its first and last taste of true love.

I would have never guessed that our first moment on my driveway that summer would turn into the moment when I'd met my future wife. I'd known when she sat next to me, and we'd shared our first few laughs, that something about her was different. I couldn't explain what it was, but I'd known that whatever light she carried, I wanted to be around it.

Always.

About the Author

Morgan Lee Miller started writing at the age of five in the suburbs of Cleveland, Ohio, where she entertained herself by composing her first few novels all by hand. She majored in journalism and creative writing at Grand Valley State University.

When she's not introverting and writing, Morgan works for an animal welfare nonprofit and tries to make the world a slightly better place. She previously worked for an LGBT rights organization.

She currently resides in Washington, DC, with her two feline children, whom she's unapologetically obsessed with.

Books Available From Bold Strokes Books

All the Paths to You by Morgan Lee Miller. High school sweethearts Quinn Hughes and Kennedy Reed reconnect five years after they break up and realize that their chemistry is all but over. (978-1-63555-662-9)

Arrested Pleasures by Nanisi Barrett D'Arnuck. When charged with a crime she didn't commit, Katherine Lowe faces the question: Which is harder, going to prison or falling in love? (978-1-63555-684-1)

Bonded Love by Renee Roman. Carpenter Blaze Carter suffers an injury that shatters her dreams, and ER nurse Trinity Greene hopes to show her that sometimes hope is worth fighting for. (978-1-63555-530-1)

Convergence by Jane C. Esther. With life as they know it on the line, can Aerin McLeary and Olivia Ando's love survive an otherworldly threat to humankind? (978-1-63555-488-5)

Coyote Blues by Karen F. Williams. Riley Dawson, psychotherapist and shape-shifter, has her world turned upside down when Fiona Bell, her one true love, returns. (978-1-63555-558-5)

Drawn by Carsen Taite. Will the clues lead Detective Claire Hanlon to the killer terrorizing Dallas, or will she merely lose her heart to person of interest urban artist Riley Flynn? (978-1-63555-644-5)

Lucky by Kris Bryant. Was Serena Evans's luck really about winning the lottery, or is she about to get even luckier in love? (978-1-63555-510-3)

The Last Days of Autumn by Donna K. Ford. Autumn and Caroline question the fairness of life, the cruelty of loss, and what it means to love as they navigate the complicated minefield of relationships, grief, and life-altering illness. (978-1-63555-672-8)

Three Alarm Response by Erin Dutton. In the midst of tragedy, can these first responders find love and healing? Three stories of courage, bravery, and passion. (978-1-63555-592-9)

Veterinary Partner by Nancy Wheelton. Callie and Lauren are determined to keep their hearts safe but find that taking a chance on love is the safest option of all. (978-1-63555-666-7)

Forging a Desire Line by Mary P. Burns. When Charley's ex-wife, Tricia, is diagnosed with inoperable cancer, the private duty nurse Tricia hires turns out to be the handsome and aloof Joanna, who ignites something inside Charley she isn't ready to face. (978-1-63555-665-0)

Journey to Cash by Ashley Bartlett. Cash Braddock thought everything was great, but it looks like her history is about to become her right now. Which is a real bummer. (978-1-63555-464-9)

Love on the Night Shift by Radclyffe. Between ruling the night shift in the ER at the Rivers and raising her teenage daughter, Blaise Richilieu has all the drama she needs in her life, until a dashing young attending appears on the scene and relentlessly pursues her. (978-1-63555-668-1)

Olivia's Awakening by Ronica Black. When the daring and dangerously gorgeous Eve Monroe is hired to get Olivia Savage into shape, a fierce passion ignites, causing both to question everything they've ever known about love. (978-1-63555-613-1)

The Duchess and the Dreamer by Jenny Frame. Clementine Fitzroy has lost her faith and love of life. Can dreamer Evan Fox make her believe in life and dream again? (978-1-63555-601-8)

The Road Home by Erin Zak. Hollywood actress Gwendolyn Carter is about to discover that losing someone you love sometimes means gaining someone to fall for. (978-1-63555-633-9)

Waiting for You by Elle Spencer. When passionate past-life lovers meet again in the present day, one remembers it vividly and the other isn't so sure. (978-1-63555-635-3)

While My Heart Beats by Erin McKenzie. Can a love born amidst the horrors of the Great War survive? (978-1-63555-589-9)

Face the Music by Ali Vali. Sweet music is the last thing that happens when Nashville music producer Mason Liner and daughter of country royalty Victoria Roddy are thrown together in an effort to save country star Sophie Roddy's career. (978-1-63555-532-5)

Flavor of the Month by Georgia Beers. What happens when baker Charlie and chef Emma realize their differing paths have led them right back to each other? (978-1-63555-616-2)

Mending Fences by Angie Williams. Rancher Bobbie Del Rey and veterinarian Grace Hammond are about to discover if heartbreaks of the past can ever truly be mended. (978-1-63555-708-4)

Silk and Leather: Lesbian Erotica with an Edge, edited by Victoria Villaseñor. This collection of stories by award-winning authors offers fantasies as soft as silk and tough as leather. The only question is: How far will you go to make your deepest desires come true? (978-1-63555-587-5)

The Last Place You Look by Aurora Rey. Dumped by her wife and looking for anything but love, Julia Pierce retreats to her hometown only to rediscover high school friend Taylor Winslow, who's secretly crushed on her for years. (978-1-63555-574-5)

The Mortician's Daughter by Nan Higgins. A singer on the verge of stardom discovers she must give up her dreams to live a life in service to ghosts. (978-1-63555-594-3)

The Real Thing by Laney Webber. When passion flares between actress Virginia Green and masseuse Allison McDonald, can they be sure it's the real thing? (978-1-63555-478-6)

What the Heart Remembers Most by M. Ullrich. For college sweethearts Jax Levine and Gretchen Mills, could an accident be the second chance neither knew they wanted? (978-1-63555-401-4)

White Horse Point by Andrews & Austin. Mystery writer Taylor James finds herself falling for the mysterious woman on White Horse Point who lives alone, protecting a secret she can't share about a murderer who walks among them. (978-1-63555-695-7)